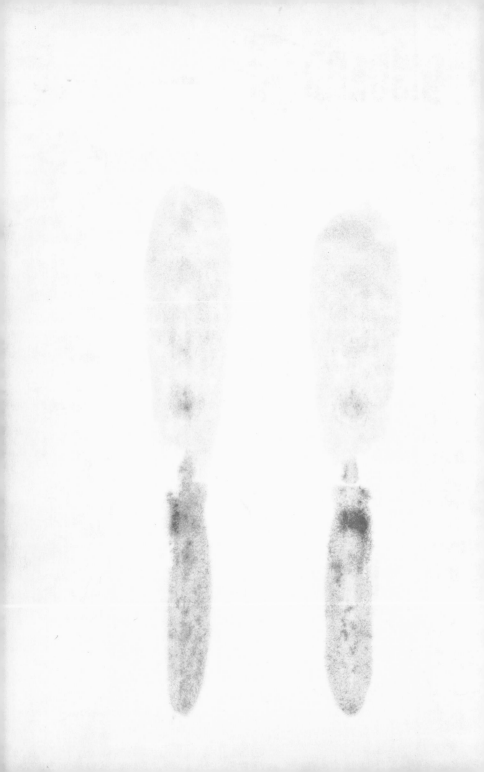

THE HUNTERS AND THE HUNTED

As Elizabeth Linington:

PERCHANCE OF DEATH
THE PROUD MAN
THE LONG WATCH
MONSIEUR JANVIER
THE KINGBREAKER
POLICEMAN'S LOT
ELIZABETH I (*Ency. Brit.*)
GREENMASK!
NO EVIL ANGEL
DATE WITH DEATH
SOMETHING WRONG
PRACTISE TO DECEIVE
CRIME BY CHANCE

As Egan O'Neill:

THE ANGLOPHILE

As Lesley Egan:

THE HUNTERS AND THE HUNTED
LOOK BACK ON DEATH
A DREAM APART
THE BLIND SEARCH
SCENES OF CRIME
A CASE FOR APPEAL
THE BORROWED ALIBI
AGAINST THE EVIDENCE
RUN TO EVIL
MY NAME IS DEATH
DETECTIVE'S DUE
A SERIOUS INVESTIGATION
THE WINE OF VIOLENCE
IN THE DEATH OF A MAN
MALICIOUS MISCHIEF
PAPER CHASE

As Dell Shannon:

CASE PENDING
THE ACE OF SPADES
EXTRA KILL
KNAVE OF HEARTS
DEATH OF A BUSYBODY
DOUBLE BLUFF
ROOT OF ALL EVIL
MASK OF MURDER
THE DEATH-BRINGERS
DEATH BY INCHES
COFFIN CORNER
WITH A VENGEANCE
CHANCE TO KILL
RAIN WITH VIOLENCE
KILL WITH KINDNESS
SCHOOLED TO KILL
CRIME ON THEIR HANDS
UNEXPECTED DEATH
WHIM TO KILL
THE RINGER
MURDER WITH LOVE
WITH INTENT TO KILL
NO HOLIDAY FOR CRIME
SPRING OF VIOLENCE
CRIME FILE
DEUCES WILD
STREETS OF DEATH
APPEARANCES OF DEATH
COLD TRAIL
FELONY AT RANDOM

THE HUNTERS
AND THE HUNTED

LESLEY EGAN

PUBLISHED FOR THE CRIME CLUB BY
DOUBLEDAY & COMPANY, INC.
GARDEN CITY, NEW YORK
1979

All of the characters in this book
are fictitious, and any resemblance
to actual persons, living or dead,
is purely coincidental.

ISBN: 0-385-15265-5
Library of Congress Catalog Card Number 78-22810
Copyright © 1979 by Elizabeth Linington
All Rights Reserved
Printed in the United States of America
First Edition

This one is for Shirley D.,
just because she's a very nice person
I'm glad to know as a friend.

Make little weeping for the dead,
for he is at rest; but the life of
the fool is worse than death.

Ecclesiasticus 22:11

THE HUNTERS AND THE HUNTED

CHAPTER ONE

Meg left the office early that Tuesday. Dr. Burton's last appointment was at three o'clock; while he was giving that examination Mrs. Wrangell came in for her new glasses. Both patients had left by ten minutes to four, and he came out to the waiting room looking tired and preoccupied and said, "May as well close up shop early."

She drove up Pacific Avenue to pick up Tammy at the nursery school. Mrs. Dean's private nursery school wasn't cheap, but it was a very good one. Clarissa Young pried Tammy away from a big picture book and said cheerfully, "Guess we're in for the usual heat wave, this time in March. Why does anybody live in this climate?"

Meg said she often wondered. She needed a few things at the market, and stopped at the Lucky on Glenoaks on the way home. Tammy used to love riding in the market cart, but now she was four she was too grown-up for that, and dawdled behind Meg along the aisles. Milk, cereal, frozen orange juice, a loaf of bread, ground round. There weren't many people at the market. When Meg pulled into the apartment driveway it was only a little after five, the sun low in the west but dusk still an hour away.

She shut the garage door, snapped the padlock, picked up the bag of groceries; they started around to the front door. On the sidewalk there Carol Sue Wiley was riding her tricycle. "Hi, Carol Sue," said Meg. "How was kindergarten today?"

Carol Sue scowled a little at her, a freckled sandy-haired little girl, and said definitely, "Yeth. All right, I guess."

Meg and Tammy walked up to the front door of the apartment. Tammy said in her funny grown-up way, "Carol Sue's a funny girl, isn't she?"

"Pretty funny," said Meg, smiling. Just lately, for reasons known only to herself, Carol Sue had taken to answering every question with a Yes first, before elaborating.

She put the groceries down again to unlock the mailbox labeled BURGESS. A couple of catalogs, a couple of form letters, a letter from Linda—good—and a long business envelope: POLLARD AND POLLARD; and her heart did something queer, missed a beat or got in an extra one, as she saw the Kansas City postmark.

Automatically she climbed the stairs, unlocked the door. Tammy made a beeline for her room, some book or toy in mind, and Meg put the groceries away. Hamburger patties for dinner, carrots and peas, mashed potatoes; lettuce and tomatoes left, and enough apple pudding for Tammy. She switched on the air-conditioning unit in the living room, and turning, met the eyes of the photograph on the end table by the couch, and a brief sharp pang of nostalgia struck her for the timeless frozen smile of the man in the photograph. Silly: life went by, you couldn't have things or people or feelings back again. And a lot of people hadn't had as happy a childhood as she had had. It was a selfish kind of nostalgia, and irrational. The feeling that nothing could ever be wrong, nothing bad could happen, if Daddy was still there.

She had loved and respected her mother, but she had been a shy and undemonstrative woman; all the warmth and loving had come from her father, and she looked away quickly from his steady, reassuring smile, sat down on the couch, and ripped open the envelope postmarked Kansas City.

The signature was *Oliver Pollard*. She remembered him vividly, a tall thin man with scanty gray hair, a firm mouth, very blue eyes, a deep voice. She read the letter and did not believe it.

. . . Will now submitted to probate and its terms to be implemented . . . question of child support will be transferred to Mr. Burgess . . . trust you will bear in mind what I said to you at the time, that as the child grows older you may wish to petition for . . . Suggest that in such case you consult your own attorney to negotiate with Mr. Burgess. He seems to harbor some extreme vindictive feeling toward you, by what he stated to me two years ago when, as you will remember, the terms of the will were first made known to him. It is possible that he may contact you; I would urge you seriously to

deal with him only through your attorney. If I may be of any help to you . . . and, faithfully yours.

The page fluttered in her hand, and she laid it down suddenly. Tammy came in clutching her big stuffed cat and said, "You goin' to fix dinner, Mama? I'm hungry."

"In a minute," said Meg. They'd let him out? Four years, and they'd let him out? And all the money— But of course the jury had made it not guilty by reason of insanity, so there was no legal reason he couldn't inherit all the money. And he was out. Free.

"Mama—"

"Just a minute," she said numbly. She had to think about this, and she couldn't think; it was too sudden and unexpected. And then she looked at Tammy standing there—four-year-old Tammy, uncannily like Meg's own pictures at that age, dark hair and eyes, fair skin, square little chin—Tammy in her crumpled blue cotton dress, one sock falling down, her braids untidy and one ribbon untied—and she thought, Dear God, no. No. Oh, no.

"Mama, we goin' to have dinner pretty soon?"

"Yes," said Meg. She got up and went into her bedroom, afraid and reluctant, after the other letter.

She hadn't wanted to keep it; it was an ugly thing; but she had realized she should keep it. In case. Just in case, She'd never looked at it again, but it was there in the bottom of her mother's jewel case under her parents' marriage certificate and the copy of the will she had made four years ago. The letter that started, *"Goddamn you."* She had wondered how he had got it mailed: didn't letters from such a place have to be censored? Another patient being released, perhaps. It didn't matter.

She held it unopened, but she remembered what was in it, and she began to feel frightened.

He was out. Free. Anywhere. Here?

Tammy. Goddamn you, all your fault—you had to have the kid—

The police, Meg thought. The police? What could they do? What would they do? She didn't know anything about the police. She'd grown up in this town, the reason she'd come back here four years ago—though by then there wasn't really anyone here for her—but about the Glendale police she knew nothing.

"Mama!"

"Yes," said Meg. "Yes, I'm coming."

At the moment the Glendale police had more than enough business on the agenda, and were feeling a little harried. Even the men riding the squad cars, who didn't come in for the sea of paperwork like the boys in the front office, were feeling that the heat wave was insult added to injury. There was a child rapist somewhere in town, and the burglary rate was soaring, and there had already been six heist jobs since Sunday.

The traffic shift had changed at four o'clock. Patrolman Stoner, cruising out on West Glenoaks, had just tagged the driver of an old Ford van who'd been doing seventy in a residential zone. The driver was Donald Biggs, nineteen, the usual long-haired teenager; his license seemed to be in order and there was no want on the vehicle, so Stoner gave him the ticket, told him he'd have to appear in court, and let him go. As he climbed back into the squad, the radio was talking about a high-speed pursuit heading for Burbank; somebody had spotted that guy there was an A.P.B. on, and he was running. Stoner just hoped the squad cars wouldn't get squashed in all the homecoming traffic; of all the damned times to be chasing somebody— On the other hand, if whoever was doing the chasing should collar him, the front-office boys would have to do some overtime.

On the whole, Stoner decided he'd just as soon be riding a squad handing out tickets as be expected to use his brain as a detective.

In the detective office at headquarters, it was getting along for end of shift. There are a lot of crimes and people police officers don't like, and a child rapist comes at the head of the list. In the last month—on top of everything else that had happened—three little girls had been raped and beaten, the youngest only six, and they had gone round and round on it and got nowhere. O'Connor and Katz had been out on the latest one all day and just come back with a handful of nothing; they had a very tentative description which wasn't going to lead them anywhere.

"Goddamn it, all up in the air!" said O'Connor, flinging himself into his protesting desk chair. He had torn his jacket off as he came into air conditioning, and the .357 Magnum bulged in its shoulder holster; at this hour of the day he needed a shave, his jaw blue, and he shoved fingers through his curly black hair, casting a bitter glance at the two detectives who'd been sitting in air conditioning all afternoon doing the paperwork.

"Not a smell of a lead," said Katz tiredly. "Except that it's the same joker on all three, which we knew anyway." The M.O. told them that. Brenda Quigley was the latest victim, and she was still too scared and hurt to tell them much. This joker wasn't using any finesse; he hadn't attempted to coax the kids into a car, just snatched them off the street by force—each little girl walking home from school alone, and on residential blocks, with no witnesses turning up at all.

It was Jeff Forbes's day off. Detective John Poor was still out somewhere on the latest heist. There had been another burglary last night; that looked very much like the same burglars who had pulled a little rash of jobs in the northwest area of town in the last few months: very smooth jobs, very pro. Varallo had been out this morning on that one, with their still-new female detective Delia Riordan. They hadn't heard anything from the lab men yet, of course. The householders had come in to make a list of what was missing; the initial report had got written.

"I might get something more out of Brenda," suggested Delia now.

"You can try," said O'Connor. From resenting the novelty of the female detective, he'd come to accept her as a good girl and a competent one; of course, she'd spent five years as an LAPD policewoman.

Varallo grinned at him. "Somebody has to do the paperwork, Charles. I'll do some legwork tomorrow and you can stay in air conditioning."

O'Connor growled, lighting a cigarette. Katz just sat back and shut his eyes. They had, of course, all the heists still to think about, witnesses to the latest one still to make statements, look at mug shots; there were the burglaries; one unidentified body in the morgue, victim of a hit-run last Saturday; and doubtless new business would be coming up, especially in a heat wave.

Delia shoved her chair back. "Well, I suppose we can call it a day. And an unproductive one it's been."

Varallo stubbed out his cigarette and stretched, watching her idly as she rummaged in her handbag for keys. They had all been rather intrigued at the notion of the female detective, when she'd got the job last November. At first glance a plain jane, their Delia; but look at her twice, there was nothing wrong with her: a medium-sized girl in her mid-twenties, roundish face, good complexion, small straight nose, blue eyes, a rather large mouth, brown hair in a plain short cut. Dress her up, she'd be a good-looking girl; but she was no nonsense, all for the job. The colorless nail polish, not much make-up, always the plain dark dresses, pantsuits. And she was good at the job too; what you could call a dedicated cop.

He stood up, reluctant to leave the air conditioning, yawning. If anybody was a dedicated cop, he reflected, it had to be Vic Varallo: twelve years on the force upstate, resigning as captain, and joining this force to ride a squad awhile before making rank again. And when the sergeant's rank had opened up, Katz had the seniority; well, Katz was a good man.

Delia had gone out. "Are you staying here all night?" he asked O'Connor and Katz. Before either one said anything, the phone buzzed on O'Connor's desk and he picked it up.

"O'Connor . . . Oh, for God's sake. Oh, hell. All right, all right."

"Now what?" asked Katz.

"That Edelman—the one fingered for the drugstore heist on Saturday. The A.P.B.'s turned him up. Tracy spotted the car, and he tried to run. Ended up ramming another squad out on Hollywood Way. Gordon was in it, and he's on his way to the hospital with a broken leg. The squad's totaled, and Tracy's fetching Edelman in."

"We're having company for dinner," said Katz plaintively. "I promised my wife—"

"All right, Joe," said Varallo. "I'll back up the boss."

O'Connor was already on the phone again, telling Katharine about it. Resignedly Varallo called Laura. Both the girls had been married to cops awhile; they knew these things came up. He wandered down to the men's room, and washing his hands surveyed himself idly in the mirror; at least, being blond, he didn't show the need of a shave. He passed a smoothing hand over his tawny crest of hair as O'Connor came in. "You ever wonder why we took on the thankless job, Charles?"

"Because we're too damn stupid to know better," said O'Connor crossly.

"All I will say," said Oliver Pollard, "is that I don't like it. Not at all."

"And that's an understatement," said his nephew. "I still can't believe they let him loose. The damn fool head doctors— It's bad enough that he gets the money. But this—do you really think he's crazy enough for a thing like that?"

"I never thought he was crazy at all," said Pollard, "if you mean that in the legal sense. It was the logical defense Morgan could go for, with Wayne having been committed before. You didn't hear him two years ago when he first learned the terms of the will, the threats he made against her and the child."

Stan Pollard rubbed his jaw thoughtfully. "I've never laid eyes on him, no." He'd only joined the firm when he passed the bar two years ago. "But a thing like that—to hold an irrational grudge that long, and you say he's not insane?"

Pollard shook his head. "Only the complete egotist—with a miserly streak too, queerly enough. Ask the head doctors why, and they'd give you the doubletalk. The only thing that matters a damn to him, or ever has, is Wayne Burgess and what he wants right now." He took off his glasses and began cleaning them slowly with his handkerchief. "I couldn't say too much in my letter to her."

"Of course not, you old fox. Put anything libelous in writing, it might be grounds to try to break that will."

"I don't think she realizes how he feels toward her."

"After all this time? That was two years ago—did he say anything about her when you saw him last week?"

Pollard put his glasses on. "Oh, no. Trying to put out the charm. But I'm not just one of the executors—I was Howard Burgess' oldest friend. He'd talked to me about Wayne for years. That one I know." He sighed. "I think. He can be erratic, but he can also hang onto an idea like death. Don't forget, by all we know, the money was the motive—and he blamed the girl then, and he blames her now for the will."

"I think I know what's in your mind," said Stan. "Do some checking up on him?"

"I would—er—feel happier if I knew where he was," said Pollard. "Maybe he's just where he said he was going. And maybe not."

"Yes, I see," said Stan. "Well, it's about a three-hundred-and-fifty-mile drive—I could probably make it by tomorrow afternoon. Just have a look around? He doesn't know me, of course."

Pollard was silent for a moment, looking out the office window. Then he said, "It's a lot farther than that to California."

"The way your mind works— And if he's not there, there are a hell of a lot of places in between.. If I'm going, I'd better be on my way."

Delia had been having trouble with the old Mercedes. It had belonged to her father, and was getting on for twenty years old; still a good car, as a Mercedes would be up to the bitter end, but it needed a lube job, probably a new battery, and some radiator work. She had an appointment at the garage tomorrow, her day off, and if it had to stay in longer than a day they'd just have to give her a loaner.

But for once it started with no trouble, and she got to Glendale headquarters a little early. The big lobby downstairs was gratefully cool—the heat was building up already. She turned to the spiral stairs, and Sergeant Duff at the desk called her name.

"I think you'd better talk to this young lady, Miss Riordan." Delia went over to the long counter. Duff, big and broad and fortyish, was looking rather perplexed. "This is one of our detectives, ma'am. Miss Riordan."

"Oh," said the girl. "Oh, thank you." She looked oddly relieved, facing Delia. "I didn't know there were women detectives. But it'll be easier to—well, explain it to you. I don't know what you could do about it, but I—but I have to ask. To tell you."

"Certainly," said Delia easily. With everything else on hand—she was due to see Brenda Quigley this morning, and there was a follow-up report to write on Sunday's burglary, and hopefully they'd get a lab report in today—but in this job it was always one thing after another. She looked the girl over quickly, unobtrusively. A pretty girl, twenty-five or so. Medium height, slim, dark-brown hair and brown eyes, a square determined little chin. She wore a plain blue sleeveless dress, carried a matching jacket over one arm, and a bone handbag: no stockings, low-heeled bone sandals. She didn't look like a flighty or stupid female. And she was frightened about something; Delia could almost smell that.

"Suppose you come upstairs and sit down and tell me what's the trouble." She led the way, the girl following in silence. In the big detective office, with the efficient strip lighting, she gave the girl a chair beside her desk and offered her a cigarette.

"I don't smoke very often," but she took it, bent to Delia's lighter. She looked around the big empty room with faint curiosity. The night watch, both bachelors, had as usual left their desks in a mess, with overflowing ashtrays. Nobody else was in yet, and the room was just a big office waiting for its staff: covered typewriters, empty wastebaskets, flat desks. "I—hardly know where to start, to tell you. There's so much. My little girl—Tammy—oh, I'm frightened for myself too, but Tammy—she's only four."

"Frightened about what? Just start at the beginning and tell me."

The girl took a deep breath. "My husband—my ex-husband. I'm afraid he's going to try to kill us." She opened her handbag and took out some papers, but just sat holding them. "I had the letter yesterday—from the lawyer, Mr. Pollard. They've let Wayne out. I didn't believe it, I don't see how they could, after only four years. The jury said he was insane, and he was in a mental hospital—institution—but they've let him out, and now he'll get all the money. And if anything's insane, that is. But you see, he's threatened to kill us." She handed Delia a letter.

It was the cautiously phrased letter of a lawyer, but this and that in it raised questions in Delia's mind. "And Wayne's letter," said the girl, and stopped, and said, "No, before you read that I'd better tell you the whole story. I'm sorry if it takes some time. You see, my parents were killed in an accident when I was sixteen, and I went to live with Aunt Ruth, my mother's sister. And she's awfully fanatical —about religion. I mean, we were Catholic too, but not like that. I don't think I'm anything now. I had Tammy baptized but I don't know why, really." She sat back and took a drag on the cigarette. "I graduated from high school here, I'd lived here all my life, Daddy was an English teacher at Hoover High—and I went up to San Jose Teachers College. That's where I met Wayne—Wayne Burgess. He was going to Berkeley, and one of the girls I knew was going with his roommate." O'Connor and Katz came in together, and the girl gave them a nervous look, moved her chair a little to sit squarely with her back to them. "I'm Meg Burgess, I didn't even tell you that, did I?" Suddenly she gave Delia a rather delightful crooked smile. "I'm awfully glad to be telling this to another female."

"Any special reason?" asked Delia, returning the smile.

"Because you'll understand how sometimes—as level-headed as a girl thinks she is—we can do some damn fool stupid things," said Meg Burgess. "I was twenty, I'd been in college two years, I thought I had some common sense. But I was just blind in love with him. I didn't know anything about him, I was just in love. He's good-looking, you know—big and dark, and he can be very charming. He's three years older, he was a senior then. He had—I found out later— quite a reputation with the girls. And of course I should've known better—when he kept up the passes—my God, me all serious and prim and eager, marriage or nothing—but of course nobody's in a state to use sense, in love like that." She looked tired now. She put out her cigarette. "You see, he wants something very much, and then when he gets it, he doesn't want it any more. I found that out. But right then I was so crazy in love that nothing else mattered, finishing college or how Aunt Ruth carried on or anything. She disowned me for marrying out of the church. And we went back to Kansas City because Wayne was going into his father's business. An accounting agency. I thought he'd just wanted to go to college in California. It was his mother told me—that he'd been committed to a—a psychiatric clinic when he was thirteen, he was there for three years. How the doctors had said he had tendencies to a schizoid personality, something like that, but he'd had treatment and he was all right now. He can be brilliant when he wants to, you know, he finished high school in only three years. But the psychiatrist said it might be better for him to get right away, be on his own. So he went to Berkeley. They were very nice people," said Meg. "They were very nice to me, the Burgesses. They worried so about him. And I found out why.

"He's erratic. He can slave at something like mad if he wants to. But he hates any work that doesn't interest him. And he wanted everything right now. Right when he wanted it. He only went for the accounting degree because his father insisted on it—he wanted Wayne to learn a job he could always fall back on—oh, he wasn't the stern tyrant, he said Wayne should come into the firm, but if he decided he couldn't stand it he didn't have to stay, but Mr. Burgess hoped he would. And there was all the money—Mr. Burgess had a lot of money. That would come to Wayne. He was the only child. I think there was farm land, and he owned the building his office was in—I don't know what else, but there was a lot."

Poor and Forbes were in now, one of them typing a report. Meg didn't seem to hear any of the background noise.

"In six months he'd got tired of me, of being married—he didn't want responsibilities of any kind. I did a lot of growing up that six months." Delia could imagine. "You couldn't ever count on him, except to *be* irresponsible and—contrary. And after a while I got to wondering—could I have another cigarette?—if I wasn't just as irresponsible, because I fell out of love with him pretty fast." Delia could imagine that too. "He hated the regular job, and he had some fairly crazy ideas, and kept asking his father for money. At the last, he had the idea of running a music store, he thought he could make a fortune selling records—look at all the teenagers, he said—he wanted ten thousand dollars to start it, he said it'd be nothing to his father, he kept asking— And then I found I was pregnant, and that was what set it all off. For Wayne."

"How do you mean?"

"Well, the Burgesses were pleased about it, and Mr. Burgess said—he was annoyed with Wayne—that settled it, it was time Wayne got over his harebrained notions, settled down to a steady job now he was starting a family, and he definitely refused to give him any money for a music store or anything else—before that Wayne had wanted to buy a silver fox farm, and after that it was race horses—and—" Meg's voice slowed and stopped. After a moment, when the typewriter clatter was broken by some cuss words from O'Connor, she said, "He killed them. That night. We'd been to dinner there, that was when Mr. Burgess said that. And I never knew Wayne had gone out again. He was like the Wayne I'd known first, charming as sin, you'd believe anything he told you—he'd make a good salesman if he wanted to work at it—we had a liqueur together, his idea, when we got back to our apartment, and I suppose he put something in mine. I went straight off to sleep and never woke up. And he went back to the house and shot them both in their sleep. He knew where his father's gun was, of course. He tried to make it look like a burglary, took his mother's jewelry and so on. But the police found one of his fingerprints, just one, made in some of the blood, and then they found the jewelry hidden in his car—he hadn't had time to get rid of it."

"This was how long ago?"

"Four years—four and a half. I was about two months pregnant, and Tammy was four the first of this month. The worst of it for me, I guess, was that I didn't have anybody of my own there—I hardly knew anyone there. This Mr. Pollard was kind, he was an old friend of the Burgesses. He's one of the executors of Mr. Burgess' will, and he got me some money. At first I didn't want to take it, but of course I hadn't anything, and there was the baby, and he said I had a claim. He got me ten thousand dollars, to pay all the medical bills, and they've been sending me two hundred a month for Tammy. Her name's Tamsen, I named her for my mother."

"They—the executors?"

Meg nodded. "You see, everything—sort of stopped. Legally, I mean. They couldn't put the will into probate or whatever it's called, because Wayne was—shut up. His lawyer claimed insanity because of his record before. And the jury believed it, and said not guilty by reason of insanity." She'd been holding the other folded paper all this time, and now held it out. "Two years ago he got the same lawyer to try to get him out—you see what Mr. Pollard said, Wayne didn't know the lawyer's address and asked to see Mr. Pollard, and it was then he found out how the will read. Only then. And he was furious. He'd blamed me at the time, you see—he said to me, it was just before they arrested him, it was all my fault for getting pregnant, if if hadn't been for that he could have argued his father into giving him that money—it was my fault he'd had to kill them to get the money—but then—"

"How does the will read?" asked Delia.

"Oh, it's all tied up. And I don't think it was because of the baby, even if Mr. Burgess had made it after we knew about that. He'd just come to realize that you couldn't ever count on Wayne, and he wanted to fix it so Wayne couldn't touch the capital. It's all in trust, I think there are three trustees, Mr. Pollard's one of them. Wayne only gets the income, but I think it's quite a lot. And he was—" Meg thrust the letter at her.

It was a single page torn from a cheap tablet, and its envelope was with it. *Mrs. M. Burgess,* an address here on Grandview. "How did he know your address?"

"I don't know—maybe the other lawyer got it for him. Wayne could have claimed he was all remorseful, wanted to make up with me—" She shrugged.

It was a brief letter, and to the point, in a distinctive square sloping backhand. *Goddamn you, you had to have a kid and that's what fouled everything up—the sentimental old bastard tying up all the money just on account of that. I'd have got it out of him except for that and I thought I'd get it in the end when I get out of here but that bastard Pollard just told me about the will and it's tied up so I can't touch it. That's all your fault, you goddamn bitch, and when I get out of here I'll pay you for it the way I paid them, you and the goddamn kid.*

"That's funny," said Meg suddenly. "I said, nobody of my own there. It was a kind of nightmare. But I haven't really got anybody here either. I came back because it was home, but I haven't. Aunt Ruth wouldn't even talk to me on the phone. I wrote her a letter and told her what had happened, but she never answered. The two best friends I had in school—Linda Dowling and Sylvia Braden—Linda's teaching in Fresno, we write letters but we're both busy. And Sylvia married a medical missionary, they're in Guatemala. And I'm alone in the office, and I don't have much time to get out and meet people—"

"You came back here and got a job, after the baby was born?"

"She was born here. I divorced Wayne. Yes. I'm a receptionist—bookkeeper—whatever, for Dr. Burton. Dr. Lane Burton, he's an optometrist, the office is in the Security Bank building. I have Tammy in nursery school, that good one up on Pacific. I had just enough money so I could stay home with her till she was two, and they took her as a favor, they don't usually take them till they're three. But Mrs. Dean's been so nice." Meg put out her latest cigarette and looked up at Delia. "I've taken an awful lot of time, I'm sorry, but—Miss Riordan, what am I going to do? I don't know if the police can do anything. But I know Wayne—and I know he'll try to kill us. Somehow. He meant that letter. He thinks everything that happened is my fault, and he's going to kill us. Or try his damndest."

They looked at each other, two girls about the same age. Only

Delia Riordan was an experienced cop, and had seen all the sordid, messy, bloody, and violent and senseless things cops always see. And as a cop she had to know something of the law. She looked at Wayne Burgess' letter, and thought about all Meg had told her; and she thought first, schizoid personality—the doubletalk of the head doctors: a type, the egotist without an iota of empathy, grasping, childish, greedy, vindictive, erratic but not necessarily irrational. He had killed, he would kill, for what seemed to him good reason. And she thought, a letter two years old: a threat two years old. A lawyer's cautiously worded letter. What did it amount to?

It wasn't anything they could act on: and even if it was, what action would be taken? Send a squad car to check on the safety of two people every couple of hours? The squad cars in Glendale were spread thin, a few of them patrolling a lot of territory. There was no justification here for using the facilities of the police—the teletypes to Kansas City—to check on the whereabouts of Wayne Burgess. The threat was an old one; and, the proverb ran, threatened men live long.

But Delia looked at that letter, and believed it. She looked at Meg Burgess, who seemed to be a level-headed, sensible young woman, and believed her. After all, she had been married to the man; she ought to know him.

"I've got to get to work," said Meg. "Dr. Burton isn't in on Wednesdays, but there's the phone to answer, appointments, the books—" She shoved her chair back. "Is there anything the police can do?"

Delia said evenly, "I don't want to give you the doubletalk." She mentioned the squad cars, the age of the threat. "About all I can tell you is, if he contacts you or utters another threat, get back to us fast. Then we can check on him, try to pick him up."

"I see," said Meg. She stood up. "You can't do anything really. I can see all that—a person might make a threat and two years later not even remember it. Only not Wayne. He meant it, and he means it. I don't know how he'll try to do it, but he will. It's Tammy I'm scared for. I—I wasn't so awfully happy about the baby, because then I knew Wayne—I was so terribly afraid she'd look like him, be like him—but she's not. She's mine. She's like me—she's such a funny, placid, old-fashioned sort of little girl. And you know, she's learning to read already, I've worked with her and she knows the alphabet and all her numbers and she can read a lot of the words in that McGuffey Reader I got at the Christian bookstore. She's—all I've got, you see, and I'm all Tammy's got. But I can see there's nothing you can do."

It was an axiom of police work, don't get emotionally involved. Delia said, "I'm sorry, Mrs. Burgess. I believe you. I can certainly sympathize with you. All I can say is—take all the usual precautions, keep your doors locked. And if he does contact you, makes another threat, then—"

"Oh, yes," said Meg. "I can see your viewpoint too, in a way. At least I've told you about it. So maybe, after Wayne has murdered us, you'll know who to look for. And maybe then they'll shut him up for good, though I wouldn't bet on that. He's so good at talking himself out of things."

"If you should hear from him—"

"Get back to you." Meg nodded. And turning away, she turned back to say, "Thank you. I don't know what for. I do see your viewpoint. It's just, you're not much help, are you?"

Delia watched her start down the stairs, and she felt savagely helpless. No, they weren't much help; and police were supposed to be.

And she had a date to question Brenda about the man who'd grabbed her off the street and raped and beaten her. A seven-year-old. Jeff Forbes had abandoned his typewriter and was on the phone, his lank length slouched in his desk chair. John Poor was just taking charge of a suspect on something, brought in by a uniformed man; he and O'Connor prodded the suspect ahead of them toward an interrogation room. Suspect on the heists, or the burglaries? It was Varallo's day off, he was probably at home spraying or mulching his roses, whatever you did to roses: an unlikely hobby for a cop, but they were human like everybody else. There was Bob Rhys, on night watch, helping his mother raise Cairn terriers. And she'd heard this and that about Lieutenant O'Connor's unlikely blue Afghan hound named Maisie.

Delia got up and went over to Forbes's desk; he was just rolling a 510 form in triplicate into his typewriter.

"What are we for?" she asked him. "Catching X's or shutting stable doors?"

"After five years at LAPD, you ask me?" said Forbes. "Why?"

Delia told him, succinctly, about Meg Burgess. "I believe her. She knows the man. And what can we do? Just damn all. So he guns down the pair of them—her and a four-year-old—so we know who to look for. What are we here for?"

"To shut stable doors," said Forbes. He passed a hand over his lantern jaw. "That's a bastard. But there's nothing we can do about it until something happens. If it does. Nine times out of ten, threats fizzle out."

"There's always the one that doesn't."

The phone buzzed on his desk and he picked it up. "Forbes . . . O.K., what's the address? We're on it." He stood up, adjusting the shoulder holster automatically. "You seem to be the only detective here, you may as well come along. Body in an alley over on Chevy Chase—funny it wasn't spotted before, middle of the morning, but I'd guess a few people did and just didn't want to get involved. People. Well, let's go look at it."

CHAPTER TWO

The body was that of an elderly man, and contrary to Forbes's pessimism, nobody might have spotted it before the trash-collection truck came by. It was in a narrow alley behind a block of small apartments on Chevy Chase, and at first glance it looked absolutely anonymous. There wasn't any obvious mark to say how he had died, and nothing of any significance around the corpse. "Sometime last night, at a guess," said Forbes. "He's stiff, rigor's set in." He squatted and investigated the pockets of the old tan pants, faded shirt, ragged jacket. The only thing on the body was a dirty handkerchief.

The trash collectors went on their way. The squad car was standing by; Forbes used the radio in it to call up the morgue wagon. But before they sent the body in, he and Delia split to cover every building on the block, see if anybody knew him. "He might have been on his way home, for all we know."

The nearest apartment was a four-unit place, and only one tenant was home, a Mrs. Willett. She came fluttering and chattering to look, said she'd never seen him before. "And of course we know everyone here, that is the Stacks and Rossiters—the couple downstairs on the other side are new, Polish or something, but they're just young people. I don't know where they work. We don't know anybody on the rest of the block, I suppose he could live around somewhere— goodness, what an awful thing—" It had made her morning.

They found eight people at home, from forty-eight apartment units on the block; nobody recognized the corpse. "So we take him in," said Forbes. "Maybe his prints are on file someplace, or eventually somebody'll miss him." It was getting on for noon then. He volunteered to write the report.

Delia had lunch at a sandwich counter on Broadway, thinking about Meg Burgess, and went to talk to Brenda Quigley, now home from the hospital. The address was on Melrose, and she went the long way round up Central to avoid Brand Boulevard; Brand, the main drag through town, was a mess these days, the long-drawn-out renovations seeming endless, sidewalks torn up and only one lane open in each direction.

Mrs. Quigley was reluctant, protective. "Just keeping it all in her mind—she's already told the other police all she could—" Delia was diplomatic. But the feminine touch didn't turn up anything new from a submissive, still scared Brenda. The man had been a big fat man, well, maybe about as tall as Daddy, and he smelled funny—dirty, and maybe like gasoline. She didn't remember anything about his clothes. She thought the car was blue. Just a car. Which was about what Varallo and Katz had heard from her already.

It added up: by the M.O., and what the other two—Sandra Tally and Alice Nutting—had said. A big dirty man forcing them into a car. It didn't offer any leads where to look, but of course they were working it in the time-honored way—the routine, the legwork. There was a list of sex offenders in their records, men to find and question: as there was a list of men with robbery records, to question on the various heists; and men with records of burglary. It was a tedious way to go at it, but sometimes it was the only way.

Delia landed back at the office just as O'Connor and Katz emerged from an interrogation room and watched an erstwhile suspect hasten downstairs. He might have looked big and fat to the little girls: a hulking lout about twenty, in ragged old clothes. "No good?" asked Delia.

"Like nine out of ten," said O'Connor sourly. "They rove around. Couldn't say where he was. Nobody else can. He could be, he couldn't be. Pedigree of indecent exposure, stealing underwear."

"Suggestive, but only just," said Katz. Delia sat down at her desk and began telling them about Meg Burgess, and in two minutes O'Connor told her to forget it.

"Nervous females, imagining things. A threat two years old yet? Lady, we've got enough to think about without reaching way out into left field. Nothing we could do about it anyway."

"Well, you needn't tell me that," said Delia. And about then John Poor brought in another possible suspect from the sex list and O'Connor joined him on the questioning. Another one who might fit the description. And another one who turned out to be a waste of time. He had the right record for it, he'd been charged with child molestation once, but last Monday afternoon when Brenda had been snatched off the street at about three-fifteen, he'd been sitting down at the California Employment Office on Colorado awaiting an interview, with several witnesses to prove it. At least that was definite: he was out of it.

When Delia started home at six-ten, through ninety-six-degree heat, she was still thinking about Meg Burgess. Which was a futile enterprise.

"Well, surprise, surprise," said O'Connor, looking up as Varallo came in on Thursday morning. "Quiet night for once. The night watch never got called out at all. That new body isn't identified yet, maybe never will be—anonymous bum. And the word is, it's supposed to go to ninety-eight today."

"You're just full of good news," said Varallo. Poor and Forbes came in with Katz behind them.

"And there's more. The paperwork's all caught up, pending something new, and we can all go out in the sun hunting the punks," said O'Connor genially.

Poor groaned and sat down at his desk. "Out of six heists, one down. And what says the rapist is in our records?"

"Not one goddamned thing," said O'Connor. "He's probably in somebody's. If we had a decent description to give L.A. or NCIC—"

That, of course, was another fact of life that just made it more difficult. No court would accept the identification of such young children; possibly they couldn't be sure of an identification themselves. They couldn't describe the car with any accuracy: two of them said it was blue, one said green; it could be a two-door or four-door—they'd all been raped in the front seat, so some evidence should show up in the car if they ever found it.

"Somebody," said Katz, "ought to mind the store in case a new one goes down."

"Many hands," said O'Connor with his sharklike grin, "make light work. There's still a hell of a list of possibles to look at."

They divided up the lists: the rest of them started out, but Varallo lingered to consult the County Guide for an unfamilar street name, the top address on his list. Spotting it, he went down the stairs fishing out his keys, and in the lobby was hailed by Sergeant Duff on the desk.

"I think you'll want to talk to this lady, Varallo. Mrs. Rohmer. This is Detective Varallo."

"Yes?"

She was a fat elderly woman in decent dowdy clothes, looking distressed; she peered nearsightedly at tall Varallo and cut across Duff's voice agitatedly. "Well, like I was just telling the sergeant, it's my brother, he's gone, disappeared, and if anything's happened to him I'll never forgive myself—I knew I shouldn't leave him alone, he's really not fit to look after himself, I mean, he's spry enough but not just, well, as mentally good as he was—only I hadn't seen May, my sister that is, in months, and I've only been gone since Tuesday, she lives in Upland—but my heavens, when I got home just now and there's not a sign of Delbert anywhere and the house wide open—"

"Could you give us a description of him, Mrs. Rohmer?" Varallo saw where Duff's mind had leaped.

"Well, his name's Delbert Crane, he's sixty-nine, about six feet, I don't know what he weighs—blue eyes, he hasn't much hair left—Clothes? Well, I don't know, he usually just wears plain old clothes, he's retired, he was a railroad engineer for the Southern Pacific, only of course it's this Amtrak thing now—"

"Mrs. Rohmer, I'm sorry to ask you, but I think you ought to look at a body which showed up yesterday. It could be—is there anyone else in the family, your husband, who could identify—"

"Oh, my heavens. A body. My heavens. No, my husband's been dead ten years. I'll come. But how could Del be dead? He doesn't have anything wrong with him—no, it's all right, I'll have to find out—"

Varallo took her down to the morgue, trusting that Dr. Goulding wasn't in the middle of the autopsy; but he wasn't in yet. Mrs. Rohmer took one look at the body from the alley and burst into tears. Varallo led her out, sat her down on the bench in the hall, and brought her a paper cup of water from the fountain.

"Oh, dear. Oh, thank you. Yes, it's him. Del." She was a sensible sort of woman; she pulled herself together and gave him the relevant facts. Delbert Crane, and he'd lived with her at her house on Stanley Avenue. He'd been a bachelor, and her children were all grown and married, and he had a good pension, it had worked out fine for both of them. "But what did he die of? Where did you say you found him?"

"We don't know yet, Mrs. Rohmer. There'll have to be an autopsy. He was in an alley behind a block of apartment houses on Chevy Chase." Stanley was just a block away, he remembered. "Maybe on his way home from somewhere—"

She stared at him and shook her head. "Oh, my heavens. Oh, dear. As if it wasn't bad enough he's dead. I knew I shouldn't have left him—but he'd seemed to have come to his senses after the policeman brought him home that time—oh, my heavens, he must have been doing it again—if I'd been there—of course I kept an eye on him—"

"Doing what?"

"A terrible thing," she said, her tears starting up again. "Always been a perfectly respectable moral man—I was flabbergasted—I thought then, he must be getting senile, and he was only sixty-nine—Why, it was last year, the police caught him—oh, dear—looking in people's windows, you know, what they call a peeping something—"

"Peeping Tom. I see," said Varallo.

"Yes, that's it. Of course he'd never done anything wrong before, and the policeman just sort of gave him a talking-to, and you'd better believe so did I, and he seemed ashamed of himself, I thought he'd had his lesson. But if he was in that alley—that's where it was before, he was looking in windows at those apartments—he must have been at it again, and had a stroke or something—"

Varallo let her talk it out some more. At least he was safe in air conditioning for another hour; a report to write on this. The old fellow, bored and nosy, out peering into windows and maybe having a heart attack. The autopsy would tell them.

When he got back to the office, before he started the report, he called back to see if Goulding was in yet, had looked at the corpse. "Just to glance at it," said Goulding. "I couldn't say off the bat. Suspected homicide?"

"Hardly," said Varallo. "Of course you never know."

He was in the middle of the report when O'Connor came back with one of the possibles from the sex-offender list, William Barger; Varallo sat in on questioning him. Barger had a pedigree of exposure, child molestation, and attempted rape; he was, expectably, an unsavory-looking character, a big paunchy man going bald at thirty, and he sat glowering at them and repeating monotonously, "I haven't done nothing lately. I'm off P.A., I'm clean."

If he was, it was only in the colloquial sense. After prodding at him for forty minutes, they left him in the interrogation room and came out to the office, and O'Connor said, "I like him, Vic. He's the right size and shape for it. And no alibi for any of them."

"Oh, yes. Which is negative evidence. I like him enough, I'll say let's hang onto him and get a search warrant for his wheels."

"Bingo," agreed O'Connor, and reached for the phone. They could hold him for twenty-four hours without a warrant. Varallo took him over to the jail and parked him. The search warrant for Barger's car came through in an hour; it was an ancient Pontiac sedan, two-door. By then Poor, Katz, and Forbes had brought in two more men to question. Varallo routed Rex Burt and Gene Thomsen out of the lab and chased them down to the garage when the car was towed in.

"And don't dawdle on it, boys. We'll have to let him go by noon tomorrow, and if there's any evidence to be got, we want it now. You know the obvious things to look for—traces of blood, semen—"

"Fibers off the kids' clothes I don't think," said Burt. "If it'd been winter, and they'd had on wool coats, sweaters, possible, but cotton dresses— Yeah. I also remember that the first kid has an unusual blood type, AB and Rh positive. That'd be a clincher, almost. See what shows up."

Nothing had by the end of shift; but lab work took time. They questioned seven men that afternoon and got nothing helpful at all. Out on the street the temperature climbed to ninety-nine; later in the year the humidity would be higher, but that was small comfort. And tomorrow, with more of the legwork to do, they'd be minus one man; it was Katz's day off. Of course they'd have Delia back; but, competent as their female detective might be, when it came to leaning on the tough louts Varallo was old-fashioned enough to think that the other sex was better equipped for it.

On Friday morning Varallo and Poor came in together to find O'Connor already in and Delia just sitting down. She said to Varallo,

"Just to round out opinion I'll throw this at you," and told him about Meg Burgess.

"Oh, for God's sake," said O'Connor in the middle of it, "I told you it's nothing. Imaginative females."

"I don't know, Charles." Varallo was interested. "Offbeat, but the girl may be absolutely right. She ought to know her own husband. But of course there's nothing we can do about it as it stands."

"I *know*," said Delia. "I just feel there ought to be something we can do, Vic. If there's anything in it—"

"Men who go around threatening murder seldom follow up on it," said O'Connor impatiently.

"*Davvero?*" said Varallo gently. "Gene Conway did, *amico*." O'Connor's head jerked around and his mouth tightened.

"Who?" asked Delia.

Varallo laughed; and of course now they could laugh about Gene Conway, who was long dead. "Before your time, lady. A fellow who held a long grudge on Charles and did his damndest to do him in. My God, he did. And at the beginning, this stubborn Irishman poohpoohing the whole idea."

"Why?" asked Delia curiously. "What happened?"

Oddly enough, even though it had come out all right in the end, none of them liked to remember that couple of weeks. Nobody said anything for a moment, and then Varallo said, "Oh, he got convinced in the end and we went out hunting him—of course the Feds were after him too, and we all sort of caught up to him at once and he got clobbered. So did my old Chevy—he was in it, with Charles taking pot shots at him all the way up Brand Boulevard at ninety miles an hour."

"Good heavens," said Delia, startled. "How many people got killed?"

"Oh, there was a siren behind us stopping traffic, and of course the Feds—"

"Insulting my marksmanship," said O'Connor.

Delia looked from him to Varallo and closed her mouth. Burt came in with a manila envelope in one hand and laid it on O'Connor's desk. "Sorry we couldn't do you any good on that car."

"Oh, hell and damnation!" said O'Connor.

"Sorry," repeated Burt. "This and that in it, but no blood, no semen, nothing to say the kids were ever near it. We didn't miss anything."

"Well, that's that," said Varallo philosophically. "He looked like a damn good bet, but if he was it, something would have shown in his car. Unless he has access to another one, and that we don't know."

"And that we'll find out," said O'Connor in something like a snarl, "but right now we'll have to let him go, damn it. You can call the jail."

Burt went out, passing Dr. Goulding in the doorway. Goulding came in, laid another manila envelope on O'Connor's desk and sat down in Katz's chair. "I thought you'd like to know you've got a homicide. That Crane fellow. Rather a funny thing."

"Don't tell me," said Varallo. "What killed him?"

"I suppose you could say he was beaten to death." Goulding stroked his bald head absently, and brought out the inevitable cigar. "The worst of the damage was done, I think, when somebody kicked him—good hard kicks. That may have knocked him down—probably did—and then somebody jumped on him. The spleen was ruptured, there are a couple of broken ribs and one of them punctured a lung. The actual cause of death was a fractured skull, but he'd taken a beating. No sign that he fought back, I think somebody just jumped him from behind, maybe."

"But there was hardly a mark on him," objected Forbes. "At least, he was stiff and he'd been there awhile, and cyanosis—"

"Yes, well, what you put down to cyanosis were some dandy contusions," said Goulding.

"Oh, for God's sake, as if we needed something new."

"Well, there's a place to start," said Varallo. "He'd been spotted as a Peeping Tom before. He may have been at it again, and maybe somebody caught him at it and got annoyed."

"Anywhere along that block," said Forbes. "Did he do much moving after he'd been jumped, Doctor?"

Goulding sniffed and regarded his cigar. "He might have crawled a little way. Or he might not. His trousers weren't torn. I don't think he'd have got far."

Part of the annoyance of the job, of course, was that they were forever having to drop one thing temporarily and work on another. Forbes and Delia looked at each other resignedly and got up.

By noon the temperature hit a hundred degrees.

Varallo didn't get home until nearly seven o'clock. It was nearly dark as he turned in the drive of the house on Hillcroft Road, and Laura had the garage light on for him. He came in the back door, and had hardly kissed her when three-year-old Ginevra pounced on his legs like a small limpet, shouting at the top of her voice, and he laughed and swung her up into his arms.

"For heaven's sake, Ginny, hush up," said Laura. "I've just got the baby to sleep. Everything's ready, Vic—you look tired to death, want a drink before dinner?"

"I deserve one after the day we've had." Ginevra squirmed out of his arms and began to pursue Gideon Algernon Cadwallader, who had just stalked in and was weaving around Laura's legs. At least that was a sign that five-month-old Johnny was sound asleep; Gideon always played assiduous watchcat until he was.

O'Connor got home, to Virginia Avenue, at seven-thirty. He opened the driveway gate and braced himself, and Maisie fell on him delightedly, shoving him against the gate. "Down, damn it," said O'Connor. He supposed he should have got around to the obedience training, but with his schedule, damn it, and overtime when they were busy, it was just too much to expect. Maisie, who was now nearly three feet high at the shoulder, pushed past him into the kitchen waving her plumy tail.

"Better late than never," said Katharine. "I was starving, but I've got your dinner in the oven. You look as if you need a drink. I don't have to ask what kind of day you had."

"By God, it's nice to get home," said O'Connor. He looked at her, his slim svelte dark Katharine, added, "Damn nice," and kissed her soundly again. All that talk this morning—he held her tighter, thinking back to that time she'd taken Conway's slug in the back, and they hadn't known whether she'd make it— She squealed and he let her go. "You can build me that drink—I want to sit down."

A raucous bellow was raised down the hall, and Katharine said, "Sorry, you'll have to wait on yourself—the offspring just woke up."

He trailed down there five minutes later to have a look at five-month-old Vincent Charles, still yelling. At least he'd learned to sleep at night.

Stan Pollard got into International Airport in Los Angeles at five o'clock on Friday afternoon. He'd never been here before, and after a look at it as the plane came in to approach landing, he decided it was a monstrosity he'd be glad to leave. A city was one thing: a conglomerate sprawl like this was mind-boggling. On the ground, out of the terminal, the astonishing heat was insult added to injury. In March! he thought. And millions of people living here voluntarily—

Fortunately he was good at maps. After a look at the one he'd bought at the terminal, he found an air-conditioned coffee shop with a vacant booth and devoted some time to studying the thing, which looked like the product of a bevy of drunken spiders. Then he found the Hertz agency and rented a car.

By seven-thirty he had found his way to Glendale and was checking in at a motel. He'd driven four hundred miles in the last three days, and by the time he'd had an indifferent meal at the nearest restaurant he was too tired, and he decided it was too late, to see the girl tonight. He went back to the motel and fell into bed.

But by ten o'clock on Saturday morning, with the help of a local map, he found the apartment and was pushing the bell. Almost at once the door was opened just a crack, and he saw there was a chain up inside. Good: a cautious girl. "Who is it?"

He had a card ready, and inserted it through the crack. "Mr. Pollard asked me to come and see you, Mrs. Burgess. I'm his nephew —partner in the firm."

"Oh." The card was taken. She unfastened the chain and let him in, immediately refastened it. She was, he thought with a little surprise, a damned pretty girl. Well, why shouldn't she be? By his pictures, Wayne Burgess was a good-looker too. He just hoped he wasn't going to scare her to death. The little girl was there too, a cute kid with big solemn dark eyes, sitting on the couch with a book and a stuffed cat.

He started out easily. "You had a letter from my uncle, I think. Now, we don't know that there's anything in this at all, maybe we're both imagining things, though that's not exactly Uncle Olly's strongest point—but after thinking it over, we thought I'd better come and talk to you about it. Your ex-husband—"

"Does Mr. Pollard know about it?" she asked. "About Wayne—" She checked herself, glancing at the child. "Tammy darling, would you please go into your room for a while? I've got to to talk to this gentleman."

"Can't we go to the park, Mama?"

"I said it's too hot for the park today. Please, darling." And as the little girl went obediently down the hall, she turned back to him. "I suppose you'd better sit down. Do you mean you know about Wayne wanting to kill us?"

He sat down suddenly on the edge of a chair and stared at her. "Does he? Uncle only knew he said so two years back. And we aren't sure where he is. Uncle thinks—well, that he could be dangerous, and you ought to know."

"Oh, yes," she said. This was an unpretentious little apartment; the window air conditioner only lessened the heat to a bearable limit. Thinking of the Burgess money, he reflected that she certainly wasn't greedy, at least. "I think you'd better see Wayne's letter. The one he wrote me two years ago."

He read that and digested it. "I think," he told her, "we'd better see the police. I don't know—"

"I've seen them." She sat on the couch with her arms folded almost as if she was cold. "A very nice policewoman. They can't do anything. And in a way you can see why. She said it was two years ago, he might not mean it any more, and unless he—contacts me, makes another threat, there's nothing they can do."

Stan read the letter again. "Well, I've got a little more to tell them. Which I think they ought to hear. By God, I do. The more I think about that, the more I think—"

"I got the chain for the door, one for the back too. But I don't know—what he might try to do."

"No," he said thoughtfully. "But you think he will try?"

"Yes," she said lowly. "As soon as I knew he was—out—when I got your uncle's letter—I knew that." He saw belatedly that she wasn't putting on an act of indifference or courage; she was scared to death, but in cold control of herself. Quite a girl, this was. "What more do you know—about Wayne?"

He told her absently. "This might put a different face on it, with the police. At any rate—"

"I don't think it will. It doesn't tell you definitely he's here, or going to do anything. You want me to come with you—but I can't take Tammy there."

"Isn't there someone here you can leave her with?"

She shook her head. "Not here. Mrs. Wiley's not very careful about Carol Sue and she's only a year older—she leaves her hours without checking. The Childs aren't home much, they have a store somewhere—and old Mrs. Kemp—no. I could"—she considered—"Tammy plays with a little girl up the block, Wanda Wyatt. Mrs. Wyatt's all right—reliable. I could see if she's home."

He waited for her to get the child, her handbag. As they went out he asked about the other tenants, and she told him the Wileys, who had the other apartment downstairs, both worked. Only old Mrs. Kemp was here all day. They were in the tiny lobby then, and a dog yapped sharp and high from behind one of the two doors. "She keeps the dog because she's getting deaf. He barks at any stranger."

"Well, that's something," said Stan.

They landed at the detective office at eleven o'clock. Delia had been out with Jeff Forbes talking to people in those apartments backing up to the alley; they hadn't got much. One woman had heard a disturbance out there last Tuesday night, couldn't say what it was, hadn't looked out, didn't know the time. They had found out where some of the tenants worked; most of them would be at work all day, and would have to be chased down. Delia was typing a follow-up report while Forbes was hunting people down at their jobs. O'Connor, Poor, and Katz were talking to a suspect in one of the interrogation rooms, and Varallo was typing a report at his desk. He abandoned it when Delia introduced Meg Burgess; he was mildly intrigued by that little tale.

Stan Pollard was brisk and forceful: not exactly a handsome young fellow, tall and bony with a long jaw, intense blue eyes, crisply conservative haircut, a good suit. "I understand you're the one Mrs. Burgess saw the other day," he told Delia. "I've got a little more to add, and maybe it'll make you think twice about this thing. Now we know that Wayne Burgess has uttered threats against Mrs. Burgess, believe he has a motive to—"

"But do we now?" said Varallo.

Pollard nodded shortly at him. "Made two years ago. Yes. My uncle's not an old bird given to flights of fancy, and he didn't like Mr. Burgess' attitude. And this was two weeks ago. He had to see Burgess—or vice versa—about the money, you see. Probate will take awhile, but meanwhile Burgess is legally entitled to some of the accumulated income. Uncle brought up the matter of that threat deliberately—sounded him about it, or tried to. And he didn't like the response he got—he said, laid on a little too thick. All the charm laid out, winsome little boy all sorry for being naughty, of course he'd forgotten all that nonsense now."

"Oh," said Meg. "You didn't tell me that. Like that? Yes, that's Wayne, covering up."

"Uncle advanced him ten thousand. To cover the probable six-month period until the estate's settled. The yearly income runs to around forty thousand—"

Varallo sat up. "Surely that's enough for anybody. So what if he can't get at the capital?"

Meg said, "You don't know how fast Wayne can go through money."

"He told Uncle—without being asked—that he wanted some peace and quiet, to get adjusted in his mind. He was going out to the old summer cabin for a few weeks, he said. The Burgesses owned it for years—nothing fancy, just a vacation spot. It's all by itself in a stand of woods, out along the Smoky Hill River. We wondered if he'd really gone there, so I went to have a look. And I don't think he's there."

"You don't think?" said Delia.

"As I say, it's a fairly lonely spot. There's a car there—a beat-up old Chevy. Registered to him. He bought it in a secondhand lot in Kansas City, paid cash for it. I found a grocery store in Russell Springs where somebody answering his description stocked up on groceries, told the clerk he was spending a vacation in a cabin in the woods. Without being asked. I prowled around there—nobody home. Not answering the door."

"I see," said Varallo. "You think that's cover."

"What else? Nominally, he's there. If anybody drops by and he's not, he was out walking in the woods. Fishing. His car's there." O'Connor had come back to the office, was sitting at his desk with one hand on the phone; he couldn't help hearing this, and directed a scowl at the little group. "But how easy just to leave it there, and walk out. Hike up the road a way, hitch a ride. To the nearest major airport."

"Where would that be?" asked Delia.

"Wichita. Go anywhere from there. Here. It's where I flew out of yesterday after a long talk with Uncle on the phone."

"That's very interesting," said Varallo, "but it's all pure speculation, Mr. Pollard, and still nothing to bring us into it. Whatever you and your uncle may think isn't evidence."

"I know that—I'm a lawyer," said Pollard tartly. "All I'm saying is, it seems to me it's a fairly good reason for you to take this seriously. Of course, this place—I'm bound to say—"

Varallo laughed. And O'Connor swiveled around in his desk chair and said in his deep voice, rather mildly for O'Connor, "Yeah, this place. You think we should go looking for evidence that this joker is here? Just drop everything else we've got on hand? Among seven million people in an area fifty miles square? If he flew in, presumably he called himself John Smith to the airline. And so what the hell if he's here? Until he makes a move at Mrs. Burgess, he's just another tourist."

And Delia said quietly, "Mrs. Burgess, you believe he does mean to kill you. Do you have any idea what he might be planning to do? Stage a fake burglary, take a shot at you from a distance—sabotage your car?"

"How the hell would she know that?" asked Pollard.

Meg said rather absently, "He won't do it the same way—try to make it look like burglary. That didn't work before. I don't know, except that I think he'll be very careful. Because if anything happens to Tammy and me, he'd be the first one you'd suspect, and he'd know that. After what he said to Mr. Pollard that time—and he won't know who I've showed his letter to. Actually I only told Linda about it, before I showed it to you."

"The only advice we can give you," said Delia, "is just what I told you before. Take precautions, don't go out alone at night, keep your doors locked—is there a good deadbolt lock on your apartment?"

"Oh, yes. There were new ones put on last year."

"And the nursery school—"

"Oh, I thought of that. Not that I think it's necessary—Mrs. Dean's terribly conscientious—but I told her my ex-husband might show up and try to get hold of Tammy. I let her think, over custody. She wouldn't let anybody even see Tammy without my permission."

"Then that should be all right. And at your job—"

"Well, I have to go to work."

Pollard asked, "So what about this fellow you work for? Could you tell him about this—maybe get his O.K. to keep the door locked?"

"Well, of course not, that's wild. Patients have to get in. No, I don't think so. He's always been very nice, but—impersonal. He's got an invalid wife, she takes most of his time away from the office, and he's going to retire next year. I—rather think if I told him, he might fire me. He doesn't like inconveniences."

"Inconveniences!" said Pollard, and made it sound like a swear word. "So Burgess is going to be very careful, and all you can tell Mrs. Burgess is to be very careful too. And for how long? Can you tell us that?" He missed the look Meg turned on him—surprised and oddly grateful.

"Nobody can tell you that," said Varallo shortly. "I see it's an invidious position—"

"I do like all the long words," said Pollard. "That is one for it, isn't it?" But he calmed down; he had the logical mind a lawyer should have. "All right, I see it. But if we're right, it's a hell of a situation for all of us." He stood up abruptly. "Just so we all understand what the situation is."

O'Connor had swiveled back to his desk and was on the phone; he didn't notice when they went out.

Varallo went back to his report. Delia lit a cigarette and sat staring at the last phrase she had typed on the 510 form for several minutes before she roused herself to get on with it.

When the night watch—which was Bob Rhys and Dick Hunter—came on at eight o'clock on Sunday night, they found evidence of a hectic day for the other detectives. Overflowing ashtrays, chairs at odd angles, a half-finished report left rolled into Forbes's typewriter, told their own story. The report, in fact, was neatly dated as of the forty-ninth of March, and Rhys said Jeff needed a vacation. But they didn't have time for any conversation; they got a call five minutes after they'd got there.

"Maybe early to yell for you guys," said Patrolman Judovic, "but we all know we've got this pervert running around, and it's a missing kid, Rhys. A five-year-old girl. We figured—"

"We're on the way," said Rhys tersely. "What's the address?"

It was Grandview Avenue, which fitted in, in a way. The other snatches had been on Melrose, Lawson Place, and Ard Eevin: the same general area northwest in the city, and this address wasn't too far away.

When they got there, it was a four-unit place, and some people were out on the street, the two patrolmen in the middle of a little crowd, and a woman carrying on loudly between sobs, and a dog barking. It was a little short-haired tan dog on the front step of the apartment, and an old lady had it on a leash.

"I do take good care of Carol Sue, nobody can say I don't, I didn't realize it was so late and her still out, just sat down to watch the TV news before I went to get her—oh, my baby—Bill, you know I take good care of our baby—"

"Then where is she?" He was a big beefy man, his voice scared and rough. "Where the hell—this goddamned sex fiend around town, we saw in the paper—you leaving her out after dark—"

"And where the hell were you anyways, watching the TV right along with me—oh, my baby—"

The old lady on the step said in a loud voice, "Riffraff! Only themselves to blame!"

"When she went to bring the kid in, she was nowhere—her tricycle just lying there." It was about twenty feet down from the entrance, lying on its side. "We've searched a couple of blocks around, as well as we could." Judovic shrugged. "Dark blocks around here, we need more manpower to cover it. The mother swears the kid wouldn't go off the block, across the street, but who knows? It was dark by seven, and she can't say what time she saw her last, except that they had dinner about six."

"Hell," said Rhys. And a girl came up to them, as they stood out of earshot of the crowd.

"Officer—I want to talk to Miss Riordan. From your headquarters. I know something about this—Miss Riordan knows—well, I have to talk to her. Please, can you call her to come?"

Rhys and Hunter looked at each other. It was the day watch that had been out on the child rapes, all three of them between three and five in the afternoon, the kids let out of the car somewhere in the same area. Rhys thought, in any case, whatever this girl had to say, it might not be a bad idea to call out a couple of the day watch. And they'd need a lot more patrolmen to cover just this block, looking. He used the radio in Judovic's squad to call Sergeant Hamilton on the desk.

CHAPTER THREE

"It was Wayne." Meg Burgess faced them tensely. O'Connor was down in the street with the other men; Delia and Varallo had come up to the apartment at Meg's insistence, and now looked at each other. "I know it! He thought Carol Sue was Tammy, and he's taken her and probably killed her. And I suppose if the Wileys knew, they'd kill me for bringing him here. But I know that's the way it has to be."

"Now, Mrs. Burgess," said Varallo, "I'm afraid you're jumping to a fairly wild conclusion there. We've had three child rapes in the last month, in just this area of town"—and that was something to do some more thinking about too—"and this is probably another in the series. There's no reason at all—"

"No," she said, "no, it isn't." She looked at Delia. "You don't know—just lately Carol Sue had taken to saying 'Yes' to whatever you asked her. I can see just what happened—he saw her out there on the sidewalk, and he thought it was Tammy—as if I'd let her be out there alone when it was almost dark—and he probably said, 'Are you the little Burgess girl?' or something, and Carol Sue said, 'Yes,' and so he took her."

And Delia had felt sorry for her, but this was wild. Wasn't it? "You can't know that, Mrs. Burgess. We don't know anything about this yet." She wouldn't listen to them; she was perfectly calm but she kept saying she knew, that was all. It had been Wayne who had taken Carol Sue.

"All I can tell you is that I know. And thank God all this commotion hasn't waked Tammy up. As if she'd have been out there—but he wouldn't know."

Varallo went back downstairs. Delia said, "As long as I'm here, let's have a look at your locks, Mrs. Burgess." Back door and front, they were good solid locks, with a generous deadbolt which couldn't be pried back with any tool.

"Don't you think it's queer?" asked Meg. "That a child should disappear from the same address where I live?"

She wasn't in any state to listen to logic, or a lecture about police routines. Delia left her to her jitters, there being nothing else to do, and started home shortly afterward. There was a crowd of patrolmen and neighborhood men out searching. But of course, she thought—which O'Connor and Varallo would be ruminating about too—if this was the rapist, it was a break in the pattern. The other three he'd snatched in broad daylight, and they'd been released not long after, in the same general area. But perverts could be erratic; after all, that was the nature of the beast.

By midnight the searchers knew that Carol Sue Wiley wasn't anywhere within a radius of several blocks. Rhys and Hunter had gone back to the office at ten o'clock when a new heist went down.

O'Connor had brushed aside Meg Burgess' wild leap with a rude word. He said now, leaning against the last squad car parked outside the apartment, "Break in the pattern—that's how these goddamned nuts are made, don't we know! She may turn up five or ten miles away in the next hour, or she may turn up— Hell! One thing I do know, Vic, we're going to do some homework over."

"Oh, by all means," said Varallo, who could add two and two just as well. They shut the search down, and went home.

Not for long. The desk got O'Connor out of bed at six o'clock. A householder up on Cumberland, leaving for work early, had found a body in the street beside his driveway, his headlights hitting it as he backed around in the street.

It wasn't light yet when Varallo and O'Connor got there; the squad car's headlights were turned on the body. "Mr. Gorman's in the house if you want to talk to him," said the uniformed man. "He was all shook up."

"I don't doubt," said O'Connor. "What the hell could he tell us?" He had called Goulding, who had cussed but would be out. They looked at the body: a very small body. Carol Sue Wiley, still in the clothes her mother had described, yellow pants and white shirt, brown sandals. She was lying crumpled up in the gutter. "Can we guess, tossed out of a car. It's dark up here." Cumberland was a quiet residential neighborhood, the street lights few and high above treetops. "Without moving her, I'd say beaten or strangled."

"And not raped." Varallo ran a hand through his hair. Her clothes didn't look disturbed. "Funny? Mrs. Burgess' wild idea—"

"The hell with that. We know, for God's sake, how these sex nuts go—from this to that. So he got his kick out of killing this time, instead—and unless we catch him he may do it again. And again. But this clinches the pattern all right, another way." Dr. Goulding drove up in his Cadillac, took a look, and said he couldn't tell them much here.

"And you'll put priority on the autopsy," said O'Connor. "Just in case anything out of the ordinary shows. I don't expect it will."

The morgue wagon came; the sun was up now, and the heat beginning to build. One job had to be done right away, and they did it: went to break the news to the parents. Then they stopped for breakfast, and got to the office a little late. It was Poor's day off; everybody else was in.

"And I'll tell you what the hell we're going to do," said O'Connor savagely. He had a stack of xeroxed pages out of Records in front of him. They were nearly at the end of their sex-offenders list, this last month. "We're going to back up a little here. Because this clinches the area six ways from Sunday, as if the Quigley kid hadn't already. Look at it." He flipped open the County Guide to the Glendale map. "Melrose, Lawson, Ard Eevin, Grandview. All right, the first three are in spitting distance of each other, all above Glenoaks, and Grandview's in the other direction, but the same area. Not such a goddamned big area. What did it look like—what does it look like all over again?"

"Somebody who lives or works there," said Katz, "as we said when the second one happened."

O'Connor was riffling the xeroxes. "So all right. We took a damned hard look at two men then—Douglas Collison and William Paley. Queer enough that two men on that list should live around there, and neither of 'em's got much of a record, but there they are. Collison on South Street, Paley on Loraine. Just blocks away. Attempted molestation, indecent exposure, but—!"

"And they were clean," said Varallo. "We looked at both cars."

Katz sighed. "There's got to be a tie-in to the area all right. This settles that. But there are other possibilities, Charles, much as I hate to mention it." He slouched back in his chair, a wiry dark man with unexpectedly brilliant dark eyes, and drew strongly on a new cigarette. "That this is his first time out. Somebody without any pedigree at all, quiet fellow who's never been suspected of any kinky ideas, husband, bachelor, church deacon maybe, all of a sudden giving in to temptation."

"Hell's fire and damnation!" said O'Connor. "Don't I know it?"

"Somebody," said Katz, "who lived around there ten years back, and roams around there hunting little girls for old times' sake."

"Damn it, we've got to work it as we can, Joe. The only way we know. All I say is, let's go back and double-check Collison and Paley, and go on from there if we have to." He got up energetically, and hitched the shoulder holster into a better position. "Occasionally we do miss things, boys."

That did happen, in the press of business. When the Tally girl had been raped, it had begun to look as if he was operating just in that area, but only begun; the Quigley girl made that almost certain, and now Carol Sue. They had got to Douglas Collison just after the second rape; O'Connor and Katz had dealt with him. His car had been clean, and he'd had an alibi of sorts for the first rape.

"Which I'm thinking twice about now," O'Connor said to Varallo as they got into the Ford. "He drives a truck for a laundry. He was on the job that day. But he could have left the laundry truck somewhere, borrowed a car from a pal—"

Whether that was so or not, their interest in Collison revived abruptly when they found him at the laundry on San Fernando Road, just back for another load, and asked him his whereabouts last Monday afternoon. "I was here. I mean on the job," he said.

"Let's see what your time sheet says," said O'Connor. They asked, and the manager said Collison had called in sick that day. "That so?" said O'Connor.

"Hell, I thought that was Tuesday," said Collison. "Oh, yeah, yeah. I was home sick. Touch of the flu or something." He was a stocky sandy-haired fellow in his thirties, with very pale blue eyes that moved constantly. He had been charged four times with exposing himself to children: no violence in his record, but as any cop knew, the sex freaks had a way of going from one thing to another, and usually bad to worse.

So they were interested in him all over again, and brought him in to talk to some more. He was nervous and shy of them; he said they'd lose his job for him. His mother could say he'd been home last Monday—all day, he'd been sick in bed. She'd been there.

He lived with her on South Street, just off Pacific. Varallo went to talk to her, and she said sure, Doug had been home all day that day. But she didn't like cops, and she'd know by the question they were trying to pin Doug down on something. She was a scrawny, shrewish-faced woman, and she said bitterly, "Always suspecting him of something—always after him. Doug wouldn't do nothing bad—just because he got a little excited a few times and—I don't know why you got to be down on him all the time."

Varallo didn't believe the alibi; it came too quick and ready. If they leaned on her a little she might admit it. He had looked over the reports on Collison, and his car was a fourteen-year-old Ford. "Would you mind telling me whose car that is in the drive, Mrs. Collison?" It was a Hornet about four years old, light blue.

"Well, it's mine, of course. No, Doug doesn't drive it. At least, not usually."

Varallo passed that on to O'Connor, and they put in a request for a search warrant on the car. Before it came through, Goulding came in with the autopsy report, and Katz was behind him.

"I've got nothing for you," said Goulding. "I didn't think I would. She was strangled manually and that's that. Short and sweet. She wasn't raped—her clothes were intact. The only other thing I can tell you, it was probably done immediately after she was picked up last night—did somebody say between six and seven? Roundabout then, or up to seven-thirty."

"Not even an attempt at rape." O'Connor massaged his heavy jaw. "So he's graduated. Just as I said."

"They will do it," agreed Goulding, who knew as much or more about the sex freaks. "The new kick. I've been looking at a city map, and it seems to me—"

"Oh, we got there a while ago," said O'Connor.

"And we can forget about Paley again," said Katz. He was leaning back with closed eyes, looking deceptively lazy. "I don't know where he was when the first one got snatched, but he didn't pick up the Quigley girl—he was helping a neighbor move. Loading a U-haul truck, with a family of five watching him."

"And he had an alibi of sorts on the second one, he was at a movie, and the ticket-seller halfway identified him," said O'Connor. "But I think I'm liking Collison all over again."

"Pray you lay hands on him soon, Charles," said Goulding quietly. "He seems to get the urge pretty damn often. He won't stop now, you know. Not until you stop him."

"Oh, you needn't tell me." O'Connor looked at Varallo. "You think, fetch Mrs. Collison in and lean on her?"

"Let's see what shows on the car." And that was at two o'clock; Goulding went out, and three minutes later the desk buzzed O'Connor and told him he had a new homicide.

Delia and Forbes had been out again on the Crane thing. It was a nuisance of a little case, no handle on it, or not much of one: the kind of simple case that often demanded the most tedious legwork.

They had split up the apartment houses on that block; most of the tenants were working people and had to be traced down on their jobs. In most cases the tenants at home could tell them where the others worked. And by noon on Monday they had just about finished talking to them. The tenants all looked like ordinary honest citizens; they had all heard about the body found in the alley, but nobody remembered any disturbance there last Tuesday night, except the one woman; nobody knew anything about it. And they all seemed to be transparently truthful witnesses, which was frustrating.

They didn't like to file cases away unsolved, and this looked like such a simple case, but they weren't getting anywhere on it, and Forbes was restless.

They stopped at a sandwich shop for lunch, and he said over coffee, "Damn it, with this new homicide and all, we'd better file this one away. We're not getting any place. I'm thinking now Crane may have been farther off, maybe a couple of blocks away, and somebody chased him."

"Mmm," said Delia, thinking about the homicide too. And she knew just what the rest of them were thinking about it, and more or less what they'd be doing. "We never found that one couple—the new tenants in the corner place right where he was found. Nobody knows them."

"What the hell?" said Forbes. "Nobody else there heard anything. I'm going back to the office, they'll be needing another hand—you can write the report on it. The final report."

"Well," said Delia, finishing her coffee, "I was trained to be thorough, Jeff." They'd been using the Mercedes; she dropped him off at headquarters and—being thorough—proceeded on to a last bit of legwork. It was so often the tiresome, time-consuming legwork that paid off in the end.

At least it hadn't got any hotter today; it had stopped at about ninety-eight.

She went back to that apartment, found Mrs. Willett at home, and asked who owned the place. Mrs. Willett didn't know, but they paid rent to the T.R.C. Management Corporation in Los Angeles.

The address was on Hill Street downtown. Delia took the freeway, where traffic wasn't bad at this time of day, and then spent the half hour she'd saved hunting for a parking space. Finally she found one, plodded back two blocks and rode up to the sixth floor in a disconcertingly silent elevator. T.R.C. Management Corporation had a slot of an office at the end of a corridor; she went in and showed the badge to a bucktoothed girl at a desk, told her what she wanted.

"*Police?* What on earth's it all about?"

"Just a little information." She repeated the address.

"For heaven's sake. We've got apartment buildings all over the place, and Sally's out to lunch—she knows the files."

"If you'd just have a look," said Delia sweetly.

"For heaven's sake—" She was gone some time in an inner office, finally came back with a file envelope. "I guess this is it—it's the only one we seem to have in Glendale. The tenants are Willett, Stack, Rossiter, and Walowsky."

"The Walowskys," said Delia. There was a name on the mailbox, of course, but that was all they'd known. "You do have references, don't you? An employer's name?"

"Oh, sure. It says here, ADAM WARWICK MEN'S TAILOR. It's on Wilshire. I wish I knew what this was all about."

"Not very much at all, really," said Delia. "A lot of police work is pretty boring." She took down the address, walked back to the car, and started for West Hollywood.

It was a severely handsome store front, just before West Hollywood turned into Beverly Hills. Wondering academically how much Adam Warwick might charge for a suit like that in the window—a poem in light-gray tweed—she went into a deeply carpeted, barely furnished small room sans counter or merchandise. A discreet bell sounded, and after a moment a suavely tailored fortyish man appeared from a door at one side. He looked very surprised to see Delia, and stared at the badge with consternation. He said, "I am with a client at the moment—I'm afraid—"

"I just want to know if Mr. Walowsky works here."

"Walowsky—yes, of course—he's one of our tailors. But police—" He had a sleek mustache, which he fingered nervously. "I hope he's not in any trouble—I can't imagine—"

"We just think he may be a witness to something," said Delia. "I'd like to talk to him if he's here now."

"Yes, well—" The man twisted his mustache, looking doubtful. "I don't know that you'd get far. George is a fine tailor, very good man and so on, but his English isn't his strongest point. He's only been here a couple of years, he's studying for citizenship, but he doesn't seem to be getting very far with his English."

"I'd like to see him." He shrugged and went away through a door at the back. A couple of minutes later another man came in there. He looked at Delia and blinked in surprise.

"Mr. Winkelman say police. To help police—me?" He was a rather handsome man, stocky and dark with friendly eyes. He smiled. "No good English. I work, work, is terrible to talk. But good citizen to be we—want to be. How help I police? You tell slow, I try." He laughed infectiously, and Delia smiled at him. "You have German any?"

"I'm afraid not." Two years of high-school German would be a broken reed.

"German, that I know. Me and my Anna, our—" he groped for the word and substituted, "mamas and papas, they come away from Communists after war—me, in Poland never was, in Germany am— am—"

"Born."

"Yes, and Anna also. Anna is more smart than me," he said. "Good well tailor not to talk must to work," and he laughed again. "Anna"—he hunted in his mind, looking frustrated, and made violent whirling motions around his head. "The ladies' hair curls Anna."

Delia nodded. "I want to ask you if you had heard anything about a body being found near your apartment. A corpse." He looked blank, and she did some groping too and said, *"Ein Mensch tot."*

"Ah? At where?"

"The alley behind your apartment. An old man." She wasn't surprised at his sudden expression of shock; he and his wife did no mingling with the other residents, undoubtedly because of the language. "He was found there last Wednesday morning, he'd been beaten to death. *Schlagen."*

He said something rapid and violent in another tongue. He looked at her with wild eyes. He said incredulously, "Dead? Not believe—dead to be."

Delia asked sharply, "Do you know anything about it, Mr. Walowsky?"

He backed away from her. He had gone dead white. "But terrible," he stammered. "Good citizen to be—forever nothing bad I do—but honest must be. For truth. But—" Astonishingly he began to blush. He looked frightened and deeply embarrassed. "But you—cannot I tell. No, no. Not to lady. You—*polizei* bring, I talk at."

"I am *polizei,"* said Delia patiently.

He waved his arms at her excitedly. "No, no—*polizei männlich!"*

"Oh," said Delia. "You stay here and wait?"

He nodded, and now he was looking morose. She looked up and down the block, spotted a public phone, and called back to headquarters. Waiting, she reflected that ideally she ought to get O'Connor to come: if anybody could be described as a male policeman, it was O'Connor. Instead she got Varallo, who said, "What the hell? We've got our hands full here, woman. What do you need me for?"

"Any of you will do, you're all the right sex," said Delia. "Why, what's been going on?"

"Just a new homicide."

They were still in the middle of taking the first statements on it, and it looked like one of those simple spur-of-the-moment homicides that could be hell to work. Of course it was early to say.

The corpse was Fred Schultz of Schultz and Moore Realtors on Glenoaks. Fifty-two, family man. He had started out for lunch late, at about one-thirty, to his car in the parking lot behind the building: a small single building occupied only by the realty firm. A minute later the two stenos and one salesman left in the office heard shots, and all rushed out the back door to the lot. Schultz was dead beside his car, and all three of them had seen a man running across the lot. The salesman chased him, but was too far behind; the man jumped into a car on the side street and took off.

"It was a two-door white Ford," he told the patrolmen first on the scene. "A two-door white Ford, I'm positive—for God's sake, I never saw the plate, it was side on to me—"

Schultz had been shot in the head and body, probably three slugs. He had fallen onto the hood of his car, and there were powder burns on him, so the gunman had been close; they towed the car in for printing. Burt said querulously they'd get to it when they could, they were still working on Mrs. Collison's Hornet. Varallo had got the address and gone to see Mrs. Schultz, who had promptly fallen into hysterics; he had to call an ambulance for her.

Now they had the two stenos, Maria Arrellanes and Louise Kelly, in making statements, and they were still pretty excited and shaken but trying to be helpful. They both said the man was tall and thin, either bald or with a short haircut, wearing a white shirt and dark pants. The salesman, Robert Garfunkel, said he was medium height— "But he ran sort of bent over, so maybe he was as tall as the girls say, but I don't think so." The girls were both small; he could have looked bigger to them. All of them said nobody would have a reason to kill Mr. Schultz, he was a wonderful man, good employer, honest, generous, always fair, everybody liked him.

Somebody hadn't. When they could talk to his wife, she might have something to offer. They'd talk to everybody he'd known, look at his finances, his recent dealings—there was never any guessing what might set off a homicide.

Meanwhile, Varallo and O'Connor had got stuck doing the spade-work on it, while the others went out to finish cleaning up the sex list; there wasn't much of it left. This second time around, they were liking Collison. Wait and see what showed on the car. But while it was significant that all four cases had occurred in that area, it needn't say X lived there. It was still up in the air.

Except for the one heister they'd turned up last week, the heists looked like lost causes, as a lot of them always were. The burglaries too, probably: no prints, no leads, most of them looking like pro jobs.

And at this end of a day, here was their female detective calling for a back-up. Varallo heard the address and swore. It was four-thirty. He'd be home late again.

He called Laura and started for West Hollywood in the Gremlin. And what the hell Delia was doing at a men's tailor shop—

She told him. "I don't know what, but he seems to know something. He went into the back a while ago and came out with a hat—apparently he's ready to go somewhere."

"Well, it's the end of the workday," said Varallo. "Now, why couldn't you have found an Italian? I don't know a word of German, and as for Polish—"

George Walowsky, however, had fetched something besides his hat: an English-German dictionary. He bowed nervously to Varallo, who put him in the passenger seat of the Gremlin and began, "You know something about the dead man?"

"I tell around—about. Yes. Terrible, terrible." He leafed through the little book. "Please, to make him dead not intend. Never. I am—was—" He scrabbled at the pages. "Angry. Angry! Yes! I could not to young lady such a thing talk. You, me, men all, yes?" He sighed. "But terrible! In prison before even citizen."

"What happened?" asked Varallo loudly.

"Was moon," said Walowsky. "Bright in window. My Anna and me, we is in bed—love make—and Anna scream, I look—is man in window see us—scare my Anna! I run out door—end door?"

"Back door."

"Ja. I catch! I am angry—angry—bad spy at us, dirty! Not mean dead make. Not know is dead."

"Well, I will be damned," said Varallo.

"Prison?" said Walowsky morosely. "I see Anna before?"

"Yes, yes," said Varallo. He got out of the car and told that to Delia. "And why the hell he couldn't have just told you—"

"What, a respectable young lady without a wedding ring? Poor man. We thought it was something like that. It'll be called involuntary manslaughter, I suppose. Suspended sentence."

"Naturally, and meanwhile there's all the damn paperwork on it, and at least a couple of court appearances. And that Edelman's due for arraignment tomorrow, somebody'll have to cover that. And now this new thing to work— You go home. I'll ferry him back to jail, and he'll make bail and be out as soon as he's arraigned. I don't know why everything has to come along at once."

Pollard had found Meg's office and insisted on taking her out to lunch. "I don't know any places. You tell me. Somewhere we can have a drink." It was a dark cozy place called Damon's, with private booths on one side. He made an issue of the drink, and she ordered a vodka gimlet.

"Now, what about that thing last night?" She had called the motel to tell him about it.

"I know it was Wayne," she said. She looked tense and tired. The air conditioning was going full blast in here, and she'd put on the jacket that matched her sleeveless dress. "They kept saying it was the same one who raped those little girls—it's been in the papers—but then this morning they came to tell the Wileys—about finding her—it was before I left for work, and you could hear Mrs. Wiley all over the place, thanking God her baby hadn't been raped. Just—killed. And that's not like the other one. He's let them go."

"That kind isn't predictable. I don't know," he said.

"I do. In my bones," said Meg. "I'm sorry for her, but I don't think she really loved Carol Sue all that much—she used to slap her and call her a nuisance. At least I know Tammy's safe at Mrs. Dean's, and when we're at home. I won't take her to the park any more—not the one across the street, there's one about five blocks away with swings and sandboxes, she loves it—but it's too hot anyway."

He wasn't sure what he thought about this conviction; it sounded irrational; the police should know their own business. She looked tired and he told her to finish her drink. The steak looked good;

she'd only ordered a sandwich. "This heat," he said. "Do you usually get it this early? Why anybody lives here—it gets hot in Kansas too but not until summer."

She laughed briefly. "I guess you're just used to the place where you grew up, take it for granted. I know, it can be awful. Any time of the year, actually. It'll cool off a little while after this, until about the end of June, and then we'll really get it—worse humidity—right through September and into October."

"My God. Eat your sandwich."

She didn't. She put it down and stared at him and said, "I just thought about something. If I said I didn't want any of the money, I could go right away somewhere, and he wouldn't know where we were. It's just because of the money for Tammy that anybody knows my address—that he knew where we are. And it's the money he minds about, really. I could take care of Tammy myself—oh, Mr. Pollard, if—"

"Stan."

"Stan—if I could—"

"You're not thinking," he said gently. "The money part, that set him off, and that's past praying for—the will, and the trust. He blamed you for making him—have to do murder. So he said. And the head doctors say he's cured?"

"But that's the way he thinks," she said tiredly. "Nothing's ever his fault. No, I see. And anyway, there's no way to tell him—I don't want any more of the money—when we don't know where he is. I don't know why you're still here. There isn't anything you can do. You must have work to do back home."

"We don't go in for criminal practice—nothing waiting that Uncle and the clerks can't handle. No, there isn't much I can do. But you're a kind of responsibility of the firm, you could say," he said lightly. "And if you think we'd let you give up any child support— No way. You come into the will too, you know."

"What?" She was surprised.

"Oh, yes. Burgess thought of everything. If Wayne predeceases you, most of it's in trust for your child or children—divided equally if there'd been more than Tammy. Two hundred thousand to you. Out of a chunk like that, you'd better believe the trustees would see you got a fair amount of child support."

She put down her coffee cup; her hand was shaking. "That was—awfully good of him. He didn't have to do that. Of course that'll never happen, but—"

"He liked you," said Pollard. "Uncle Olly said something on the phone the other day. That Howard Burgess had told him if anybody could straighten out Wayne, it was that nice girl—she was a good girl. And Uncle thought a good deal of Burgess, you know. I think he feels you've been left to the executors as a kind of responsibility."

She laughed. "I don't need anybody responsible for me."

"Well, we might have a different opinion about that."

"And I've only got an hour for lunch."

The man with murder in his mind sat on the park bench across from the little apartment building. It was very hot and still; there was a dim hum from traffic on the boulevard a couple of blocks away. Nobody else was in the little triangle of park here, this hot day.

He was coldly furious at himself for such a stupid blunder. He had meant to plan it out so carefully, a plan nothing could go wrong with, and then for a moment's temptation—! It was all right, it couldn't put him in danger, but he'd been a goddamned fool to do it. Hadn't he thought from the start—when he knew they'd let him out—*Accident*. Accident, the thing to keep in mind—something that looked natural. What the newspapers would call a tragic accident.

Nothing so crude as that— He'd sat here across from the apartment, looking over the terrain, on and off for a week, trying to come up with the perfect plan. The one great miraculous stroke of luck he'd had—and it had been a hell of a chance to take, but too good to pass up, and he'd gambled and pulled it off—but he'd always been lucky.

Usually he'd been lucky—until he'd met up with this little bitch, little prim prude bitch—sweet-talking him into marrying her, and that was his first big mistake. And then she had to have a kid, so the old bastard wouldn't part with any more money, and tied it all up like that. That had been a hell of a shock, finding that out. All her fault. And it might seem all for nothing now, to pay her out for it, but nobody took him for a sucker like that and got away with it.

But it had to look natural. Because he wasn't sure he'd convinced old Pollard— Little bitch and her kid get knocked on the head, they'd think of him right off. Damn fool to write that letter. Damn fool to talk to Pollard a while back. But water under the bridge.

That damned *kid*. He'd just been starting back to the car, almost dark, when he'd spotted her there riding a tricycle. Dark in five minutes, and not a soul around—and it was the goddamned kid who had fouled everything up, almost the kid's fault more than Meg's— Goddamn it, she'd *said* she was the Burgess kid, and such a sweet chance—

The wrong one. Another kid. He'd stayed away from here until this morning, probably cops around yesterday. Today she wouldn't be going to work; and he knew the comings and goings of the other people there now. Everybody else going to work except the old woman. The old woman went out with the dog every morning about nine o'clock, and the days he had watched, she'd never been gone less than an hour.

And then, goddamn it, an hour ago the little bitch had come out with the kid and driven off in the old green Chevy—as he'd watched her before, followed her— The other kid, the wrong one; he hadn't known any other kid lived there, and damn it, she *said*—

Water under the bridge. The wrong way to do it anyway. There had been a vague idea in his mind then, make it look like suicide, over the kid—but forget it. It had to be something ordinary, simple, all straight in his mind before he moved on it.

The old woman came out with the dog, across the street, and started up toward the boulevard. That damned dog, he had found out, yapped as soon as anybody put a foot on the walk up to the building.

He had built his cover; nobody could ever prove he'd been here. He had found anonymous shelter—that flicked across his mind half contemptuously, he'd always been good with the females—

Except for the little bitch.

And there would be a way to do it. A good simple way. Natural. Accident. The erratically bright mind moved hard and cold as a diamond. There was a gas line to the apartment. There was food poisoning. Something to hit them both together. To pay them out—pay them good, the little bitch and her kid, for getting across Wayne Burgess and what he wanted and what was his right.

There'd be a way to do it—

Mrs. Collison's car was innocent of any incriminating evidence. Burt broke the news to them first thing on Tuesday morning, and O'Connor turned the air blue and then shut up looking guilty; he still sometimes forgot they had a female in the office.

"Don't mind me," said Delia imperturbably. "I knew all the cuss words before I went to school."

O'Connor eyed her with momentary curiosity. She'd have learned a lot of cuss words in five years on the LAPD, naturally. In the five months she'd been with them, she hadn't mentioned a word about her background, family; all business, their Delia.

"So we forget Collison," said Varallo. "It looks more and more like a maverick, Charles. Not in anybody's records, possibly. And how to get any lead—"

O'Connor said a few more things. There had also been another heist overnight, at a drugstore on South Central. The loot had been a little cash and a lot of miscellaneous drugs—barbiturates, Benzedrine, Quaaludes, Valium.

Katz went to cover Edelman's arraignment. They hoped to talk to Mrs. Schultz sometime today. Varallo talked briefly with the D.A.'s office about George Walowsky; it was Forbes's day off, but he thought Jeff would be amused about that, and called to tell him. "Well, for God's sake, of all the silly things," said Forbes.

But of course, if the routine was tedious, sometimes it paid off with prompt results. The drugstore clerk came in to make a statement and look at mug shots at nine o'clock. At nine-thirty he said, "That's him. I'd swear on a stack of Bibles."

The mug shot was that of one Esteban Morales, record of narco dealing, shoplifting, petty theft, and pimping. The last address was Eagle Rock. Varallo and Poor went out to see if he was still there, and found him just concluding a deal for all the dope from the heist. The buyer was subsequently found to be in Pasadena's records, Ernesto Medina, possession and dealing. They called up a squad to take them in.

"Dirty goddamn fuzz!" said Morales bitterly. "Ten minutes and I'da been long gone—have to come louse up everything—"

"That's right," said Varallo. "We're the original spoilsports, *amigo.*"

CHAPTER FOUR

Just before noon, Varallo tried to see Mrs. Schultz at the hospital, and was foiled by the doctor, who told him that she had a heart condition of some standing, had suffered a slight attack yesterday, and probably couldn't be interviewed for another twenty-four hours. However, also at the hospital was the Schultzes' married daughter, Roberta Stinson, who talked to him in the waiting room on that floor: a plain, sensible young woman, upset and grieving, honestly bewildered.

"I just don't know what to tell you. As far as I know, Daddy didn't have an enemy in the world. In business, or any other way. He's never had trouble with anyone, of any kind, that I can remember. I just couldn't believe it when the police called—and then Mama—well, they were always awfully close, it's no wonder. The doctor says she'll pull out of it, but—" She and her husband lived in Northridge, and they usually saw the Schultzes several times a month; they'd have heard about any trouble, business or personal. "There's nothing to tell you," she said. "There couldn't be any reason for someone to shoot Daddy."

After lunch, Varallo collected Delia and they heard that all over again from the Schultzes' neighbors, up on Matilija Road: a nice upper-middle-class street, the Schultzes' house Norman provincial painted a neat gray with white trim. The Schultzes had lived there twenty years, and the neighbors who were home all said the same things. Not the kind of neighborhood where people ran in and out of each other's homes, but they all knew Fred and Rena Schultz. Couldn't imagine any reason—Fred a nice easygoing fellow, never got across anybody. Nobody had ever heard of him having a serious fight with anybody, he and his wife got along fine, married son and a daughter and a couple of grandchildren—nice ordinary people.

"Well, somebody thought he had a reason to shoot him," said Varallo when they compared notes back at the car. "He sounds too good to be true."

When they got back to the office, Burt had just sent up the report on the slugs, which Goulding had dug out last night and sent to the lab. That didn't tell them much. Three slugs out of a Colt .38 revolver, a gun, whether old or new, never much used.

And O'Connor and Katz had finished looking at the men on the sex list. The last few had been like most of them, no really suggestive evidence, here and there an alibi, some of them without access to cars. Something helpful still might come in from the lab: on the first three cases, the rapes, Burt had sent the victims' clothes for more sophisticated examination at the LAPD lab. That was about the top crime lab anywhere; if there was any useful evidence they'd find it, but it would take time; there'd be a backlog of lab work to do, down there.

"So we start all over again," said O'Connor, "and thank God for computers. Damn the general-area bit—the reason for that we'll find out when we lay hands on him. Go back to the M.O., daylight snatch and rape, and ask the computers—LAPD, Pasadena, Burbank."

"And environs," agreed Katz. It would be easier if the city—which wasn't that small a city, a hundred and forty thousand—was isolated in the middle of rural country; as it was, it was just one more suburb of a hundred and fifty suburbs, all running into each other to form the great spreading metropolitan sprawl that was Los Angeles County; and it was a very mobile county. With a set of wheels, available to nearly every resident, you could get from Santa Monica to La Crescenta, Long Beach to Burbank, in a couple of hours.

The computers would make it easier: but the LAPD records alone might turn up another fifty or sixty men to look at, question. The city fathers had voted in an extended police budget, and with any luck they should have double the number of plainclothesmen next year, which was no help right now.

Varallo sat down and lit a cigarette, and Delia started a follow-up report on Schultz. Ten minutes later they were called out on another burglary.

It was a newish house up in Chevy Chase Canyon, and as soon as they got there they put it down to a pair of slick pros. There were always burglaries happening: in the last month, twenty-five or so. Most of them were hasty break-ins after quickly grabbed loot, and now and then a stupid punk whose prints were on file left one and got picked up—mostly to plead guilty to a reduced charge and be out in a few months. A lot of the jobs, by their very anonymity, had to be filed away as unsolvable. But in the last month there'd been four— this made the fifth—with the same earmarks of very slick pros.

The houses had all been in wealthy sections of town: upper Ross-moyne, one of the newly opened canyon roads. The burglaries had been daylight jobs, and evidently cased, the householders known to be out. The break-ins had been neat, effected with a glass-cutter on rear windows, sliding doors. Two of the houses had not been over-looked by neighbors, one on a deeply wooded lot, the other a new house with no others nearby; at those places large items had been taken: TVs, stereos. At the others, only the portable valuables: jew-elry, cash, fur coats, expensive cameras. The large items said there were at least two men.

This was in the pattern, except that for once they hadn't got much loot. The householder was Warren Fielding, a gloomy youngish man who said this was all he needed. He was a stockbroker with Fuller and Power downtown, and feeling like hell, he said, with a cold start-ing; he'd come home early, to find this.

The house was up for sale; his wife was in the process of divorcing him, and he'd already sold some of the furniture. What the burglars had got was a transistor radio, a tape recorder, a portable TV, and a diamond ring that had belonged to his father.

On the other four jobs no latent prints had shown up, but they had to go through the motions; they got Burt out to dust everything, and he wouldn't finish that today. They got back to the office at five-thirty, and Delia said she'd write the report in the morning.

"I hope to God it cools off someday," said Varallo. Nobody else was in at all.

Delia stretched and picked up her handbag. "I'll be glad to get home tonight."

"Fed up with the job?"

"Not really. Just tired."

Meg got home to the apartment at five-thirty. Tammy was a little cross and fretful, unusual for her; she'd got her dress dirty at the school playground, and she was a funny, fastidious little thing; she wanted to change it, and ran ahead while Meg shut the padlock on the garage. She was halfway up the stairs as Meg opened the mailbox, took out a handful of mail. There was a letter from Linda— she'd written Linda about Wayne last week. Linda was a better correspondent than she was.

Wayne— But she felt very safe and secure as she locked the door, fastened the stout chain. "I want to put on the pretty blue dress," announced Tammy, heading for her room.

"No, you don't, it's clean. Put on your pink robe, funnyface." Tammy was grown up for four, she could manage the couple of buttons involved. "And put your dress in the hamper in the bathroom."

"*I* know," said Tammy. Meg smiled at her father's photograph as she switched on the air-conditioning unit. She went out to the kitchen to start dinner; no real hurry. There was leftover asparagus, and new potatoes: the lamb chops all ready to broil. She wouldn't coax Tammy to eat a salad tonight. She put the asparagus and the potatoes on the stove, turned on low, frowning as she got them out of the refrigerator. Something wrong with the refrigerator, it wasn't as cold as it should be: overworking in the heat wave. She set the table in the kitchen, and went back to the front room to look at her mail.

She heard Tammy fussing around in the bedroom, then in the bathroom; talking to that stuffed cat she was so crazy about.

She started to read Linda's letter.

Mostly she liked the job, which was a good thing; but any job had its ups and downs, and tonight Delia was tired, and a little tired of the tedious, unglamorous job. Traffic was thick as usual through the Atwater section, and backed up at Riverside Drive just into Hollywood; she had to wait at the intersection through two light changes. It was nearly dark, but still stickily hot. With relief she flicked on the left-turn signal and turned off Los Feliz onto Waverly Place; half a block up, she turned into the drive of the familiar old two-story Spanish stucco with the red tile roof.

She went in the back door and inhaled thoughtfully. Lemon-butter sole ready for the last light broiling, which meant a really big tossed salad, everything in it and Alex's special dressing, and probably cheese cake to follow. She went down the hall and looked into the living room. The air conditioning made a grateful hum, and there was just a circle of light in one corner where they sat over a chessboard, absorbed. They looked up as one man, and Steve said, "You're late."

"Traffic."

"Anything turn up on that homicide?" asked Alex.

"Absolutely nothing. Well, the ballistics report." Yes, it was a good thing that on the whole she liked the job.

Alex Riordan, losing his first wife after twenty years of childless marriage, had married a girl half his age, only to lose her in childbirth a year later. They had managed somehow, he and Delia, with a succession of housekeepers, until that year Delia was thirteen and he was sixty-five. He'd been full of plans for her first time of entering the junior target-pistol competition—he'd started her with a gun on her seventh birthday. Then, just two days before his official retirement, he'd gone out on his last call—Captain Alex Riordan, Robbery-Homicide, LAPD—and taken the bank robber's slug in the spine. That had been a bad time, for a while, and then they'd found Steve. Ex-Sergeant Steve McAllister, LAPD, just short of twenty-five years' service when he lost a leg in an accident; a widower with a married daughter in Denver. The three of them had been together for thirteen years now. The new leg didn't hamper Steve from manipulating Alex's wheelchair, and Alex had always liked to cook.

Of course it had had to be this job, for Alex.

They were both immensely proud of their Delia, the youngest female around to achieve detective rank, which she was aware of; and they'd have died before telling her so, which she knew too.

They talked about homicide over dinner, the latest one in Glendale leading to inevitable reminiscences. She felt better, getting the usual kick out of both of them—Alex handsome as the devil with his mane of white hair; Steve square and solid, waving his knife fiercely as they argued about some case back in 1947.

After dinner they went back to their chess. Delia stacked dishes in the dishwasher, started it going, and went upstairs. She meant to wash her hair and do her nails tonight. But at nine-thirty, just as she'd finished pinning up her hair, the phone rang in the hall and she had a premonition. She went out to the extension and picked it up, and Sergeant Hamilton's voice said her name. "Damn!" said Delia.

"I'm sorry to bother you," he said. "But this Mrs. Burgess just called—"

When Delia, with her hair tied up in a scarf, got to the emergency wing of Glendale Memorial Hospital, she found Meg sitting huddled on one of the benches in the waiting room. She was white and shaking; Delia touched her arm and she looked up.

"I don't know how he did it," she said. "I don't see how. I'd just been thinking—safe, all locked in. It's Tammy—but the doctor promised she'll be all right. I was never so scared—"

"Just take it easy and tell me what happened."

Meg nodded tremulously. "But I don't see *how*. How Wayne could— We came home—just as usual—and had dinner. About six-thirty. Tammy usually just plays around with toys, until her bath at seven-thirty. I'd been straightening up the kitchen—and when I went into the front room I found her unconscious on the floor. I tried to— but I saw it was something—I called the paramedics, and they took her right in, in the ambulance, I rode along—oxygen, and then— The doctor said she'll be all right." Meg swallowed. "But he said an over-dose of barbiturates or something like that, and that just couldn't be—"

"Do you have anything like that at home?" Meg shook her head.

Delia had a little argument with a nurse before the badge produced the doctor, a brusque middle-aged man. "The child will be all right," he said shortly. "We got to her in good time. Asleep now. We pumped her stomach. Know exactly what drug? My dear woman, lab analysis takes time. Whatever brand of sleeping tablets she found in her parents' bathroom, I suppose. Why people have to be so damned careless— We'll keep her overnight, but she'll be fine in the morning."

Meg had come up to them in the corridor, heard that. "You'll watch her?" she asked fiercely. "G-guard her so no one can get to her?"

The doctor looked at her impatiently. "No one can interfere with patients. I'd just advise you to put a lock on your medicine cabinet, madam. This kind of thing happens too often, and we're not always in time to save a child's life."

"But there wasn't anything—she couldn't have got—"

"I've heard that before," he said with a shrug. "Just be thankful we got her in time, and be more careful in the future."

Meg was reluctant to leave, but Delia got her out to the car. "Now let's talk about this, try to figure it out." On the way to the apartment she asked a few questions, got Meg calmed down a little. "What did you have for dinner?"

"Lamb chops. Asparagus. New potatoes. Tammy had milk, I had coffee. But there couldn't be anything— Tammy's never been mischievous, getting into things. And there wasn't anything—"

"You'd have noticed if the apartment had been broken into—that is, any attempt—" That was the first thing in Delia's mind: those excellent new locks.

"Nothing like that. Of course not."

"Well, we'll have a look around." She parked in front; they went into the lobby, and the dog uttered a series of shrill barks. But even over the barks they heard the loud voices from behind the opposite door.

On the stairs Meg said thinly, "Ever since it happened, the Wileys fighting—blaming each other for it—and it's all my fault. Just for living here. They'd kill me if they knew."

"Don't be morbid," said Delia shortly. Meg unlocked the door and they went in. This was an ordinary middle-income apartment, a good-sized living room with beige carpet, rose-beige drapes, a couch, two upholstered chairs: a small TV in one corner. A hall led off to the upper left, leading to the kitchen, Delia remembered: two bedrooms and bath between on the other side of the hall. At the rear of the kitchen a solid door gave onto a small square wooden porch with stairs down to the little paved rear yard, the four joined garages.

The kitchen was neat and clean, the wastebasket beside the refrigerator only a quarter full. Delia made for the bathroom. It was small and square, with a tiled counter holding a box of bath powder, a couple of bottles of cologne, hair spray. Delia moved them all, after examining the medicine cabinet, and said, "Mrs. Burgess. You said you didn't have any sleeping tablets, anything like that."

"No, I—oh, my God!" said Meg. "Oh, my God. I'd forgotten that was there. It wasn't there, it was on the top shelf of the medicine cabinet! But Tammy wouldn't have—she never—"

"How long have you had it? What was it? Do you remember how many tablets or capsules were left?" It was a plastic prescription bottle, neat label pasted on. It was empty. It had been in the corner behind the box of bath powder.

"Nembutal," said Meg. "It was Nembutal. I had an abscessed tooth out—just before Christmas—the dentist gave me a prescription. But I had only to take one—I don't know how many were left, but it was nearly full. I—you don't just throw things away. Sometimes I get sinus headaches, I thought—"

"You didn't think of locking it up somewhere? With a four-year-old—"

"No, I didn't," said Meg, and briefly she was angry. "Because it never crossed my mind Tammy would ever see it. She's strictly trained to leave the medicine cabinet alone, even if she could reach it, which she couldn't. She's never been a climber, she's afraid of heights. I'd forgotten it was there myself."

Delia went back to the kitchen. "What did Tammy have for dinner that you didn't?"

"I wasn't very hungry. I had a lamb chop and some potatoes. The asparagus—she had some, and I threw the rest out. It had been in the refrigerator for four days—and there's something wrong with the refrigerator, I think. What are you looking for?"

Delia had the wastebasket on top of the counter; it was a little round metal wastebasket, and she looked into it, and very carefully lifted out a half-crumpled sheet of paper. It had been torn from a tablet of typewriter-size stationery. There were just visible a few yellow grains clinging to it. "What is it? What are you—"

"Don't touch it. Did you run the dishwasher?"

"There wasn't enough in it. Did he? Did he *get in*—somehow? Oh, my God—"

"Take it easy," said Delia. She had been sorry for this girl, but she felt slightly impatient with her now. She found the phone and called the night watch. She got Rhys; Hunter was out on something. He said he'd be right up, and got there in ten minutes. They exchanged a few opinions about this while Meg sat watching them miserably. Rhys maneuvered the sheet of paper into an evidence bag. He went into the rear bedroom, and Delia sat down beside Meg on the couch.

"Do you have paper like that, typewriter size in a tablet? Where is it kept?"

"My little desk—in the bedroom."

"Well. Do you ever pound or chop things when you're cooking—seasonings, whatever?"

"I don't know what you're talking about. I really don't. Parsley," said Meg. "Pound what? Sylvia sent me one of those mortar and pestle sets for Christmas—silly—something you use once in a blue moon. Before it turned so hot I got a little ham—I broke up some cloves for the sauce—but what's that—"

"When you came in tonight, exactly what did you do?" Dully Meg told her. "I see," said Delia thoughtfully. "Mrs. Burgess, where do you keep that mortar and pestle?"

Meg put a hand across her eyes. "I don't—I never—I think it's in the right-hand cupboard under the counter."

Delia went to see what Rhys was finding. He was in the child's bedroom, looking in a dissatisfied way at a set of toy dishes on the floor near the bed, stuffed animals ranged on a shelf. "Nothing here heavy enough that I can see."

"Maybe it's even simpler," said Delia. They found the mortar and pestle on the bottom shelf in the kitchen cabinet, a primitive-looking pair in rough stone.

"Better bet," said Rhys. "Have a look." There were two or three yellow grains in the bottom of the little bowl. "I suppose she'd seen it used. Funny what kids will get up to."

Delia opened the dishwasher and spotted the pan which had held asparagus, the child's dish. "Waste of lab work," said Rhys disparagingly. "It's plain enough what happened."

"I think it might set her mind at rest." She couldn't take time to give Rhys all the background now. She went back to Meg. "Listen," she said. "This was a bad thing to happen, but it wasn't anything to do with your ex-husband. It was just an accident, and I'm afraid it was partly your fault. I know, you just didn't think, because Tammy'd never shown any interest in the medicine cabinet before, you thought you could trust her to leave it alone. You never thought about that old prescription. But a four-year-old isn't really reliable, and they can be inquisitive."

"You think *Tammy*—did that? Put those tablets—" Meg shook her head. "Oh, no, she wouldn't—she hates taking medicine—"

"Children do imitate what they see. She'd seen you preparing things in the kitchen—maybe just recently using that mortar and pestle, for the cloves with the ham. And adding things to pans on the stove. You were busy reading your mail. And for once Tammy did get at the medicine cabinet, and got hold of that Nembutal. Probably she was playing house, the way little girls do. She took a piece of paper from your desk—I'll bet she's seen you using a cutting board—and found the mortar and pestle to break up the tablets, and dropped them into the pan of asparagus. By the time you came to finish getting dinner, the fragments were dissolved. No, you wouldn't have noticed even the larger little pieces—you'd added margarine or butter, hadn't you? and that would be the same color."

"She couldn't do all that. She wouldn't. It was Wayne—somehow—"

"Now just think a minute. Nobody can get into this apartment when it's locked. They're good safe locks, and we're telling you there's been no attempt to break in." Rhys was watching them, head on one side, faintly curious; he looked, Delia thought irrelevantly, rather like one of his mother's Cairn terriers, a slim middle-sized man with terrier-alert eyes, suppressed energy radiating from him. "You've got to believe evidence, you know. We've found the paper, and the mortar, with traces of the tablets on both. It was Tammy. There wasn't anyone else here. It was a terrible thing to happen, but she's going to be all right, and you'll be more careful after this. It was just very lucky that you didn't eat any of the asparagus, or nobody might have found both of you until it was too late. But it's all right now, you see?"

Meg drew a long shaky breath. "The locks," she said. "Oh, that's true—you said so before. You'd know about locks. He—couldn't—have—got—in. I still can't believe Tammy— But he couldn't have got in. I was so frightened—I guess I just wasn't thinking. Because—besides the locks, there's Mrs. Kemp and Petie."

"Oh?" Delia was at a loss.

"Her dog. She's inquisitive, if you like—she keeps her door open a crack, and every time Petie barks she looks to see who's come in. And if anybody—had been up here, trying to get in, Petie'd have raised the roof and she'd have come looking. I just wasn't thinking. But Tammy's never done anything like this—"

"There's always a first time," said Delia. "And there could be a reason of sorts. You've been upset and worried, and she'd sense that. It just might have prompted her to do something she'd never thought of before. Children are strange little creatures—she might have thought she was helping you in some way."

"Yes. I see."

"Now do you feel better? We're going to do an analysis, and prove all that to you. That it was just an accident. And Tammy's going to be all right. Do you think you can get some sleep now?"

"Yes, thank you. I was—so scared—but it's all right now. I—have to believe evidence, don't I? And heaven knows I'll be more careful."

Delia got home at midnight, yawning her head off.

On Wednesday morning, with Varallo off, there was a new one to work. A Mr. and Mrs. Kirby Cooper had been held up on the street coming out of the Center Theater last night. They'd be coming in to make a statement, look at mug shots.

The computers at LAPD and elsewhere were grinding out new lists for the Glendale boys, and a batch of xeroxed pedigrees was awaiting O'Connor when he came in. He passed half of them over to Katz and they started scanning them rapidly, looking for any M.O.'s that might match their rapist however faintly. Twenty minutes later he said, "I'll be goddamned. This might say something." Katz looked up. "Ralph Kleinman. Nothing matches to a daylight snatch, but we busted him the first time, eight years back." He got on the phone to Records downstairs, and presently said, "Sweet Christ, have we got a break at last? Thanks! What do you know, Joe, he was living on Kenilworth then. Smack in the middle of our area."

"That might be gratifying. What did we bust him for?"

"Grand theft auto. He was eighteen then. He graduated to attempted rape, contributing to delinquency, possession, two counts of rape—a twelve-year-old, a fourteen-year-old. I don't know," said O'Connor wryly, "that you'd call 'em children at that age, but— He seems to prefer the juveniles of his own sex, but you never know how these freaks will go. I think we have a look for him first. Last known address is Romaine in Hollywood." But as they got up, Thomsen came in.

"We've finished going over Schultz's car. There were some dandy clear latents on the left-front hood, three of 'em. Not in our records, so we sent them off to the Feds. They look male, but that's just an opinion."

"Well, for God's sake, we didn't think he was shot by a transvestite," said O'Connor.

"They're not, of course, Garfunkel's, or the two girls'."

"I'm glad you checked that." He and Katz went out, leaving Poor and Forbes looking over the new list interestedly. Five minutes later the Coopers showed up and Delia talked to them.

"This used to be a nice quiet town," said Cooper indignantly. "Reason we moved here twenty years back. Now all these aliens coming in, and probably half of them illegal—my God, I never thought I'd see the day I could walk down Brand Boulevard and never hear a word of English! And God knows there are enough punks around who were born here—"

"Well, that's one thing we do know," said his wife amusedly, "that he wasn't a foreigner. No accent at all when he said, 'This is a hold-up,' and pointed the gun at us."

"Where was this, in the parking lot?" The Center Theater, a popular little legitimate theater, had its own lot.

"No. We were late, and it's a popular production, the lot was full. I found a place on the street, around the corner on Lexington. Of course the crowd coming out went the other way, there was just us went around the corner there—he was walking down toward us, and I think it was a kind of spur-of-the-moment idea, when he saw us. He stopped and pulled the gun. Oh, it was a real gun all right, enough light to see that, and I wasn't about to argue with it—never know whether these punks are hopped up." He'd got about twenty dollars in cash, a couple of rings from Mrs. Cooper, neither very valuable, and Cooper's watch, also of small value. They'd got a fairly good look at him, felt they might recognize a picture.

Delia typed up a list; it would be added to the hot list sent to all pawnbrokers. Automatically the proceeds of the burglaries were on that list too, and once in a while something turned up that way. Their slick pro burglars, of course, would have a tame fence. She took the

Coopers down to Records and they started looking at mug shots of men with robbery records. They seemed to be enjoying themselves, hobnobbing with police.

An hour later, as she was on the phone with a P.A. officer in San Diego—they'd mislaid a burglar, whose wife happened to live in Glendale, and wanted somebody to check if he was here—the Coopers came back upstairs. They'd picked out two mug shots; both were of men in their early twenties, with little records which said that either could have pulled the job.

"Just hope you get him," said Cooper. "Only then some fool judge will hand him a suspended sentence because he grew up in a slum, or his mama and papa were mean to him."

"Well, we're only here to arrest them," said Delia dryly.

Meg called Dr. Burton and begged off work; her little girl was sick, but she'd be in tomorrow. She'd never asked for a day off before.

He said kindly, absently, that was quite all right.

At the hospital there were forms to fill out, the impersonal questions to answer. Tammy looked fine, if pale, but she was sleepy and cross. She wouldn't remember much about it, said the nurse, she'd only waked up a little while ago. Better keep her in bed today, very light meals.

It wasn't the time to try to talk to Tammy, ask her about the pills in the medicine cabinet. And very likely when she did, Tammy wouldn't remember. Meg was feeling too tired to think about it. Thinking of Delia's quiet firm voice last night, she felt desperately confused and a little worried about herself. She had forgotten all about those safe, secure locks. Like a fool; like a stupid hysterical heroine in a Gothic novel.

Tammy ate a little soup and went straight off to sleep. And now Meg had to talk to somebody about it, and she called Stan Pollard.

He shot over in a hurry, and asked a good many questions. "My God, of course you would think— You must have had a night. What a thing to happen—"

"You don't know what a fool I feel like now. You see, she's always been such a good child—I never had to worry about her getting into things the way a lot of children do. She's never gone in for little fibs, or mischief of any kind. I just—jumped to the conclusion." She took the offered cigarette. "I'd been—so scared."

"Well, naturally—"

"No, I don't mean it that way. I mean, of Wayne. I never knew just how frightened of him I was until I got that letter. Your uncle's letter telling me he was—out. I'd been frightened before, you know—and I don't think I could ever make anybody understand—what a—a *strange* thing it was to be frightened of Wayne. The man I'd married —the man I thought I loved. But loving isn't the same as being in love." She was talking almost to herself, looking at her cigarette. "That night, at dinner at the Burgesses, I actually thought it might be all right—Wayne might grow up and get some sense. I'd found out about him then, and I wasn't in love with him any more, but I was trying to make it work, I don't like the idea of divorce. The church hanging on, I suppose. They were so pleased about the baby. And it was then Mr. Burgess said—just sensible and friendly, you know—better Wayne should stick to a job he knew, starting a family—and Wayne never flared up or talked back. I was surprised. We went home to the apartment, he was in a good mood for once, laughing about some silly joke—I forget—and he said, 'Have a little drink before bed'—it was crême de menthe—"

"Look, is it such a good idea to go over all this?"

"I was undressing, he brought it in. And I thought he wanted to make love to me, but I was so sleepy. He went to work the next morning, just as usual. It was about noon the police came and told me—they were dead. And how. And I knew right away—it was Wayne. I knew. And I was so frightened—*that they wouldn't find out!* And the next day, when that police lieutenant came, I felt—that's the very worst thing—I felt as if I'd died and come back to life, because I didn't have to go on with Wayne. That they knew, and were going to shut him up somewhere. It was as if I'd never known him at all—a little evil dirty man I didn't know, nobody I'd ever really known—and all the while I was so ashamed of feeling that way, when the baby—"

"Now, for God's sake stop thinking about it," said Pollard.

"No, I've got over that now. Because Tammy isn't his, she's mine. But you see, I'd been afraid of him—when the lieutenant was talking about rights, and a lawyer, and Wayne just looked at me and said, 'It's all your fault'—but they took him away and locked him up. And then, when I found out they'd let him go—I tried to be sensible, I tried not to go to pieces, but I guess I just held it all in so tight, I couldn't help acting like a perfect idiot." She laughed shakily.

"Look here," said Pollard briskly, "you know what I've been thinking? The police are probably quite right. Uncle Olly's emotionally involved in all this, and so, God knows, are you. And I guess me, now. And just on account of that old letter, and what this—this nut said to Uncle, we've all been building this up out of nothing, see? All of us just getting the jitters. You said, everybody says, he's erratic. Maybe he's forgotten he ever wrote that letter. So maybe he's not at that summer place on the river—he got sick of it, and the car was dead, so he left it and hitched out. Maybe he's sitting at a night club in K.C. right now."

"I don't know, I don't know," said Meg. "It's just—I felt like such a fool, forgetting that he can't get in here. I just realized you can't let being frightened—sort of paralyze you."

"No," said Pollard gently. "You know, one thing you've needed for a long time is somebody to talk to."

"Oh, I know that." She was surprised that he should know it. "Letters aren't the same, are they?"

"Suppose I fetch in a couple of steaks, and some salad makings, and so on. Couple of drinks before you cook the steaks. How does that strike you?"

"Just fine," said Meg. "I don't know why you've stayed around."

"You're a responsibility of the firm."

About four o'clock a new call went down: a brawl at a bar on South Central, with a corpse. Forbes had just come back from an abortive hunt for one of the possibles on the Cooper hold-up, and Delia tagged along with him, though he wasn't eager for her company.

"Questioning drunks is no job for a female," he said.

"Oh, it isn't that I enjoy it," said Delia amiably, "but more experience is always useful."

As a matter of fact, none of the witnesses were drunk. The bar was a respectable neighborhood place, not a joint, and the whole confused affair posed a little mystery.

The bartender's name was Albert Smith. "Look," he said, "sometimes guys get a little excited. Especially these Mexes, Italianos, right? It don't necessarily mean nothing. Now these fellows, Al Montez and Steve Aguino, they're regular customers, perfectly good guys —both in steady work. Al works nights at Lockheed, Steve's in construction, but the job's stalled some reason so he ain't working right now. So they get in an argument, they aren't nowhere near drunk, just excited, so I says to cool it, boys, step out awhile and don't bother the other customers, see?" He was a fat, earnest, hairy man in a dirty apron. "So they go out. Next I hear shots, so I go out too. And there's Al dead on the sidewalk. That's all I know. "

Steve Aguino told them some more, excited and shocked. "Sure I'm mad at Al—he owes me fifty bucks from last month, claims he's still short, but my wife knows his wife and she tells me they're not hurting for groceries—T-bone steaks and imported wine in her grocery cart, Marie runs into her at the Safeway—so I tackle Al and he tells me about his kids' dentist bill and inflation—we're out here on the sidewalk arguing and, by God, all of a sudden this strange dude just walks up and shoots him—who in hell he was I got no idea, never saw him before—"

There were two other witnesses, who'd been waiting for a bus on the corner: a teenage boy and an elderly man. They both said the same thing. They'd noticed the two men on the sidewalk, hadn't paid much attention, when a man had come up—they thought maybe from the used-car lot next to the bar—and started shooting. They'd been too surprised to do anything, and the man had walked back into the lot. He'd been kind of medium-looking; all they agreed on was that he'd had on a tan shirt and tan pants. They'd never seen him anywhere before.

"Well, talk about a handful of nothing!" said Forbes. When they thought about all the paperwork on it, talking to the wife, everybody he knew, they felt tired. But it had to be done.

Heading back to the office after the morgue wagon had left, toward the end of shift, they came on an accident at the corner of Lomita and Brand. There was a parked squad car behind an old Ford sedan smashed against the light pole, and a new Chevy slewed up over the curb; an ambulance was just arriving. They stopped to see if it was going to be a felony charge for them to handle.

Patrolman Neil Tracy was on it. "These goddamned idiots," he said. "Nah, it's nothing much. I spotted him in the Ford doing about sixty on San Fernando, and took off after him. He ran. Up to ninety — I ask you—he got this far and missed the turn, sideswiped the Chevy. The driver's got a broken arm, is all—mad as hell, of course. The speeder claims he was just scared when the siren blew. There's no want on the car and his license looks O.K.—name's Donald Biggs."

They went back to the office and called it a day.

CHAPTER FIVE

By the last half hour of the day shift on Thursday, they were sitting around the office talking to pass the time until they could knock off.

"God only knows," said O'Connor forcefully, "we see a hell of a lot of homicides done for no reason at all, but the goddamned idiots usually think they've got a reason. I refuse to believe that inside three days two maniacs picked two perfect strangers to gun down with not even an imaginary reason."

"And even stranger things than that have happened," said Varallo, "but I don't think so either. I just don't see anywhere else to go on Schultz or Montez."

John Poor said from his desk across the room, "And if you ask me, we'll be beating the bushes for this rapist for the next six months, unless we get a break—or he does something stupid the next time."

There was a little silence while they contemplated that. Another one: another five- or six- or seven-year-old snatched, raped, and/or killed. But that one was just a ghost out there somewhere; for all their experience, the technical aids they had these days, the computer-produced lists of known criminals, they still couldn't make bricks without straw.

They had been round and round today, in the various tangles, looking for leads. They had talked to Schultz's partner again, and looked at all the recent business deals Schultz had been involved in. They had talked to the rest of his friends and acquaintances they hadn't seen before, and it was all a great big blank. Montez looked just the same: a quiet family man living a humdrum life with a prosaic wife and four kids. He hadn't had any trouble on the job or anywhere else, with anybody, as far as his wife, his employer, his immediate close friends, knew.

O'Connor, hot on locating Ralph Kleinman, had found his parents still living at an apartment on Kenilworth. He was the youngest of three sons, and they had written Ralph off by what they said. Kleinman was in an architect's office downtown. "I don't know why," he told O'Connor sadly, grimly. "Bad company, weak character, just words. He used to come for money, and this fool of a mother of his giving it out." But he gave his wife an affectionate look; she just shook her head at him. "I finally told him, 'You want to be a bum, you can live like one.' We haven't seen him for a couple of years—don't know where he's living."

Katz had found a lead of sorts in Hollywood. The last time Kleinman had been picked up—for narco possession—a pal had been with him, Ron Sayers, who also had a small pedigree. The Hollywood precinct had an address for him, a two-room apartment on Harold Way, and he wasn't averse to helping Kleinman into a little trouble with the fuzz. "Hey, man," he told Katz, "that damn dude walked out of here with all that high-class grass I'd just got hold of. Where to, that I can't say—he lit out somewhere last weekend, but he hadn't been paying his share of the rent, so what the hell?" He said Kleinman had a job at a porn theater on the boulevard.

Walowsky had been arraigned this morning, and Varallo had covered that. The charge was involuntary manslaughter, with a low bail set. Walowsky had been surprised at getting off with a minor charge; he'd made bail and was out.

The autopsy on Schultz had just come in. He'd taken two bullets in the body, either of which could have proved fatal, and one in the head which had killed him instantly.

There were, just for openers, about twenty men from the LAPD list they wanted to find and talk to, but they could only accomplish so much with the men and time they had.

O'Connor was talking earnestly with Katz, Poor and Forbes were just leaving, and Varallo was just standing up, when the Memorial Hospital called. Mrs. Schultz could be interviewed now, at any time. So there'd be some overtime to do tonight.

At least it hadn't been quite so hot today. Maybe the usual March heat wave was going away.

Varallo went home, too tired to do more than glance at his yard full of roses—after drastic pruning in January, they all badly needed spraying for aphids now, and God knew when he'd get at it. He went in the back door, kissed Laura and said, "I sometimes think you're right, I needed my head examined, volunteering to be a cop all over again."

Laura laughed, turning back to the stove, her bright brown hair in its new shorter cut a little disheveled. "Honestly, Vic. Now, with the seniority building up, it's a fine time to realize that." And belatedly discovering that Daddy was home, Ginevra came running to pounce on him. Varallo swung her up to his shoulder and marched down the hall, to find the baby peacefully asleep, with Gideon Algernon Cadwallader grooming his gray tiger stripes while he played watchcat.

"Dinner in ten minutes—and don't wake up the baby," called Laura firmly.

When visiting hours opened at the hospital, a calm-eyed nurse led him to Mrs. Schultz's room, drew the curtain between her bed and the second in the room.

She was a thin blond woman, once very pretty, now looking tired and ill. She looked up eagerly at tall blond Varallo there at the bedside and asked, "What have you found out? I'm so sorry I've been laid up like this, it was just the shock—but I've wanted to see the police, ask—because I can't imagine—"

"Well, we haven't found out much, Mrs. Schultz. We've been anxious to talk to you, ask if you can suggest anyone who might have had a grudge against your husband, think he had some reason to kill him."

She frowned at him, shaking her head. "That's stupid, there isn't anybody like that. He was the best man in the world. He never had trouble with anyone that I can ever remember. I just don't understand how it could happen."

"Can you think of anything at all," persisted Varallo, "maybe something very minor, just lately, any little problem that had come up—little difference of opinion?"

She was still shaking her head. She said, "He was annoyed about the bill for the roof, but that's silly. Nothing."

"What was it?"

"Nothing," she said faintly. "They gave him one price, and then the bill—Fred was annoyed. I don't remember the name, he always

took care of things like that. But that couldn't be anything to do with
—I don't understand how it could happen. It's silly to talk about—
enemies. Fred? He was such a good man." Her blue eyes were un-
blinking on Varallo, then suddenly filled with the easy tears of weak-
ness. "Please, you've got to find out who did such a terrible thing."

"We'll try, Mrs. Schultz."

O'Connor went home, was fallen upon by Maisie, and complained
to Katharine about the thankless job. "Overtime, and at a porn theater yet."

Katharine was amused; under the very tough exterior Charles Vincent O'Connor was the ultimate puritan. They shut Maisie outside
while they had dinner; she was tall enough that she didn't have to
beg, simply lifted what snacks she fancied. Nobody but them, said
Katharine, would get stuck with such an animal, and if she had time
she'd try the obedience training herself, but with the baby—

He didn't bother to shave again; the porn theater could take him
as he was. He met Katz at headquarters and they took O'Connor's
Ford over to Hollywood. When they found the place, he said, "Goddamn it, Joe, I remember going to movies here when I was a kid—
neighborhood place, second and third runs." A good many of the little movie houses had been taken over by the hard-porn purveyors.

There wasn't an usher to take tickets, just the ticket booth with a
clerk, a pimply-faced youth. He didn't look at all upset when O'Connor flashed the badge; these places didn't have to be nervous of the
law any more, with everybody's rights so tenderly considered. "Kleinman? He don't work here any more."

"You sure about that? Is there anybody else here who knows
him?"

The kid shrugged. "Mr. Durran's in the office, I guess—the manager. You want I should ring him and say you wanta see him?"

"That we do, sonny boy," said O'Connor.

In a couple of minutes a slender little man, dapper in gray Dacron,
appeared at the one entrance of the place, came out to them, identifying them at a glance. "The fuzz interested in Kleinman?" he asked.
"What for?"

"That's our business. We understand he had a job here."

Durran stepped to one side of the open lobby as a couple of cus-

tomers approached the door. "That's right, he was a part-time pro-
jectionist up to last Saturday. I don't know anything about him and I
don't give a damn. I get paid to run this place, but I don't want anything to do with the gays or freaks."

"Which one is he?"

"Both, I'd guess." Durran hunched his shoulders eloquently. "I'd
heard he goes for the kids."

"Did you fire him?"

"No, he quit. And when I say I don't know where he is—" Durran
paused, considering. "Well, for what it's worth, I think it's possible
he's taken up with a new bosom buddy. The guy showed up here
twice to meet him when he got off work—just last week. I heard
Kleinman call him Lloyd once. A guy about forty, drives a Jaguar,
and he's got about five C's of clothes on his back from a high-priced
tailor. I heard him say something about a beach house up Malibu.
Could be Ralphie's got a thing going for him there, doesn't need the
regular job."

"Could be," agreed O'Connor. "Thanks so much." In the Ford, he
said to Katz, "I am not going to bother the sheriff's boys about that
tonight. If they can tell us anything, I'd rather have the excuse to
drive down there tomorrow."

And tomorrow was Katz's day off, but he said thoughtfully, "We
may have a little something here. I'll be in. Take a bet they know
Lloyd?"

"No bets. We usually end up doing it the hard way."

When Delia came in just behind Varallo on Friday morning,
O'Connor was already in and on the phone, Katz watching him
sleepily. There wasn't a sign of Forbes or Poor; they'd have gone out
hunting without bothering to check in.

O'Connor slammed the phone down and circled thumb and forefinger at Katz. "There you are. The sheriff's boy picked up the
ball right off. Ralphie's new friend is probably Lloyd Bunting, he's
part owner of a gay bar in Manhattan Beach. They suspect very
strongly that he's also mixed up in producing the kiddie-porn movies,
but they've got no handle on that yet. He's got a condo on the beach
in Malibu, which just shows you how crime pays. Let's go ask him if
he knows where Ralphie is."

"Ought to be twenty degrees cooler down there anyway," said Katz. They went out in a hurry. O'Connor hadn't even glanced at the night watch report.

Varallo picked that up and looked at it. "Another quiet night for once. Attempted heist at a downtown pharmacy, the clerk scared him off with a gun. Nothing for us. Hit-run on San Fernando, victim not hurt much. Paperwork. Where the hell do we go on Schultz and Montez?"

"I know," said Delia. "And that was something else. You'd think, a fairly busy street like that, middle of the afternoon—but only those two witnesses. The maddening thing is, there were two men in the office of that used-car lot and they never even looked out—thought the shots were backfires. And evidently he got away across the lot. The Schultz thing—it seems to me you've gone everywhere you can."

Varallo sat back and lit a cigarette; goofing off, but he wanted to think. And he wasn't sure just what there was to think about, on either Schultz or Montez. And he didn't get paid to sit and daydream. He'd just squashed out the cigarette when Burt came in.

"We finally got a kickback from the Feds on those latents off Schultz's car. I don't know that it means much to me—it may to you." He laid the telex in front of Varallo.

The prints had been made by Paul William Gibson, and the reason the FBI had them on file was that Gibson had put in a tour in the Navy twenty-two years ago. Aside from that, he was apparently clean, no criminal record anywhere.

"And who the hell is he?" asked Varallo.

"For all we know, the mechanic who serviced Schultz's car the last time," said Burt. "I just lifted the prints, I never told you it was the gunman who made them. I'll say one thing. The car had been washed recently, and polished—those were the only prints on the outside of it. Not even any of Schultz's."

"So let's see if we can locate Mr. Gibson," said Varallo, and reached for the phone book. A moment later he said, "Well, just fancy that."

"What?" asked Burt.

"I think we may have hit a jackpot. Delia, you can come along and get some more experience." They left Burt eying the phone book.

Far out on East Broadway, Varallo slid the Gremlin into the curb in front of a small frame building standing alone at one side of a big market parking lot. A sign on the roof said ROOFING. There was another sign propped against the building beside the door which said PATIO ENCLOSURES AND ROOFS. The door was open, and they went in.

There was a man sitting at a scarred golden-oak desk in what was evidently the first of two small rooms. He was a stocky, heavy-shouldered man with sparse sandy hair, a bulldog-jowled face. He looked up from a ledger and assumed a friendly smile. "Howdy, folks. Do something for you?"

Varallo showed him the badge. "I think you could tell us something about how Mr. Fred Schultz got shot the other day. That is, if you are Mr. Paul Gibson?"

"Yeah—that's me. I don't know what you mean. What the hell do you mean?" The smile had vanished.

"Mr. Schultz," said Varallo. "How he happened to get shot. I think you were there at the time."

Gibson made a sudden jerky movement, and then sat very still. "I don't know anything about it. I saw about it in the papers. I didn't know the guy."

"Oh, I think you did. Mrs. Schultz will remember your name, and there'll be an invoice somewhere. You did some roofing work for Mr. Schultz and he was unhappy about his bill, wasn't he?"

"I never overcharged him," said Gibson sullenly. "It was a mistake."

"I see, you can explain that. Can you explain how your fingerprints happened to show up on the hood of Schultz's car—his otherwise very clean car—right after he was shot?"

Gibson leaped to his feet and hurled one loud ugly expletive at them. "The luck!" he said in something like agony. "The luck—Christ damn it, nothing goin' right the last year! Now—oh, Christ, I never meant to kill that guy!" He collapsed into the chair again, and suddenly he began to pound one fist, futilely, on the arm of the old wooden chair. "This is a little business, I'm in the red already, and alimony and support to pay, I got to live somehow— All that goddamned stupid girl's fault—I shoulda checked the ad but I never, and she left out where it was supposed to say 'plus labor.' So I get three good jobs last week from that ad—and these two goddamned lazy

guys I hire, can't depend on 'em, half the time don't show, I had to
go out on all the jobs myself, and then they're all raising hell about
the bill—what the *hell,* they think they get a roofing job just for the
cost of the materials? But it said in the ad, they tell me, and I go
right up in the air—was it my fault? I been so damn worried—I was so
damned mad, I just blew up—and they all said, report it to the Better Business Bureau—my God—"

"And Mr. Schultz?" said Varallo.

"Oh, my God. He was the third one. And I heard that's the trig-
ger, you get reported three times, they lift your business license.
What the hell could I do? Lose everything— I just—I just went to see
him, I thought I'd try to explain—and I saw him come out the back
there—"

"How did you come to have the gun on you?"

Gibson was in better control of himself. He said, "I had an idea—if
he wouldn't back down, I'd shoot myself. Last straw, way everything's gone— Oh, hell. Oh, hell. I never thought about fingerprints."

They found the gun in the top drawer of the desk; it hadn't been
cleaned. Varallo called up a squad car to take him in; he wouldn't
say another word, and refused to put all that in a statement, so
Varallo booked him in at the jail and started the machinery on the
warrant.

"This is one report I won't mind writing," he said to Delia. "And
it's a toss-up whether the D.A.'ll call it One or Two. But I certainly
don't buy Mr. Gibson's pathetic tale all the way. He had the gun on
him when he went to see Schultz. And one shot I might swallow as
spur-of-the-moment, but not three." He rolled the triplicate forms
into his typewriter. "Of course, at the last minute it may have been
pure impulse, seeing Schultz come out alone. And of all the stupid
things to do—" He looked at Delia seriously and added, "But then
they are stupid, ninety-nine out of a hundred of them we see in here,
or they wouldn't mess up their lives the way they do."

"I don't know what you're talking about," said Ralph Kleinman
contemptuously. "The fuzz tried to hang a few on me, but it was just
harassment." He seemed to savor the word, repeated it. "Harassment."

"Come on," said O'Connor coldly. "You like the little girls,

Ralph. Also the little boys, but we're talking about the girls. Sandra Tally, three weeks ago last Tuesday. Alice Nutting, eight days later. Brenda Quigley, a week ago last Monday."

He shrugged. "I don't know what you're talking about."

They had found Kleinman alone, here at Lloyd Bunting's Malibu condominium. It was a very lush one in this expensive beach area, a top-floor unit with a view for miles out over the Pacific, with government-owned empty beach across the highway. But as they talked to Kleinman, certain speculations were raising doubts in both their minds. Kleinman's official mug shot hadn't been taken to flatter, but face to face with him they could see why the prosperous Bunting—granted that the sheriff's boys were right about him—would have taken him under his wing. Ralph Kleinman had the sharp, distinctive good looks of a young Spanish grandee: square cleft chin, a cap of thick dark hair, arrogant nose, sensuous mouth.

"When was the last time you were in Glendale?" asked Katz.

"That dismal burg? Years. I forget."

"Never picked up any little girls there to play with?"

"Oh, get lost," said Kleinman. "I don't have to pick kids any-place—" He stopped.

"What are you driving these days?" asked O'Connor. There was a ten-year-old Ford registered to him, but it hadn't been visible in the underground garage.

"If it's any of your business, my car got totaled by a drunk last week—sitting out there in the road. It's junked. I'm waiting for the insurance. Look, you got nothing on me and I don't have to answer any questions." He hadn't asked them in, and now he stepped back and shut the door.

"Second thoughts," said Katz sadly. They sank back down in the elevator and on the highway got into the Ford. "If we hailed him in and asked for alibis, any of those times and places, I bet Mr. Bunting could find forty people to swear he was at a party. I think maybe Ralphie's got a nice new job acting in Mr. Bunting's movies."

"And," said O'Connor, "so Ralphie goes for the kiddies—knocking around Hollywood, mixed up with the hard-porn field, he needn't have gone out of his way, gone over to Glendale, after them. Damn it, Joe, I've got hypnotized by that area aspect. It says nothing, Kenilworth Avenue. Coincidence. Damn it. And—"

"Twenty degrees cooler down here anyway."

"—Would you have a guess, even if it was worth it, what the lab could do with a junked car, even if we could find it?"

"I can hear what Rex Burt would say," said Katz.

Meg got up with a sinus headache on Saturday morning. Let the first heat go on long enough, and it was inevitable. She'd meant to clean the apartment today, but it would just have to wait. She managed to get breakfast for Tammy, and however she felt she'd have to go out to the market this afternoon. She settled Tammy down with the little dollhouse. "Please, you just be quiet and good this morning, darling. Mama doesn't feel good."

"You sick? Like me that time? You goin' to the hos-bittal like me?"

"No, of course not. Just try to be quiet, Tammy." Tammy didn't remember much about the hospital, just being scared when she woke up there. Meg took some decongestant and three aspirins and huddled on the bed with the drapes drawn; she slept a little, and the headache was better but still there by noon, when Tammy came in clamoring for lunch. She'd been good all morning, was restless, wanted to go out now, to the park.

Meg took some more aspirin and dragged out to the market. Her mind wasn't working quite right with all the dope, she had to stop and think what she needed, and Tammy was full of bouncing energy, finding pretty new boxes to dump into the market cart, until Meg could have screamed. "We don't need that, Tammy, put it back."

And it was cowardly of her, but she just couldn't cope with an energetic Tammy today, and you couldn't leave a four-year-old to her own devices for hours, even cooped up in an apartment. Tammy had been good all morning, that was enough to expect. After they got back and Meg had put the groceries away, she got a children's aspirin down Tammy and persuaded her to take a nap with Mama.

Her head was still pounding dully. She lay awake in the darkened room, the child's even sleeping breath light on her cheek, and she felt the fear move somewhere deep inside her. The fear of Wayne.

She didn't think he'd forgotten writing that letter. She didn't think he'd forgotten anything. His queer twisted egotistic brain still blaming her for what had happened—only this time he'd be more careful, so that no one would know—

She could almost feel him there, somewhere out there, thinking and planning how to get at her and Tammy, so secret and cunning that no one would ever know he had done it.

The man with murder in his mind sat in the dark, rather dirty booth in the corner of the bar and stared at his glass of beer. He was remotely aware of the talk flowing over and around him, inane talk of inane people, but he let it flow past.

"And I said to him, 'Mister, if you think I get to keep all my tips you got another think coming—'"

"That's tellin' him all right, when I was working at Barney's in Hollywood, honest to God, you wouldn't believe what we hadda put up with—"

He'd missed somehow; he didn't know how. Figured on getting them both at once, but it had gone wrong. He'd been nervous of hanging around, in case of police, that next day, but there hadn't been anything in the paper. And that day he'd seen them both—her coming out, coming back with the kid. What the hell had gone wrong he didn't know, but he had missed.

"Drink your drinkie, honey. Only young once."

"Hey, go easy on the sauce, girls, this stuff costs money. We ain't millionaires, are we, Ricky?"

"What? No," he said inattentively. Contempt flickered over him for these little boorish people—anonymous cover, he needn't give it much attention, just enough to keep in sweet with the woman. The idea had struck him the first time he had seen the woman, at a bar very much like this one. He'd always been good with women, understanding the types they came in with a sure touch: that type he recognized cold and clear. An easy, shallow, silly woman, easy in more ways than one, an easy mark. About thirty-five, and been around, but never learned much; feed her the flattery, the little attention, and he was in. She'd been minus a boyfriend at the moment, and nothing as good as him had ever come her way before; she hadn't been coy.

She was a little blowsy, skin starting to sag, and not too clean; if it wasn't for the cover, he wouldn't have gone within a mile of her. But there was the shabby, untidy three-room apartment on a narrow street in a poor section of town, a place where nobody noticed comings and goings, or cared about morals or hours. No sweat, she had swallowed the little tale, down-and-out actor trying for TV bits, agent coming up with something any day now. She was a stupid bitch, but useful here and now.

The other one— And he wondered who the man was. Coming that day, and to see her, because they'd come out together, gone up to the market on the boulevard, gone back there. He didn't give a damn about the bitch picking up a boyfriend; he just wondered, because it might be a complication.

Have to try another way. Only one thing had worried him a little— what had she been thinking, about that? What the hell had happened? But there she was, acting just as usual—getting groceries at the market, going to work— It had come to him that the stuff hadn't been strong enough. Maybe old. Not enough of it. So she hadn't noticed anything.

There would be a way. There'd be another plan to make. Only he had to be right out of it. He was never here. Even the damn trustees couldn't look at his bank account; he'd deposited that ten grand all right, but taken out nine in cash the next day. Three hundred for the old clunker he'd left back there in the woods, and he'd picked up a slightly better job here for four; at least it ran. And not from a used lot, either, where they wanted to see a license, send in a new registration; he'd watched the ads, found a private party. Just a little possible danger there: the car was still registered to that owner, and he didn't have a driver's license, of course; but he was being very careful indeed not to invite a traffic ticket. He touched the money belt under his clothes.

But time—time. He couldn't expect the cover he'd arranged back there to last forever; or the cover here either. Come up with another plan, a good foolproof one, and *do* it, and get away. His mind moved over possibilities, sharp and quick.

"Ricky, gimme a cigarette, I'm all out."

"Just one more and Gus and me better cut out—"

"O.K., O.K., just one more, I guess I can run to that."

Fix the little bitch and the kid: it was an obsession doubled in him now, because he had missed the first try.

Sunday was supposed to be O'Connor's day off. He took Maisie up into the hills above the college in the morning, let her gallop around for a couple of hours to work off some of that excess energy. But there was a lot of unfinished business on hand, and he went in at one o'clock.

Poor and Forbes had just brought in a man off the new list and were questioning him. Everybody else was out but Delia. There had been two new heists overnight, at an all-night restaurant on Colorado and a bar on Broadway. Witnesses had come in, made statements, and she had two of them looking at mug shots right now.

Before Poor and Forbes let their man go, Varallo came in with another one. This was groping in the dark, but the only way to go at one like this. This possible was Roy Nealy, and he had a pedigree back to fifteen, various sex offenses; in the last five years he'd been picked up four times for indecent exposure, twice for attempted child molestation; on both counts it had been in broad daylight at a public schoolground, which was about the only reason Varallo had brought him in.

And on such a chancy thing as a sex count, and on a long hunt like this, they might have expected it to happen at least once; but it was annoying when it did.

They got him into an interrogation room, sat him down, and Varallo started the ball rolling. "We want to ask you some questions about little girls, Roy. You like little girls, don't you?"

He nodded reluctantly. "I got to get to work," he said. "I got a job." He was a man about forty; he hadn't much education or, by his looks, apparent intelligence. He had held jobs as a common laborer, was oftener unemployed. He was as tall and lank as Forbes.

"You ever been in Glendale before?" asked O'Connor.

"Yeah. Sometimes."

"Remember just when? What about a week ago last Monday?"

"What happened then?"

"A little girl got raped here, Roy. A little girl six years old. That's one of the things we're asking you about."

"Oh," he said.

"Do you know anything about that, Roy?"

He debated with himself. Then he said slowly, "Yeah. Yeah, I guess I do."

"Suppose you tell us about it. Will you do that?"

"O.K., I'll tell you. I did it. It was me."

They didn't look at each other. "Where did it happen, and when?" asked Varallo.

"I don't remember that. But I did it. She was pretty, all blond and little, and I think she had on a—a—a blue dress. And I saw her—walking along the street, just walking along, and I—" He thought about it. They waited. "Yeah, I went up behind her and I grabbed her and pulled her in behind some bushes right there and I did it to her. She was screaming and hollering like anything—" He was excited, talking about it.

They went out to the corridor and O'Connor said disgustedly, "First one of those we've had." The compulsive confessors could clutter up an investigation now and then.

He was just off P.A. After some delay, Varallo got hold of his parole officer, who said, "Oh, has he? Again? You wouldn't think it to look at him, but Roy's got a little imagination. You can probably alibi him if it worries you. I got him a job selling papers on the corner of Ivar and Hollywood, he's there all afternoon and evening. Oh, he can drive, but he hasn't got a car right now."

"Thank you so much," said Varallo.

The only good thing about the day so far was that it was cooler—a good ten degrees cooler. Now they'd got the March heat wave over—only March itself had gone last week—they'd get the cool, overcast skies through most of June, and then summer would come in with a vengeance.

They told Nealy he could go, and he looked surprised and went. O'Connor and Varallo lit cigarettes, and Delia said, "That's a funny sort of thing, isn't it? Alex told me—I mean, a detective I knew in L.A. said during that Black Dahlia case they had over a hundred fake confessions."

"Little before my time, but I don't doubt," said O'Connor. "Notorious case like that—if it isn't the nuts, it's the publicity hounds." The phone buzzed at him and he picked it up.

Sergeant Duff was excited enough that his voice reached all of them. "Lieutenant—he tried to snatch another kid just now, and she got away from him! Tracy's there, he just called—"

"Goddamn!" said O'Connor. "What's the address? By God, are we going to get a break at last?"

The three of them rushed out on it. It was East Dryden, an unpretentious frame house, but of course right in that area. The calmest person in the group was the little girl, Mary Lou Turner. Her father was alternately raving about sex fiends and beaming pride at her for her guts and sense; her mother was getting over an attack of nervous weeping; a younger sister was staring in awe; and an older brother was saying, "Now, if she'd just had a baseball bat with her—"

Mary Lou was nine, and small for her age, a slender whiplash of a child with the same bright-red hair as her father and siblings, greeny eyes under sandy lashes, and a businesslike manner. "Now you just tell the policemen what happened, and they'll catch him and put him in jail," promised her mother generously. "Don't be nervous now, honey," urged her father. "Aw, such a big deal," said her brother, eying Varallo and O'Connor with awful secret admiration. Sister just went on staring.

"I'm not nervous," said Mary Lou. "There's nothing to be nervous about. I got away from him, didn't I?" And of course this could be just a wild coincidence, some other joker making a grab for a little girl right here; but it was the same area, and she looked younger than she was. And when he hadn't got hold of her, hurt her, the chances were she'd remember more than the little girls who had been raped.

She looked at Varallo and O'Connor politely, at Delia with interest. "Are you a policewoman? I think that'd be kind of interesting."

"I'm a detective," said Delia. "Sometimes it is. Now we'd like to hear all about what happened to you, Mary Lou."

"All right. I wasn't really scared. I don't seem to get scared very much," said Mary Lou.

"The red hair," murmured Varallo. "Naturally."

Yesterday Mary Lou had been up at the school playground: Mark Keppel Elementary School, where she was in the fourth grade. The playground was open, not fully fenced, and she'd been there with her best friend, Marcia Hansen, as kids sometimes did on weekends, playing on the swings. Their mothers had let them take their lunches, and she'd left her lunchbox there, with the thermos in it. And today being Sunday, her mother hadn't missed it, until Mary

Lou remembered and went back to get it. It was only four long blocks up there. She'd found the lunchbox right where she left it, beside the swings—"Which," said Mrs. Turner, "is a miracle in itself, the pilfering that goes on in schools these days"—and started home. And she'd got about halfway, was on Palm Street about the middle of the block, when a car came up behind her and stopped at the curb, and a man got out of it and grabbed her.

"I guess it was lucky I wasn't wearing pants," said Mary Lou gravely, "because my dress wasn't so sort of thick, you know, and he hadn't got a really good hold, just on my skirt, and it tore when I pulled away. And he got in front of me and grabbed me by both arms, but I kicked him in the shins as hard as I could and he yelled—I know how that hurts, and I had on my patent-leather shoes that are real hard. So he let go, and I ran as hard as I could—I remembered how Mother always said, anything like that happens, run to the nearest house and ring the doorbell, ask for help. So I did, but there wasn't anybody home. But I guess he thought somebody might be, and he got in the car and drove away. So then I just came on home. When he let me go the second time, I nearly threw my lunchbox at him, I thought that might be a good idea, but I remembered how much it cost and how Daddy was worried about the taxes, so I didn't." And she hadn't screamed at any point, to attract attention from neighbors who were home.

"That's just fine," said Delia. "You were certainly very brave and sensible. Do you remember what he looked like? Could you describe him?"

"Oh, yes. He was about," said Mary Lou thoughtfully, looking at O'Connor, "as tall as you, but not so, you know, broad. He was kind of narrow in the shoulders, and then he had a fat stomach. He had brown sort of hair, not much, I mean not long at all, and he had glasses on. They were the kind without any rims. And when I kicked him and he yelled, I saw he had a gold tooth on one side."

"I will be goddamned," said O'Connor, and Mrs. Turner bristled at him. "I don't suppose you could say which side?"

Mary Lou thought. "He'd just let me go then, so my right'd be his left. The left side, I guess."

"Sweet Jesus Christ!" said O'Connor, and Mrs. Turner opened her mouth to utter what would undoubtedly be a sharp reprimand.

"You're a pretty smart detective, Mary Lou," said Delia hastily. "You've been a big help. Thanks a lot."

"Well, that's good. I'm glad I could help you. I hope you catch him," said Mary Lou politely. "I don't know why he should try to grab me, he must be crazy or something."

"Yes, he is. Do you remember anything about the car?"

"Well, no," said Mary Lou apologetically. "I didn't get a good look at it. I think it was blue, but I'm not sure."

"That's fine, you've given us a lot," said Delia.

"By God," said O'Connor, "that's a damn definite description, and the only one we've had. That is one damn smart kid. It's got to be our boy, Vic."

"Outside of a wild coincidence. Gives us a hell of a lot more than we had."

"So we have a damned good look through the list—by God, feed it into the computer and sift through every record we've got available— This has got to narrow it down, and that kid deserves a medal—"

"Unless," said Varallo, "he's not in anybody's records, Charles."

It started out to be a quiet night; Rhys and Hunter didn't have any calls until eleven-twenty. Then Patrolman Morris called in and said they'd better come look at a corpse. It was, he said, kind of a funny story.

They went out to hear it. The night had cooled off considerably, the way the climate here was given to extremes, and there was a chilly little wind. Morris had said the corner of Pacific and Elk. When they got there, there was a dead man in the street, the squad car, and an Olds sedan slewed into the curb, passenger door open, with a woman sitting in it crying.

"You never," said Morris, "know what the drunks will do."

The woman pulled herself together and talked to them, hiccuping and distraught. She said she was Mrs. Peter Lyman—Myra Lyman— and the man was her husband. They'd been at a restaurant out on Colorado, and he'd had too much to drink, in fact he was pretty drunk, so she'd been driving them home. And just as they got here— they lived at an apartment on Pacific a couple of blocks away—all of a sudden he'd yelled that she was driving too fast and opened the door and jumped out. She'd been going about thirty-five, she said.

"Well, a funny one," said Dick Hunter. "These drunks. He's dead all right, I suppose he fell on his head."

"I wasn't going too fast," she sobbed, "and he *said* I should drive—"

CHAPTER SIX

One thing immediately apparent was that the description given them by Mary Lou Turner didn't fit any of the men out of Records they'd talked to so far. And computers were useful only up to a point.

"When you come to think," said Varallo, "while it's a definite description in a way, Charles, there's not much there that a computer could evaluate. Except for the general size, the gold tooth, the—and all things considered—"

O'Connor said querulously, "Hell, yes, of course there's that—if he is in anybody's records, he might have got mugged and booked before he acquired the gold tooth or started to go bald, but for God's sake don't be a wet blanket, Vic."

"The one thing in my mind," said Katz, "is that it's just a week since he began getting his kicks out of killing instead of rape. And there wasn't much time between them before. He got stymied yesterday—how long will it be before he gets the urge again?"

That was a thing to think about; but they could only work with what they had. O'Connor was on the phone to R. and I. at LAPD headquarters. Varallo said Delia could stay in and take the statement on that drunk last night. There were a few people he hadn't talked to about Montez. They should be getting an autopsy report sometime, not that it would tell them much they didn't know. Thomsen had had the slugs from Goulding, and identified them as out of a Harrington and Richardson nine-shot revolver.

The witnesses to the latest two heists, at the bar and the all-night restaurant, had positively picked two mug shots: Frank Rinaldi at the bar, Terence Jones at the restaurant: both black and with appropriate records, latest addresses in Eagle Rock and the Atwater section, respectively. Forbes and Katz went out looking for them now.

Myra Lyman came in at nine-thirty, and told Delia three times over what had happened last night. "I don't believe it yet. Honestly, I woke up this morning, I don't know how I slept at all, the other bed empty, I thought I'd dreamed it. Just yelled out at me, driving too fast, and jumping out like that—and all of a sudden he's dead! It's crazy." She was about thirty-five, a thin blond woman with sharp features, but good-looking, superficially smart, and conventional in a navy suit and white blouse. "We were married twelve years," she said. "It'll take some getting used to."

Delia asked the necessary questions to get down in the statement. Lyman had worked at the Sherwin-Williams paint store on Wilson; she was a sales clerk at a gift shop in La Cañada. "Well, no, he didn't tie one on often, I guess that was partly it, it didn't take much to reach him, see. It didn't get him excited, he just got quiet—he said I'd better drive, he hadn't said a word all the way home, and I thought he'd passed out. And then all of a sudden he starts to yell and got the door open—I nearly had a heart attack—"

She watched Delia type the statement, read it obediently, and signed it. Delia explained about the mandatory autopsy, that she'd be notified when she could claim the body.

"Well, thanks," said Mrs. Lyman. "I didn't know that. I never had anything to do with the police before. I suppose I'd better think what to do about a funeral." She trailed out looking rather forlorn.

Just before noon, Katz and Forbes came back. Forbes hadn't had any luck locating Rinaldi, but Katz had found Jones, peacefully passed out on the daybed in his rented room with an empty fifth of gin beside him. He had brought him in and lodged him in jail until he was conscious enough to question, which would probably be tomorrow. They started out for an early lunch together, leaving Delia alone in the office. Ten minutes later as she realized it was after twelve, fished her handbag out of the bottom drawer and stood up, the phone buzzed at O'Connor's empty desk.

"You've got a new homicide," said Sergeant Duff.

"Where and what?" asked Delia crisply. She was secretly rather pleased that nobody else was in: the first time she'd go out alone at the start of a case, and she'd better not do anything stupid or they'd never let her forget it.

It was Adams Square, over southeast in an old part of town. Four streets came together at odd angles, and there were two service stations cater-corner from each other, a half block of business on one side, a good-sized single building opposite. Patrolmen Harper and Gallagher were riding herd on an excited little crowd of people on the sidewalk, on the corner. They looked disappointed to see her, and she used her briskest manner.

Gallagher left Harper minding the crowd and gave her a rundown briefly. "It's the market owner, guy named George Mihardis. About sixty. It looks like the heister came in—these people say he'd be alone in the store till a clerk came on at one—pulled the heist, and Mihardis got his own gun and fought back. We don't know if the heister got shot. Don't know if anybody can give you a description, but the mechanic at the Seventy-six station saw him running away."

Delia told them to stand by. Sergeant Duff would automatically send out whoever came in first from lunch, but that might be a little while. She went into the market, which was an independent neighborhood place, occupying the largest space in the little half block of one building: a drugstore on the corner, then the market, then a dry cleaner's. It was a large, clean, bright place looking well stocked and maintained: a liquor section, three long frozen-food cases running the length of the store, two checkout counters and cash registers.

The body was lying just to the right of the front door, prone and facing the door, right arm flung forward. Still clutched in the right hand was a gun: Delia bent to look, and it was an old Luger automatic. All she could tell about the body was that it had curly black hair just going gray; the man had been big and broad-shouldered, not fat. She measured distances with her eye, quickly. He'd been at one of the checkout counters, the heister had put the gun on him, he had produced his own and started to follow the man out. And been unlucky.

She went out and asked Gallagher who had called in. "Me," said a voice from the little crowd. "My God, we got to depend on female shamuses now? No offense, lady, I'm sorry—I'm all shook. My name's Sid Harris, I got the Seventy-six station across there. My God, George—the nicest guy you'd want to meet—had that market for over twenty years, everybody around here knew him, I can't get over it. I was in the garage working on a brake job, I hear shots, I come out and see this guy come flying out of the market with a gun in his hand—he runs around the corner and I get over here about the same time as everybody else, and there's George dead, my God—"

"Everybody else" turned out to be the pharmacist from the drugstore, three girl clerks, the attendant from the other station, a husband and wife from the dry cleaner's. They had been at the back of the shop, were slower coming out after hearing the shots; of course the heister had been running that way, and they'd just missed seeing him.

Directly across from the market was the larger building. It bore a sign on its front: CHRISTIAN NEWS PRESS. It also bore a sign on the front door which Delia could just make out: CLOSED. HOURS 1–8 P.M.

She told Gallagher to call in for a mobile lab unit, and started to question Harris; but of course within half an hour Varallo and Forbes landed on the scene and took over. Burt and Thomsen arrived in the mobile lab truck and Varallo emerged after ten minutes in the market to say, "You'd better go and see his wife, Delia." He passed over the address. "She won't be able to tell us anything, but she's got to know."

All I'm useful for, thought Delia, is to tactfully break the bad news. The feminine touch. But it was all part of the job.

The address was on Glenwood Road, a pink stucco Spanish place in a neatly landscaped yard. The woman who came to the door was ageless, a tall, deep-bosomed woman with classic features, a coil of hair on her neck, very dark eyes; she looked incongruous in a simple cotton dress and cardigan. Delia broke the news tactfully, and went in to stand by. But Helena Mihardis was dignified in her grief, in control of herself.

"Would you like me to call someone for you?"

"It would be kind. My son Demetrius. How good that he is near—he has just been transferred from the Long Beach store." He was in personnel at Buffums' department store at the Galleria. While they waited in the neat, conventionally furnished living room, Mrs. Mihardis talked, not talking to Delia as a person, but to herself, of the years that had brought them here, the work and sacrifice and success and comfort. The son and daughter to take pride in—"My daughter is married to a fine man, a doctor, they live in San Diego. They give us three beautiful grandchildren. Demetrius will marry soon." And presently she said, "So he will have a second funeral mass now. Life is strange. Fate sends, we take. Over thirty years ago, thirty-five, he was partisan—at home in Greece—fighting the Communists after the war is over. For months he is missing in the mountains, he and Demetrius, his great friend, and it is accepted they are dead. There was a funeral mass said for him in our village. And then he came back—they had been held prisoner, but escaped. Demetrius died later of wounds, and George vowed to name a son for him, a braver man than himself, but I do not know about that."

The son, striding in, embracing her, looking fiercely at Delia, had the face on a Greek coin. "Of course he couldn't stand still for the dirty little thief—he wouldn't have been Papa if he had. Goddamn the bastard. And there wouldn't have been fifty bucks in the register, on a Monday morning. My God, my God. Why the *hell* couldn't he have let the bastard take it and run? Not worth his life—my God, he was only fifty-nine—"

"We must call Hermione," she said.

Delia explained about the formal identification of the body; he said he would come in.

She went back to the scene, but the only activity going on there was by Burt and Thomsen; the witnesses were being taken to headquarters in relays to make statements. She went back to help out on that. They were busy taking those the rest of the day, and no clear leads developed.

The heister had been too far away from Sid Harris for him to give any useful description. "But I got the feeling he was young, the way he moved. Did George get off a shot at him? I bet he did—the shots sounded different, a couple kind of light and sharp, and then some a lot deeper, you know?" Mihardis had got off three shots; they had found the ejected cartridge cases. "God, I hope he winged him! He was running fast enough, but it could be—I was too far off to see any blood."

The station attendant across the street had seen about the same thing; he said the heister was wearing a navy jumpsuit, and looked medium-sized. He'd run around the corner and there was the sound of a car starting up, but of course nobody had been able to see the car, it had been on the side street, Park Avenue.

There might be some lab evidence on the scene; wait for it. But for whatever it was worth, they had to take statements from everybody there, file an initial report. Toward the end of shift, Varallo got on the phone to Goulding, asked him to get the slugs out and send them over to the lab.

"I've just got them," said Goulding. "They look like twenty-twos to me. Three of 'em."

O'Connor had been gone all afternoon; at a guess, he was down in R. and I. at LAPD headquarters.

At six o'clock the witnesses had all gone, and only Varallo was left finishing the report, swearing as he occasionally struck two keys together. Delia had just said, "See you in the morning," and was on her way out when the phone buzzed on her desk.

Resignedly she turned back and picked it up.

Meg had got home with Tammy a little early. She was feeling a hundred per cent better for the cool weather, down in the sixties today, and a slight chance of rain, which of course would be the last of it for this season.

She was thinking about what she'd said to Stan. You got in a rut, you stayed in it out of inertia. She'd come back here automatically because she thought of it as home, but it wasn't any more; it had been home, when Mother and Daddy were alive, in the old house up on Mountain Street. Aunt Ruth's had never been home, with the dark rooms, the fragile antiques you had to be careful of, all the religious statues. The only family she had left, but—she had realized slowly—Aunt Ruth didn't want to be family to anybody; perhaps she had been glad to seize any excuse to push Meg out of her life, which was bounded by the church and her precious house full of treasures.

She and Tammy could go anywhere. Up the coast where it was cooler. It was unlucky that Linda was in Fresno; that was even hotter than Los Angeles. She could get another job, maybe one in a large office where she'd get to know more people. Only it would cost some money; there'd have to be enough to live on until she found the job, found somewhere to live. There was only about three hundred and fifty dollars in her checking account. She'd start to save right away, save as much as she could every week.

Tammy had learned a new song in nursery school, a monotonous little jingle about some kittens, and she'd been singing it all the way home. Meg hardly paid attention; her thoughts were racing on to the future.

And then they went in the front door, and all that went away from her and her mood changed in one heartbeat. The door to the right-hand apartment was open, and Bill Wiley stood there. He was a big man with heavy shoulders, a heavy unhandsome face under short-cropped hair; she had the vague impression that he worked at some construction job. He was just standing in the doorway, and his eyes looked bleary. He looked at Meg and said, "There she is, drunk again."

Carol Sue's funeral had been this morning. He had come to tell her last Friday, and she'd sent some flowers.

"Drunk again," he repeated. "She's got a guilty conscience, and so the hell she oughta have—leave Carol Sue out in the dark so that sex fiend could get her."

"I'm sorry," Meg started to say inadequately, but he pulled the door shut and lumbered out, pushing past her. Tammy was already up the stairs, singing her little song.

Meg thrust the key in the lock soberly, and inside immediately put up the chain. Tammy made for her room. Meg realized she'd forgotten to check the mailbox, but there probably wasn't much there. She went out to the kitchen, trying to think what to have for dinner. There was some ground beef in the freezer—there were always instant mashed potatoes. Peas or something, and open a can of fruit cocktail for dessert. Not very inspired, but she was feeling depressed again, after that little scene downstairs. And that, she thought, *was* all my fault. Just for living here.

She opened the refrigerator and exclaimed in annoyance. It was barely cool, and certainly not running. The freezer seemed to be all right. She moved things around in the refrigerator, looking; but if nothing else had gone, the rest of the half-gallon of milk certainly had—she picked up the cardboard carton and could feel the soured curds swishing inside. "Damn," she said to herself. Tammy would just have to go without milk tonight, and she'd have to use dairy creamer in her coffee. She poured the soured milk down the sink and ran the disposal. The wastebasket was full and she carried it down the back stairs to empty into the big trash bin. The trash collectors would come by tomorrow morning.

She'd have to call Mr. Glidden, the landlord, about the refrigerator.

Just as she shut the back door and fastened the chain, she heard Tammy's little startled cry, and hurried into the living room. "What is it, T— Oh, Tammy!" Her father's photograph was lying face down on the bare floor beside the end table, beyond the edge of the inadequate carpet. There were shards of glass all around it.

"I didn't break it, Mama!" Tammy sounded frightened. "Honest, I didn't! It—it jumped all by itself—it just jumped off the table and broke itself!"

"Oh, Tammy," said Meg wearily. "It's all right." It was just the glass; it wouldn't cost much to replace. She picked up the frame and photograph and put them into the drawer of the end table, went to the kitchen broom closet to get broom and dustpan to sweep up the glass.

It was as she leaned in to reach the broom that she noticed the cardboard box in the corner of the narrow closet. It was beside the extra box of detergent there, a box not quite as big as the box of detergent. It was white, with a large red X on its side, and below that was printed RED X SURE POISON—and below that in smaller letters, FOR MICE, RATS, ALL RODENTS.

An hour later they were still arguing at her, going over the same things, and she was saying the same things back. Stan Pollard and the nice policewoman who had believed her about Wayne, at first.

"I ought to know. I do know. I never bought that, at the market or anywhere. There've never been any mice here. Why should I? If I had bought poison for any reason I'd never have put it there, on the floor, with Tammy around."

"That Nembutal—" said Delia.

Meg put one hand on her head as if to hold in the pressure of anger. "Just listen," she said. "Words of one syllable. When you're used to a baby crawling around, you just automatically put dangerous things up high. Bleach. Ammonia. Lysol. Anything. It gets to be a habit. But that's beside the point. I did not buy that poison, and if I had I wouldn't have put it there."

"Now listen, Meg. You told us about Saturday—"

"I told you *all* about Saturday." They had led her back to her latest trip to the market, of course, and the sinus headache, Tammy and the market cart, the aspirin. "Whatever either of you may think, I am not an absolute fool. Yes, she put things in the cart and I took them out. Three or four things, not dozens. Yes, I had a bad headache, but I wasn't out of my head. I was mentally competent enough to drive the car to the market and push the cart around and pick out what I needed. *Just* what I needed. Yes, there were two large bags of groceries, but I'd have remembered seeing that when I was taking things out. You don't think Tammy got there first and put it in the closet, do you? Well, *do* you?"

"Mrs. Burgess, what I think is possible," said Delia, "is that you mistook it for a box of detergent. The box is very similar to the brand you use, and colored the same, red and white. That's where you keep detergent, isn't it?"

"An extra box, yes. But my brand of detergent doesn't have a big red X on it."

"You had this headache," said Stan.

"Will you both," said Meg forcefully, "please stop talking to me as if I was Tammy's age! My God, if I'd only kept the market receipt! That would have told you—what price is on it?" She had refused to touch the thing; it was sitting on the coffee table in front of him.

"Four fifty-nine."

"Well, then. You'd have seen there wasn't an item priced like that. Only I threw it away. And I really can't help it if you think I'm a hysterical fool, but every single bit of food in this place is going out—because that damned box has been opened, and God knows where some of that poison might be."

"Oh, now, Meg. Look," he said. "We made you look—Miss Riordan showed you. There is no way anyone can get into this place when it's locked. You've been keeping the windows locked when you're gone, and they're good tight locks. There isn't a window onto the back porch, and the rest are all on the second floor. Anybody'd have to use a ladder, and break a window to get in—and don't you suppose he'd have been seen?—Mrs. Kemp's dog barking up a blue streak at him, and the old lady yelling 'Burglar!' "

"You believed me," she said. "You believed me about Wayne.

You came out here to warn me about him. Why don't you believe me now?"

"Because this just isn't possible," he said patiently. "It's not physically possible, Meg. Surely you can see that?"

"I don't know how he did it. I can't be sure. One thing I *am* sure of: I—did—not—buy—that—poison. Tammy didn't put it in the cart and I didn't overlook it, I didn't put it in the cart, and I didn't put it in the closet thinking it was detergent. And I don't know that some of the food here isn't loaded with it, and neither do you. And I'll tell you something else—yes—yes—" She sat up with a jerk. "It was Daddy who made me find it—he warned me! Tammy said the picture just jumped off the table and broke—so I had to get the broom for the glass—" She saw them look at each other, and sat back, breathing fast.

"Mrs. Burgess. You're working yourself up to a nervous breakdown over this. I understand that you're very frightened of this man, but you mustn't let yourself get irrational about it. Now we're pretty busy right now, at headquarters. But I'm going to have a detective come and take samples of all your food, for analysis. It may be a little waste of time for us, but at least we'll prove to you that it isn't possible for anyone to get in here."

Meg said miserably, "I don't know," and it didn't mean anything.

"Now all right," said Stan. He leaned forward from where he sat opposite her and took one of her hands. "Is it remotely possible that anyone else could have a key to this apartment?"

"Just Mr. Glidden. The landlord."

"Well, do you think Mr. Glidden could be bribed by Wayne Burgess to give him a duplicate key?"

In spite of herself, Meg laughed. "He's about sixty and he was a sergeant of Marines, and he was a professional boxer and still keeps in training. If anybody offered him a bribe, he'd—he'd punch him in the nose."

"Well, then. Has anybody ever had a key to get in here? Workman? Plumber, electrician—"

"No. Mr. Glidden does a lot of things himself. Once when I had to have a plumber, he came and let him in and stayed until he was finished."

"All right. Former tenants?"

"The locks were changed when I moved in, and then he put new ones, better ones, in last year, because there'd been an attempted break-in at the Wileys'."

"Now don't you see that you've just proved there is absolutely no way anybody could get in? Do you leave your keys lying around? How many are there?"

"No, of course not. Just the car keys, the house key, a key to the office—I'm usually there first, and Dr. Burton doesn't come in on Wednesdays. They're all on one ring."

"Where do you keep them at the office?"

"In my handbag in a drawer of the desk."

"Take your handbag with you when you go to the ladies' room?" She nodded. "All *right*," he said.

Delia got up. "There'll be a detective here later to take samples. I didn't tell you, did I, that our lab did find out there were particles of crushed Nembutal tablets in the asparagus, and on the paper, and on the mortar and pestle. I'll see you get that and the dish back."

And Tammy appeared in the hall, clutching her stuffed cat and looking cross and sleepy. "Aren't we ever goin' to have dinner, Mama? I'm awful hungry—and I played with the dollhouse like you said, an awful long time, and I'm tired playin'—"

"Oh, my God," said Meg. "The time—darling, I'm sorry—" She looked at Stan wildly.

"You get ready," he said. "We'll go out and have some hamburgers."

He half-shut the door behind them and said to Delia, "What about this? It's wild."

She looked tired. She said, "I think she's held this fear in so closely, she's seeing bogeymen around every corner. Of course the fear for the child would be the worst. I think that poison got there by accident when she picked it up thinking it was detergent, or possibly Tammy did put it in the cart. Certainly the flap's a little loose. You often get a box like that—of anything. The stock clerks slit open cartons with a special knife, and the top boxes get in the way sometimes."

"Hell, I don't know," said Stan. "We haven't seen a sign of the damned fellow—if he were going to make some move, wouldn't he have by now?"

"How can anybody know that? I'll send a detective up," said Delia, and turned away.

Tammy was thrilled with the bright little restaurant and the novelty of the cheeseburger. But she fell asleep in the car on the way back to the apartment, and Meg said, "Poor baby, I'll just get her undressed and into bed."

She was still in the other room when the detective came, an alert-looking slim man who said his name was Rhys. He had a lot of plastic bags and bottles with him, and he took a sample of every item of food in the refrigerator, in opened boxes and jars. Stan watched him, and told him what this was all about when Rhys asked.

"So that's it," said Rhys. "What a hell of a situation."

"You can say that again," said Stan.

When he had gone, Meg came out to the living room and said, "I'd have had to throw out most of that anyway. The refrigerator's on the fritz."

"Now look here," he said. "Would you trust me with a key? I'll tell you what I'll do. Just so you can be a hundred per cent sure nobody's getting in here, I'll stay here all day. How's that?"

"What on earth would you do?"

"Catch up on my reading. Catch up on my sleep."

"You can't do it forever," she said. "You don't believe anybody got in, do you?"

Stan looked at her. He wondered if he and Uncle Olly had been making fools of themselves. He wondered if Wayne Burgess was within a thousand miles of this place. And then he wondered if her female intuition was telling her something. He also wondered how Uncle Olly was getting on with the Chalmers suit, and the Graftons' divorce, and a few other things he'd shoved off on him when he got that plane out of Wichita.

He knew he could be half in love with this girl if he let himself. He didn't know what to do for her. She didn't seem to be a hysterical type, but she did seem to be obsessed with fear of the man.

He decided he'd better have a talk with Uncle Olly and hear what he thought about it.

Delia was feeling a little out of sorts on Tuesday, what with missing lunch yesterday and not getting dinner until after eight last night. She was usually resigned to the fact that the men were chary of letting her help question the punks; maybe in time— But today she was amused at the way things fell out. O'Connor was busy on the newest sex list again; he went out about ten and didn't come back. It was Forbes's day off. Poor brought in a possible heister a little later, looked mildly disconcerted to find only Delia in, and let her sit in on the questioning, but it didn't take long. He was one of the two the Coopers had picked out, and he said he'd been working that night, the bowling alley down on Glendale Avenue. The manager backed him up and they let him go.

Poor went out again, and a couple of minutes later Katz came in towing a big black fellow who was obviously suffering from quite a hangover. Katz looked at Delia just the way Poor had, but he hadn't any choice; if a suspect came apart and admitted anything, it was a good idea to have a witness. They took him into an interrogation room and Katz briefed Delia: Terence Jones, the heister identified by three witnesses at that twenty-four-hour restaurant.

They went the route with the monotonous repeated questions. Terence didn't know nothing about a heist. He'd been clean since he got off P.A. the last time. He didn't have no gun, and he never was at that place.

"Come on," said Katz. "Unless you've got a twin brother, how come all those witnesses picked you out?"

"I don't know."

He couldn't be much more distinctive; he had a puckered scar on one cheek, two front teeth missing, and a cauliflower ear.

"Where'd you get the bread to tie one on?" asked Katz. "You haven't got a job and your landlord says you're behind on the rent."

"Thass my business." He was nervous of Delia; the usual kind of fuzz he was used to, not the female type.

She looked at Katz. "I don't know, Joe. They could have been wrong." Katz opened his mouth at her; she cut across his words. "That one witness—the cashier—said the heister was about the ugliest black bastard he'd ever laid eyes on, and no more brain than an ape, to walk in without a mask wearing a face like that—"

Jones began to look mad.

"And wasn't he right," said Katz. "Or don't you think this one is ugly enough?"

"It isn't that," said Delia, "but he told us the heister cut the phone cord so they couldn't call in, and this one looks too stupid to do a thing like that."

Jones looked madder and confused. "I ain't either stupid. I never done that—that bassard's a liar!"

"Well, he was smart enough to get away with about five C-notes, so the cashier said," said Katz.

Jones let out a roar. "You crazy or somethin'? It wasn't no more than a hundred—" He stopped, looking even more confused.

"And thank God they're mostly fools," said Katz in the corridor. "It does make the job so much easier."

After lunch at the place on Broadway, Delia went out to do some legwork. It wasn't that she felt she'd really get anything, but she'd run out of paperwork at the office and it was, after the long heat wave, an invigorating day with the sky a deep blue, a cool wind, the temperature a nice sixty.

She went down to that bar on South Brand and talked to the bartender again, of course futilely. She went to the used-car lot and talked to the owner and his salesman, who told her that people used the lot as a shortcut from Brand to the side street Garfield, and vice versa. Nobody thought anything of it. They were, they said as they'd said before, sorry as hell they hadn't realized those were shots, gone out to look—they might have seen the guy, given a description. Hell of a thing, that fellow getting shot like that.

Delia came out to the sidewalk and looked across the street. Everybody along here had been talked to. There was an old tan brick building across there which housed a liquor store, a dry cleaner's, and a musty-looking secondhand shop on the ground floor. And whoever was there would have been questioned, without result. She was vaguely reminded of the business block where George Mihardis had died yesterday: and of course some of the men had been out today on that, looking at M.O.'s in Records—not that there was any distinctive M.O. on it. But there was a second floor to this building, and now she noticed curtains at the windows up there. She wondered: apartments?

THE HUNTERS AND THE HUNTED

She walked across the street and investigated. There was, around at the side of the building on Garfield, a narrow entrance, a solid door marked *102–106*. It was unlocked. Inside there was a tiny square of cement at the foot of a very steep dark flight of wooden stairs, and two mailboxes set in the wall. One bore no nameplate, but the other had a neatly lettered one that said MAINWARING.

She climbed the stairs. At the top was a little landing, a blank wall ahead of her, and a door to the right and left. The right-hand one was just a door, but the left one had another nameplate on it, and it said MAINWARING. Delia knocked on it.

"Who is it?" came a cheerful voice inside instantly.

"Police," said Delia.

"Oh, just a moment." There was the sound of a wheelchair—quite unmistakable to Delia, who had lived with one for fourteen years—and then the door swung open.

The little woman in the wheelchair was merry-faced, white-haired, with very bright brown eyes. She had some knitting in her lap, pink wool. She was wearing a pretty blue dress with a real lace collar. She looked at Delia and said, "Gracious, you're not police, are you?"

"Yes, I am." Delia showed her the badge.

"Well, come in. That's very enterprising of you," said the old lady. "I was a suffragette in my day. Is it an interesting job?"

"Tolerably," said Delia. "Did you hear about a man getting shot across the street the other day?"

"Ah, it's about that. I wondered if I ought to call the police, but I felt sure that someone closer by would have provided you with the evidence. Besides, there's no denying it would be difficult for me to get out to give evidence," and she twinkled at Delia cheerfully.

"Do you live here all alone—is it Mrs. Mainwaring?"

"That's right, my dear. No, indeed, my daughter lives with me. My daughter Joyce. It's really quite convenient, if not exactly grand." In fact, this little living room at the front of the building was surprisingly comfortable and pleasant, a faded old oriental rug on the floor, tapestry-covered couch, a couple of upholstered chairs, some pleasing flower prints on the walls. There was a door at either end of the room, one to a hallway, the other to a glimpse of a bright-looking kitchen. "The man who owns the liquor store keeps the rest of this floor as a storeroom. We're quite private up here. Joyce was left a widow rather young, and we always got along well, which is not always the case with one's children—I love Tom and Margaret dearly but I could *not* live with either of them—so we're quite comfortable here. Joyce is in the cosmetics department at the Broadway in the new shopping center. The rent here is astonishingly low, and after all, if one is comfortable *in* a place, what does the outside matter? May I know your name, my dear?"

Delia told her. "You can manage by yourself all day?"

"Oh, yes. So far. Let us trust, up to the end." She was knitting briskly without looking at her work. "This wretched diabetes—they had to amputate one of my feet, you see, but I manage—with the crutches I can get back and forth to the bathroom, get the meals—Joyce fusses, but I really like to do that. I can do a great many things. One does learn to cope when one must. My dear—what have I said? You're crying—"

"I just got something in my eye," said Delia. She got out her handkerchief and dealt with it. And she was, here and now, a full-fledged detective, about the youngest female one around, on a job; she pushed memory away to the back of her mind . . . The memory of a thirteen-year-old Delia, very scared and hurting and alone, there in the hospital room where Alex was long and flat in the bed, all the love and home and family she had. And the doctor taking her into the corner of the room, a big flabby man who called her "My Dear Child," and saying she must be prepared, they would do all they could, but he was afraid— And Alex dragging himself up in the bed and throwing the glass at him, shouting thickly, "Goddamn you—think you kill me off—before I raise my girl? Go to hell, you bastard!" The glass had missed the doctor, which Delia had violently regretted.

"I saw an article in the paper about the shooting," said Mrs. Mainwaring.

"Yes," said Delia. "We don't know much about it yet. Did you see anything, Mrs. Mainwaring?"

"Why, yes, I did. I sit by the window most of the time, not only for the light, but to watch the people in the street. We have a television set in Joyce's bedroom, but I really don't care much for it. I don't mind at all not getting out, you know—Joyce changes our library books twice a week. But you want to know about the poor man who was shot— Yes, I saw it. Or rather, I looked up just afterward, when I heard the shots. It was still rather warm, and the window was open."

"And what did you see?" Delia didn't expect anything useful. She'd enjoyed meeting Mrs. Mainwaring, Mrs. Mainwaring was a darling, but of course she wouldn't have seen anything they didn't already know about.

"Well, I heard the shots and looked up. Or rather, of course, down. I saw the man lying there, and some other men rushing up to him, and I thought, Goodness, he's been shot—and I saw the other man walking away, just putting a gun in his pocket. He went through the used-car lot to the side street. I couldn't give you any description of him, it was much too far away and he had his back to me. I expect you have a description from witnesses nearer by."

"Not very good," said Delia. "He went onto the side street, Garfield?"

"That's right. He got into a parked car there and drove off. Dear me," said Mrs. Mainwaring, "I have just realized that possibly nobody else noticed that—from here, of course, I had a view over the lot. The car," she added brightly, "was a Lotus Elite, that two-door sports coupe, and it had a custom paint job—bright kelly green. It doesn't come in that color from the factory, or rather didn't. This one was either a 1952 or 1953 model."

"What?" said Delia. "You're sure—but how—"

"Oh, quite," said Mrs. Mainwaring. "You see, my husband was quite a connoisseur of automobiles—what do they call it, a car buff? He always kept up with all the makes and models. So I took an interest too. Remember that, my dear, when you marry—common interests make a marriage very solid. Henry and I were married forty-eight years, very happily—very happily indeed."

CHAPTER SEVEN

"Now isn't that something!" said Varallo, amused and intrigued. "I like your old lady. A Lotus—that was a little British racer, wasn't it? Not just a dime a dozen, especially now. Even without a plate number, we could brief Traffic at roll call to be on the watch for a thing like that—most of the men know something about cars. I'd take a bet there wouldn't be more than one Lotus drifting around this town, and maybe in the whole county."

"Well, that was what I thought," said Delia.

O'Connor came trudging in looking surly and discouraged, heard about that, and grunted, "Could be helpful. Do you know that the computers have turned up—out of sex records countywide—just one character with a gold tooth in front, and he's got a solid alibi for Alice Nutting and Brenda Quigley."

"*Che peccáto,*" said Varallo thoughtfully.

Katz said from his desk, "Dentists don't put them in any more, do they?"

"So he had an old-fashioned dentist. Where are you getting on that new homicide?"

"Nowhere," said Varallo. "There isn't a smell of a lead anywhere. Burt said they picked up a lot of latents, on the counter and register mostly, they're still sorting them out."

As if on cue at hearing his name, Burt came in with a manila folder, and Varallo said, "Good—you've got something for us on Mihardis, Rex?"

"That?" said Burt. "For God's sake, it'll take another day or so to process all those. No, what is in that I thought you'd like to see pronto is the lab report from LAPD. Those jokers take their time but they are good—well, they've got the equipment. Here you are." He handed it over: the downtown lab report on the rape victims' clothes.

Varallo spread it flat on his desk and the others crowded around interestedly. It was long and meticulously detailed. Analysis of particles of soil on soles of shoes—particles of dust from skirt, Subject B—fibers from underpants Subject A identified as from twill fabric most often used in automobile upholstery, manufacturer unidentifiable. The most definite finding was substantially detailed last. On all of the underclothing, in however minute quantity, they had picked up fibers of a coarse knit synthetic fabric, identified as most likely from some article of men's wear, probably trousers, possibly a jumpsuit: the contents were broken down. On all of those particles were present definite traces of concentrated fertilizer. There was a list of unpronounceable contents, percentages, a brand name; the fertilizer was manufactured principally for use on lawns, and was of a concentrated type used mainly by large gardening-service outfits, not individual home owners.

"What the hell?" said O'Connor.

Varallo rubbed his nose. "Well, it's the time of year to fertilize lawns, Charles," he pointed out. "And through at least some of that area are people who can afford the hired gardeners."

"And that could be the connection to the area," said Katz. "So we go and ask."

"Sweet Christ!" said O'Connor. "Everybody there? It takes in at least seventy square blocks!"

"Well, this is the first strong lead we've had, isn't it—that looks like a real lead. And it does so often come back to the legwork," said Katz.

Burt said to Delia, "We're halfway through your little job. I'll let you know when we're through."

"And what did that mean?" asked O'Connor as Burt went out.

"A little waste of the lab's time," said Delia equably, "reassuring a citizen. We're supposed to be here to serve the citizens, aren't we? That frightened wife expecting her ex-husband to murder her."

"Oh, for God's sake," said O'Connor. "Now what the hell are we going to do with this, boys?"

Wednesday and Thursday the relentless routine went on—on Mihardis, on the various other heists, on the rapist. Looking at the men with the right records to have pulled the market job, hauling them in and questioning them—other men on other jobs.

As a first cast at using the new information from the LAPD lab, Varallo saw all the families involved and asked whether they had a regular gardener. The Tallys had, and the Nuttings had: the others, in slightly less affluent homes, did their own yard work. The Tallys employed a Japanese gardener named Sam Nagao; he had a good many weekly jobs in Glendale, Burbank, Hollywood, but he worked alone, didn't employ any helpers. The gardener the Nuttings had worked for an outfit called Garden Boys; it was based in Burbank, owned by a man named Field. He employed five men, and Varallo met all of them; not one bore even a faint resemblance to the description.

As a last thought, he went to that apartment on Grandview and asked there. The old lady with the dog was the only one home, and she told him the owner, Mr. Glidden, came to cut the little strip of lawn every week; there wasn't much landscaping there to take care of.

So they would have to cover it block by block, find out what professional gardening services came regularly to take care of yards there, and eventually get a look at all the gardeners. But even the first half day of that legwork was slightly encouraging; in most cases, two or three people on a block could tell them which neighbors hired the professional gardeners, which cut down on the calls and the time.

Paul Gibson was due to be arraigned on Wednesday morning, and Varallo had to cover that; being out, he stayed to help out on the legwork. Drifting into the office at five-thirty, he said to Delia, "At least it's nice weather to be out on the street."

Delia was just sitting there smoking a cigarette and staring into space. "Yes," she said. "I was just wondering—did Burt send Carol Sue Wiley's clothes to LAPD too?"

"I don't think so. The first three, there just wasn't the ghost of a lead—that was why we needed all the help we could get. Why?"

"I don't know," said Delia. "No reason. That one was the break in the pattern."

On Thursday Burt and Thomsen finished processing all the prints they'd picked up in the Mihardis market. None of them were in their records or LAPD's, so they were sent off to the FBI, which had a lot more prints on file than any police department.

That afternoon, Varallo and O'Connor had just ended a session with a possible suspect on Mihardis; there was nothing to say either way whether he was the boy they wanted. They were just sitting there smoking when one of the sergeants from Communications came in with a report. Varallo glanced at it idly; it was the autopsy report on Peter Lyman, the drunk last Sunday night.

A minute later he said, "*Che diavolo!* I will be damned!"

"Now what?" asked O'Connor.

"This Lyman—his wife said he jumped out and landed on his head. He didn't. He got run over. Twice, Goulding says—wheel marks on abdomen and lower legs, which wouldn't happen in one pass. He was drunk as a skunk, blood level way up. Cause of death, massive internal hemorrhage."

O'Connor held out his hand mutely, and read. He said, "The things we do see. Cluttering up the really important jobs," and of course he was thinking of the man going around raping little girls. "I suppose we'd better go see this woman."

"I suppose we had. Where is she?"

"Delia took the statement."

Varallo looked it up. The place, when they found it, was a very classy boutique shop on Foothill Boulevard in La Cañada. Inside there were glass display cases at random angles, at the moment no customers, two women talking behind a rear counter which held a cash register. One was stout and friendly-looking, one thin and blond. O'Connor produced the badge and asked for Mrs. Lyman. "That's me," said the blonde.

"We've got just a few more questions for you, Mrs. Lyman, if you don't mind."

"Red tape," said the other one, nodding. "I know how it goes. You might as well take the rest of the day off, Myra, business is slow anyway. And cheer up, dear, better times coming. We all go through the bad patches."

They rode in silence all the way back to headquarters, and settled her down in a chair beside O'Connor's desk. "Is it about—getting the body for the funeral?" she asked. "I suppose I have to sign things."

"Well, that can wait a little," said O'Connor, giving her a rather

ferocious grin. "You told us that your husband jumped out of the car
without warning, was presumably killed when he landed on his
head."

"That's right," she said nervously. She fingered the single strand of
pearls at her throat.

"Then how do you suggest he got run over? We've just had the autopsy report, and that's what happened to him. You said you stopped
the car immediately and got out."

"Oh," she said weakly.

"There will, of course, be laboratory evidence to pick up on the
car—blood and so on," said Varallo.

The string of pearls snapped and the pearls made a little clatter as
they scattered on the floor. She didn't move to pick them up. Her
pretty, if sharp-featured, face suddenly looked pinched and drawn.
She asked, "Could I have a cigarette?"

Varallo gave her one and lit it. "How about it, Mrs. Lyman?"

She smoked for a little while in silence. Then she said, "That policewoman told me how there had to be an autopsy. I never knew
that. I've been worried about it ever since. Not that it could have
made any difference, I mean even if I had known about it, because I
wasn't thinking very straight. I suppose I'll have to tell you about it."

"I think you'd better," said O'Connor grimly.

"Well, it happened just the way I said. He was drunk, and he
jumped out. What I didn't tell you is that he was a lush—he was getting worse and worse. He'd got fired the week before for being drunk
on the job, and that wasn't the first job he'd lost. I was sick to death
of him, him stealing my money to get liquored up. It happened just
the way I said, only he wasn't hurt—the drunks never do, do they? I
stopped the car and looked back, and he was sitting up against the
curb, I could see in the street light there, starting to get up. I saw he
wasn't hurt at all, and I don't remember planning to do it, you know,
I just did it—there wasn't another car in sight and it's a quiet block
along there, and I backed up around him and just gunned the motor.
And when I looked back then, he—he was still moving, so I did it
again. And then a car came around the corner and the people
stopped—and I told them what I told you—and they went to the
nearest place to call the cops. That's all." She put out her hand for

another cigarette. "Except, ever since, I can't tell you what an awful relief it's been to get *rid* of him. And I never thought about his insurance until afterward, but—I always thought I'd like to have a shop of my own—like the one where I work. I suppose I never will now."

She agreed dispiritedly to sign a statement on all that; Varallo typed it up, and then took her over to the jail. When he got back, O'Connor had started the machinery on the warrant. "That's a funny little thing," commented Varallo. "I wonder what they'll decide to call it—first or second or voluntary manslaughter. I don't suppose they could prove malice."

"And it's a first count on her. I know what I'd like to call it," said O'Connor, "but they won't. She'll get a three to ten and be out in the minimum time. But after all, Vic, there is such a thing as divorce."

The monotonous routine went on, sorting out the gardening services. So far they had found four different ones contracting to maintain yards in that area on a weekly basis. The latest one they'd come across employed fifteen men, who were scattered all over the place every day, Sunland to Eagle Rock; it would take time to get a look at all of them.

Late Thursday afternoon, an urgent A.P.B. went out to all police forces countywide. Yesterday night an LAPD traffic man had been shot down while responding to a robbery taking place, and was D.O.A. at the emergency hospital. Evidently the witnesses had made a mug shot, and the call went out on William Gully, male Caucasian, 21, five-ten, a hundred and sixty, brown and blue, armed and dangerous: driving a white 1972 Chevy, new plate AGO-710. There were still two different kinds of license plates in Califorina—the old orange-on-black, the new gold-on-blue.

Before that, they had the kickback from the Feds on those prints from the Mihardis market. Only one set was known, and they belonged to a Sidney Harvey Harris who had done a stint in the Army during the Vietnam War. Varallo dropped in to the Seventy-six station to ask him about it, and he said, "Yeah, I'd been in the market just that morning to pick up a six-pack of Pepsi. Say, haven't you found out anything about that S.O.B. yet? I sure did hope, maybe George winged him—"

Meg had called Mr. Glidden about the refrigerator, and he had come to look at it. "I kind of think," he said, "it's seen its best days, Mrs. Burgess. Getting on for sixteen years old, and there were three, four tenants using it before you. I'll figure on getting a new one. Got to keep the place up."

"Oh, thank you," said Meg, surprised.

He called her on Thursday night to say the new refrigerator would be delivered the next day; he'd come over and let the deliverymen in, and lock up.

"Oh, you don't have to," said Meg. "A—a friend of mine's at the apartment most of the day, he can let them in, but thank you."

"Oh, that so?" She felt his curiosity through the line, and just thanked him again and hung up.

On Friday afternoon Forbes and Varallo had just come in with another man to question when they got a buzz from the desk. "Maybe we're about to drop on some pro burglars," said Duff. "One of these Neighborhood Watch citizens just blew the whistle—they're still there, and Tracy and Gallagher on the way."

"Address?" snapped Forbes.

"It's Whitehaven Terrace, just off of—"

"I know where it is." He scribbled down the house number. "Come on, Vic. We may get a break on the housebreakers."

They took Forbes's Pontiac. That would be the right area for those pros, one of the wealthier sections of town. They made it in a little over fifteen minutes: off Mountain into the Rossmoyne area, the little streets were narrow and winding. When they spotted the address, one squad car was sitting parked three doors down with somebody in it. The house indicated was an old two-story Spanish nearly hidden behind well-grown pine trees, a tall privet hedge. At the entrance to the drive Tracy was talking with a stout woman in a pink pantsuit. He nodded as Varallo and Forbes came up.

"This is Mrs. Draper. Detectives Varallo, Forbes. I've got one of them, and Gallagher's after the other. We tried to come up quiet, but it could be they were upstairs and spotted my squad as I came round that corner—Gallagher was coming in from the other side. We were just moving in when we heard them split out the back, and took after them. I got this one, and Gallagher ought to be back any minute."

"I knew it!" said Mrs. Draper triumphantly. "I knew they were burglars! There was a talk at the Tuesday Afternoon Club about five months ago, it was the Chief of Police, all about crime prevention, and he mentioned this Neighborhood Watch. And it seems every paper you see, there's nothing but burglaries. So we all got together —well, Dorothy Morrison and I really organized it—and set up a kind of schedule, to keep an eye on the neighborhood. You know, when anyone's going to be away, or—"

"Here's Gallagher," said Tracy.

Gallagher, who could profitably have dropped a few pounds, was blowing and puffing. "I chased him—all the way over—next block," he reported. "Ran like—a damn deer. I figure he—left car—block or so away—heard an engine start up. Long gone."

"Well, we've got one," said Varallo.

"—Knew the Schuylers were going away for the weekend, in fact they left this morning, and so I was going to keep a special watch. And of course I live right next door, and I just happened to look over here about thirty, forty minutes ago, and saw these two men going up the walk. And I waited, and they didn't come back, the way they would have if they'd just gone up and rung the bell and got no answer. So I called right away—"

"And we're very much obliged, ma'am," said Gallagher gallantly, having recovered his breath.

"So let's have a look," said Forbes. They went around to the rear of the house and found a neat square of glass cut out, low down, on a sliding glass door, just big enough for someone to reach in and dislodge the steel bar which held the door shut. The door was open, and they went in to a large dark formal dining room.

The slick pros had methodically begun their work upstairs, in the master bedroom. There was a shabby suitcase open on the bed, and it contained a few portable valuables: a few pieces of jewelry, a new transistor radio, a tape recorder, a fur stole. There would be more loot in the other bedrooms, downstairs; silver, whatever. "But we do have to tie it up for the courts," said Forbes. "We'd better get somebody up to print all this. And let's hope the one we've got will tell us who the other one is."

Tracy had just slapped the cuffs on that one, stashed him in the squad cuffed to the rail in back, before he decided it was too late to help out Gallagher, and then Mrs. Draper had hailed him. Now they went out to the squad to see what they had, and met a little surprise.

The burglar sitting helpless in the back of the squad car was a good size, maybe five-nine, a hundred and forty. But as he lifted his head to stare at them, they saw a round beardless baby face, freckled and snubnosed; he couldn't be over fifteen.

"My God," said Forbes. "What the hell is this?"

Tracy unlocked the chain. "What's your name?" asked Varallo.

The boy gave him a defiant stare. "Go to hell, fuzz."

They ferried him back to headquarters, took him up to the office. He looked around fearfully, and surprise showed in his eyes when he saw Delia, but he wouldn't talk. They made him sit down. And then he looked at the men around him, Varallo and Forbes looming over him, wiry dark Katz, O'Connor just coming over curiously, jacket off and shoulder holster bulging—and he started to cry, the tears welling up; he snuffled and smeared a hand across his eyes, angry and ashamed, furious at himself for looking like a fool little kid. He said thickly, "All right, I'll talk. The hell I'll talk! Him runnin' off and leavin' me like that—what the hell do I do now anyways?"

Varallo gave him a Kleenex and a cup of water. "What's your name?"

"Dan Dunning."

"How old are you, Dan?"

"Fourteen."

"And who was with you on this caper?"

"The same one been with me on all the jobs we ever done. Here and lotsa other places. My dad. Pat Dunning. He's about the best in the business, he knows all the tricks, see? They only caught up to him twice and he done time in a real tough academy back in Texas, but nobody couldn't break him. Not Pat. He was gonna teach me be the best damn houseman inna whole country. We been doin' all right." It came out in a little rush.

They looked at each other. In this job, there wasn't often anything new coming along. Sometimes they got little surprises.

Delia came over and sat down in Katz's chair. "Where's your mother, Dan?"

"Who needs her, lady? She was nothin' but a donegan worker when he met up with her, he said, an' that's no class—she got on the sauce a long time back, she's been useless four-five years, I guess."

Cops necessarily understand criminal jargon, and that drew a graphic little picture for them. No, a high-class pro burglar—a house-man—would look down on the humble female who earned her keep picking up handbags in ladies' restrooms. Maybe that was why she drank herself to death.

"Don't you go to school?" asked Delia.

"What for? I never been to no school. Pat and me, we just move around. He hadn't no call run off and leave me like that! He hadn't no call!"

"So tell us where to find him," said Forbes.

"Sure I tell you. We been at a place, the Melville Hotel, some-place in this burg, I dunno where exactly. He said he was Pat Smith inna book you gotta write in."

They would be doing some overtime on this. Varallo and Forbes went out in a hurry; O'Connor went down to Communications and sent a query off to NCIC. Promptly the computer produced Pat Dun-ning's record. Dan hadn't been told the whole story: the fuzz had caught up to Pat Dunning plenty. He had a record, of housebreaking mostly, a few other things—petty theft, arson, two counts of assault—in Texas, Arkansas, Arizona, New Mexico, and Nevada. He was cur-rently not wanted anywhere, so if they got him they could keep him.

"And added to that should be contributing to the delinquency of a minor," said O'Connor, passing the telex over to Delia in the office.

"I've been talking to him. He's completely illiterate," said Delia. "Never been to school at all. Can you believe it?"

"Easily. He may be no worse off than the illiterates the public schools keep giving diplomas to," said O'Connor. "I'd better call Katy. I suppose he'll have to go down to Juvenile Hall. We're not supposed to keep minors in jail with all the hardened criminals."

"You won't need me, will you?"

"Why? You got a date?"

"Just," said Delia, "an errand."

"So go, go. We'll do just fine without you."

It would make her late, but Delia drove over to the apartment on Grandview. It was six-thirty; when she parked the Mercedes in front, just behind her a car pulled out from the curb, and she recognized

Stan Pollard at the wheel. So that quixotic young man was keeping his promise, guarding Meg's apartment during the day.

She heard the chain unfastened, and then Meg opened the door. "I've brought back your dishes," said Delia, "and our lab report. I'd like you to look at it, Mrs. Burgess."

"Well, all right. I was just starting to get dinner—"

"It won't take long." Meg stepped back and Delia went in, taking the loose pages of the report from her bag. "I think it's all pretty clear, though there are some abbreviations. What it amounts to is that every food sample taken here was perfectly all right. No trace of any poison."

"I see," said Meg. "In fact, I was imagining things."

"That's what it looks like, doesn't it?"

"Well, thank you," said Meg. She looked at Delia steadily, a little flushed. "I know you think I'm a fool, and maybe I have overreacted on this thing, but you see, I know Wayne, and I know he's out there somewhere, thinking and planning how to kill us. How to do it and stay safe himself. I don't know how he'll try, but he will." She brushed a lock of hair back from her forehead. "Stan's staying here days now, so I can be sure nobody's getting in. But that can't keep up—we're nobody of his, he's got a job back east. I'm going to get away from here when I've saved enough money—I've been thinking about it, trying to make some plan. I think it'd be best to go up north somewhere, and just—just not tell Mr. Pollard where. Just forget the money for Tammy—so then nobody would know where we are, there'd be no way for Wayne to know. And we can start all over. I can find another job, take care of Tammy." She smiled at Delia, the crooked little smile that lit up her rather grave face. She said, "I'm really not a hysterical fool, Miss Riordan."

Delia felt oddly disturbed about that, all the way home. There was a niggling little something at the bottom of her mind, about Meg and her problem, but she couldn't pin it down.

Varallo and Forbes picked up Pat Dunning in his room at the Melville Hotel, a fleabag just over the Burbank line. He was surprised and grieved to see them. "I never thought Danny'd split on me," he said aggrievedly. "I was just figurin' how to get him out—bail prob'ly wouldn't be much. He oughta knowed I'd see he was O.K."

"What did you expect when you cut out and left him holding the bag?"asked Varallo reasonably.

"Jeez, it was just such a surprise was all—no sweat, a sweet peaceful job, and all of a sudden we notice the squads turning in from two sides—I thought Danny was right behind me, wasn't till I got to the car I see he isn't— Who the hell blew the whistle, anyways?" They told him, and he looked disgusted. "Hell, when people start gangin' up on you, it ain't fair." He was a stocky barrel-chested fellow in his fifties, with restless eyes. "Listen, what's gonna happen to Danny, you take me in? You can't put a kid in the slammer, I know that—"

Something more traumatic would happen to Danny, perhaps. He'd be declared a ward of the court, and social services would try to place him in a foster home. Some of those were good, some indifferent; but either way, they could see Danny having quite an impact on a more or less ordinary household. And the chances were pretty slim that Danny's values and ambitions would get turned around. Of course there was always the millionth chance.

It was after eight o'clock when they finished the paperwork on it. O'Connor had pulled rank and gone home an hour ago. By the time Varallo got home he was starving. The house was deathly quiet; the children would be sound asleep. Laura was stretched out on the couch with what looked like a new detective novel.

"*Che giorno!*" said Varallo from the door. "What a day!"

She jumped. "I never heard you come in. I'll bet you're starved. Something break?"

"Yes, we got a pair of burglars. Rather an interesting pair." He told her about it over a brandy and soda while she warmed up dinner for him.

About ten-thirty, Patrolman Robert Bruce McLeod, cruising out near the Burbank line, got sent to a family disturbance. It was a small apartment house on Grandview, down a fairly dark street; as he parked the squad he could hear the fight all right, a man cussing and yelling, a woman yelling back. It was one of the ground-floor apartments; he knocked loudly on the door with his nightstick, and the voices died down for a minute. The door opened.

"I'm afraid you're making a little too much noise, sir," said McLeod. You were supposed to be diplomatic, when it was possible.

The man was big and broad, and he had some drink in him but he wasn't drunk. Behind him McLeod could see a woman, rather plump and slatternly, and she had the start of a black eye, a cut on one cheek.

"Sorry," said the man. "Little family argument, officer. That's all."

"Are you all right, ma'am?"

She had more of a load on than he did. "Yeah. Yeah, I'm O.K. Jus' leave us alone."

"Well, just keep the noise down, please. It's getting late and your neighbors would like to get some sleep."

"Yeah, sure, sure—we'll cool it, officer."

"Just see you do, sir." McLeod went back to the squad. If he had to make a report about that, he'd have a guess that the man had been knocking her around. But she'd had a chance to yell for help if she thought she needed it. He wondered why he'd ever thought this would be an interesting career. It was, in fact, a very good way to lose all your faith in the essential goodness of mankind. Why the hell, he thought, couldn't people behave themselves and keep out of trouble—it wasn't as if it was such a damn difficult thing to do. Remember a few rules, keep a few simple moral standards. But so many of the damn fools—well, practically all of them you saw on this job—would go to getting drunk, getting greedy, getting covetous of somebody else's wife, and dodging any common responsibility for themselves and their actions, and you had a mess—a big fat mess with innocent people getting hurt. Patrolman McLeod had an orderly mind, and all of this annoyed him considerably. He had thought lately that maybe he ought to get out of this job before he got any older, and get into something peaceful like—well, what, for instance?

The trouble was, in almost any kind of job you had to deal with people—human beings; and nobody who had ever been a cop, even for only three years, would ever be able to believe again that the majority of humanity was good, kind, responsible, brave, and generous.

As the night wore on, and he met two other patrolmen to break up a brawl in a bar, and later went to another family disturbance where a husband, who had unexpectedly returned home, had found his wife entertaining company, he got to feeling more depressed. It would be some help if he was a cop someplace where they ran two-man cars; at least he'd have somebody to talk to.

The radio was his only company. About midnight that A.P.B. was broadcast again, for William Gully, wanted for shooting that LAPD man. That one they wanted bad, and no wonder.

The monotonous routine went on, the garnering and sifting of facts here and there. In that northwest area, perhaps a third of the householders had a hired gardener; they had come across some duplications, but there were a lot of gardening services around, and to work this at all they had to it thoroughly. It was the strongest lead they had.

The chances were that the Mihardis homicide would be filed away unsolved. There just wasn't any lead at all, no description, nothing. The lab said the three slugs out of Mihardis were .22's from an old Smith & Wesson. A lot of those would be floating around.

Traffic had been briefed about that old British racer, the Lotus painted kelly green, but nobody had spotted it yet.

Detective Bob Rhys left for work at seven-thirty that night. People —including his mother—kept asking him why he didn't get married, but whether it was inertia or whatever, he was quite contented with his mother's comfortable old house, and her comfortable company, and the dogs, and maybe always would be. After all, he'd turned thirty-one last month.

It had been rather a hectic day. He shaved again and got dressed, and said, "See you in the morning." She said, "Don't interrupt me, I'm counting drops for her milk supplement, goodbye." Rhys went out and got in his Chevy sedan.

As he drove down Verdugo Road he was thinking, smiling a little, about the new litter of pups born this afternoon, and how life was always a miracle, a most surprising miracle. A handful of new life, the puppies, each of them hardly as big as his palm, but wriggling and blindly sucking and padding paws in the air, full of new life and eager to get on with living. Three new puppies, reaching for life with such tremendous hope.

He caught the light at Glendale Avenue, where he'd be turning to go down to Lexington; and as he waited for it to change, all of a sudden his idle gaze focused on the car ahead of him: on the plate number. It jumped out at him: AGO-710. His mind went cold. That A.P.B.—William Gully, who'd shot the LAPD man. A white Chevy, sure. It had its right-turn signal on, same as he had.

Unfortunately, of course, driving his private car, he couldn't tell anybody about it. All he could do was follow it, and hope to spot a squad car somewhere on the way.

He stuck behind the Chevy down to Broadway, where it turned right. At least after dark Gully wasn't apt to realize he was being tailed. Rhys was trying to remember traffic patterns, from his days riding a squad—cruising a certain area, you'd hit the same places roughly once an hour, but he didn't know what the pattern was for downtown now— And the Chevy wasn't exactly downtown now. It was away out on Broadway. Then it turned on San Fernando and came back into town again. It was ambling along, being handled all right; Rhys stuck with it, constantly on the lookout for a squad car. There was never a cop around when you needed one, he thought bitterly. If the Chevy pulled over, parked, get out fast and try to take him—but it didn't. It went out to Chevy Chase and turned left there up to Broadway again.

Rhys decided that the driver was lost. What the hell was Gully doing in Glendale? He didn't know the town, anyway. He went back up Broadway to Brand, turned left and suddenly picked up speed. Recognized some landmark?—knew where he was now?

Where the hell were all the squad cars? Supposed to be covering this town night and day— William Gully armed and dangerous. Rhys felt for the gun in the shoulder holster, loosened it. It was regulation to carry it; in the six years he'd ridden a car in uniform he'd had to pull the gun just three times, and never since he was in plainclothes. You had to keep up a certain score, but he wasn't the top marksman O'Connor was.

Lomita, Chestnut, Maple. Traffic was light for a Saturday night. Windsor. And there, by God, coming toward him in the opposite lane, was a black-and-white squad car—been down to the Glendale line at San Fernando Road, and on its way back—

He leaned on the horn, and it blasted loud. It was the only way open for him to do it, and pray the man in the squad was quick on the uptake. The driver's window was already down. He braked to a violent stop as he hit the horn, and leaned out the window, fishing desperately for his badge—dark, but the arc lights shadowless—

The squad braked. Rhys leaned half out the window, stabbing his left hand urgently ahead, and yelled, "Gully! Gully!"

He never knew if the driver saw or recognized the badge. The red light and siren went on in two seconds; the squad pulled around in a great U-turn, traffic suddenly frozen, and Rhys gunned the Chevy after it.

The other Chevy had gained on them, but he could still spot it eight lengths ahead, and its right-turn signal was flashing—Los Feliz coming up—

The driver of the squad had spotted it now. The siren screamed like a banshee, and as the Chevy made the turn it suddenly took off like a scalded cat. That driver knew the siren was for him, now. Rhys floored the accelerator, tailing the squad, and suddenly he heard a crackle of vicious little spats, and thought, by God, he's shooting at the squad—

Traffic stood still for them. They would be out of Glendale and into Hollywood in thirty seconds.

The squad—and whoever was driving it knew what he was doing—put on a burst of speed and pulled alongside the Chevy, which took nerve at eighty miles an hour. It edged the Chevy right and right, that driver chicken as it nearly scraped his paint, and just at the next traffic light the Chevy went roaring up over the curb and fell on its side and slid smoking along the sidewalk. Rhys stood on the brake. The squad shrieked to a stand, and a man crawled out of the Chevy and fired at the driver of the squad as he emerged. The uniformed man already had his gun out, and shouted, "Hold it! Right there!"

Gully fired again, and the patrolman staggered and went down. Gully was sidling across what seemed to be a parking lot, he came into the inadvertent light of flashing neon, and it burned into Rhys's mind, inconsequent, ridiculous—UNCLE JOHN'S PANCAKE HOUSE—and he put the Police Positive at arm's length and fired it three times, and Gully went down.

He ran to the patrolman. He saw then that it was Stoner, and said his name.

"He got me in the leg. I'm O.K. Did you get him?"

Rhys went to look. It was William Gully, by the description. He

lay flat in the flashing light of the pancake sign. One of the three
shots had got him between the eyes. William Gully, twenty-one.

The great big miracle of life, thought Rhys, and they threw it
away.

The man with murder in his mind was thinking savagely, how the
hell had he missed this time? How the *hell*? Both of them should
have been dead—but they weren't. There was no way they could be
alive— Kids, they always drank milk, didn't they?—and the bitch always put a quarter cup of it in her coffee. Foolproof—but something
had gone wrong. What?

Behind him on the bed the woman slept gracelessly, snoring a little. His anonymous cover. But time—time!

And who the hell was the man? He didn't give a damn what boy-
friends she picked up, but why the hell was he *there*? The devil's own
luck—right there in the hall, when he'd heard him talking. Talking on
the phone. *There.* He'd watched, and the bastard had been there next
day, and the next. All day. Why?

Whoever he was, he was at a motel downtown. The Golden Key.

But how he had missed getting them twice— The first idea, when
he'd spotted that Nembutal, he'd got from something he saw in the
paper at home, a kid playing house, put Grandma's heart medicine in
with some saccharin tablets and nearly killed a whole family. What
one kid did, another might do.

He couldn't figure what had gone wrong. But small cold triumph
rose in his mind—she didn't know. She couldn't know, or there'd
have been cops swarming, that next day.

Still time. All quiet, his cover holding. But it had to be next time.
It had to be. Sure and no mistake. That bastard, whoever he was, get
rid of him—and the damn dog in the apartment. Then he would have
time to do what he had to do—

Because his time here was running out, he had to get them for sure
the next time, the little bitch and her kid—

He began suddenly to think of fire, crackling up through that
building, exploding—

CHAPTER EIGHT

On Sunday morning all the talk was about Rhys taking that gunman —just a fluke Gully had been wandering around over here, and spotted: a damned good job. The desk had checked the hospital about Stoner; he'd taken a bullet in the thigh, and would be O.K.

The boss would be in later: out running after that dog of his up in the hills.

On a Sunday the routine on the gardening services was all but shut down, not everybody home, and the offices of those outfits closed. Katz went out to poke around, but the rest of them were concentrating on the heisters.

Overnight, a citizen had been mugged on the street, up on North Glendale Avenue. He hadn't been hurt enough to need an ambulance, but a report had to go in; Varallo called, and went to see him in midmorning. The address was on Randolph; his name was Roger Keeler.

"The damn punks!" he said. He was sporting a black eye and kept feeling the back of his head as if he had a headache. He was a middle-aged man, a little too fat. He was, he said, a C.P.A. with his own business. "And this time of year, with the deadline coming up, we're swamped. I was at the office overtime every night last week, catching up. Came out about eleven, locked up, and I was nearly to my car when they jumped me—"

"More than one?"

"I think so," said Keeler. "I think there were two of them. Came up from behind, chopped me across the neck and knocked me against a light pole there—how I got the eye—and when they hit me again, I guess I hit the sidewalk and knocked myself out. Just a couple of minutes, but of course when I came to they were gone. I never got a glimpse of them, couldn't tell you a thing." They had got about eleven bucks and his watch, which was an old Bulova.

There wasn't much to do about that kind of thing. An anonymous deal; and here, even the watch was anonymous. No initials or any other marks. They got the muggings now and then, and it was usually the late-teen juveniles, no way to come down on them.

He came back to the office to write the inevitable report on it, and found Delia alone, sitting at her desk smoking and staring into space. "And what are you brooding about?" he asked, uncovering his typewriter.

She said, "A very niggling little thought, Vic. About those two things happening in succession, sort of—ordinary in themselves, but are they a little queer together? Or just—the kind of thing that happens?"

"Just what are you talking about?"

"The Nembutal. The mouse poison." Delia told him about that, succinctly. "She said the child had never shown any tendency to investigate the medicine cabinet, get into that kind of mischief. You know, if Mrs. Burgess had eaten the rest of that asparagus, they'd probably both have slept away and never been found until it was too late."

Varallo thought it over, smoking thoughtfully, and said, "Woolgathering. In a way, the one cancels out the other. There's always a first time for kids to get into a new kind of mischief, and after all, there wasn't any mouse poison in any of the food, was there? But she's nervous, and more so on account of the Nembutal bit, seeing bogeymen the way you told her. She picked that up by mistake. Because if you're supposing there's anything sinister about either thing, you're supposing the ex-husband has a way to get into that apartment. In other words, a key. And you've found there's no possible chance of that."

"That's so," said Delia. "Security there pretty tight. Yes, I see what you mean. You're probably right, and I'm just woolgathering."

About two o'clock the desk got a call from a Dr. Gunther at the Memorial Hospital, who reported a patient with a gunshot wound. Standard procedure, and in a good many cases it turned out to be some idiot practicing a quick draw; but sometimes it didn't. Only Varallo and O'Connor were in, and they abandoned the small-time heister they were talking to and shot down there. They hadn't got to first base on the Mihardis homicide all week.

They saw the doctor in a slit of an office, and he said the slug had been in the shoulder, high up, and still in. "Since when?" asked O'Connor.

"I'd estimate five or six days. It was a little mess. Looked fairly suspicious to me, though kids get to horsing around, but when the father said it was a knife wound—" He shrugged. O'Connor demanded the slug, and Gunther produced it silently in a plastine envelope.

"Oh, yes," said O'Connor, and sighed deeply. The slug was a little flattened, but both he and Varallo could make an educated guess that the lab could pinpoint it as coming from that old .380 Luger. He raised cold eyes. "So where are they?"

William Siegler, in the waiting room, acknowledged the badges with bewilderment. "What do the cops want? Say, what's all this delay, anyway? Rudy isn't hurt bad, is he?" Varallo said they just wanted to ask a few questions. "What the hell about? I don't get this. I got nothing to hide, but it's nothing for cops either. Look, I been away all week, I get home, the wife says Rudy's not feeling good, off his food. Whenever that kid's off his food, something's wrong, so I talk to him, and it turns out he and some pal was fooling around throwing knives, you know the things kids get to doing, and just by accident he got stuck, been trying to take care of it himself. I thought it looked kind of nasty, maybe infected, I told him he was a damn fool not to see a doctor, and brought him down here—and now all of a sudden cops show up, why the hell?" Siegler was a long-distance trucker, away from home most of the week. He said Rudy was their only kid, in his first year at Glendale College. And why the hell the cops wanted to know—

Rudy wasn't exactly a kid, sitting on the examining table in the little cubicle. He looked a good six feet, solidly built. He was, they had heard by then, nineteen. He was buttoning his shirt over the thick bandage on his right shoulder when they came in, and he shied away from the badge like a nervous pony.

"We'd be interested to hear how you picked up the slug, Rudy," said O'Connor, standing over him. He bent the hungry-shark grin on Rudy, who looked back as if he was hypnotized. He was an ordinary good-looking youngster, dark-haired, with blunt regular features, but now he looked witless with fright.

"I—it was just an accident—friend of mine and I just fooling around—"

"First with knives and then with a gun, hah? Dangerous," said O'Connor. He upended the envelope and dropped the slug into his palm. "It's in pretty good condition. I don't think our lab will have any trouble identifying it as out of George Mihardis' Luger. We know he got off three shots at the heister. What about it, Rudy?"

The youthful face was a mask of futile rage and terror. "How'd you—" And then he said with a sob of frustrated fury, "Him! Him always saying can't afford, can't afford—you got to have money, just ordinary stuff like gas for the car, take girls out, everything—he thinks I can get along on like a little kid's allowance, and that damn old clunker all he says he could afford, it's always needing something —all Mom ever says, ask your dad—how do they think I'm gonna get *along* on peanuts— I had to—"

"So you decided to get some the hard way," said Varallo. "How did you happen to pick that market? We know you did, so don't waste our time."

"God's sake, why the hell I let him bring me here—giving me hell all week, but I could've stood it—"

"And possibly died of blood poisoning next week," said Gunther, an interested witness.

"God's sake! Mom goes there sometimes, she's always saying groceries up so high now, I thought there'd be a pile—and not a big place, just one guy there—I know where Pop keeps that twenty-two— And then that old bastard had to pull a gun and shoot me! He kept on coming and coming—he was gonna *kill* me—so I— And I never got a dime—" He sucked in his breath and let it out with a little hiss. "I never got a dime," he said dully.

They had a little session with the father, who was belligerently incredulous. They took Rudy back to headquarters, started the paperwork, applied for the warrant. Rudy wouldn't say another word, which probably didn't matter.

"And you know it'll be a charge of second degree," said O'Connor. "Goddamn it, just the kind of irresponsible brainless lout who might end up on the Ten Most Wanted list some day, and he'll be out in three years! I get fed up, Vic. I get tired. Goddamn it."

"At least we caught up to him, Charles. He didn't quite get away with it."

On Monday morning, with Poor off, the legwork on the gardening services got under way again. Varallo teamed up with Katz, and Delia was out with Forbes in another section of the area. He and Katz split up this section half and half, roughly a six-block square, Kenneth to Olmsted, Graynold to Highland, and started to ring doorbells.

In the first six blocks, he racked up three more single gardeners who worked alone, and two more gardening-service outfits. He hit the last house on Norton just before noon, and a harried-looking woman said, "If that's not like police, wasting time on idiotic questions like that! You taking a survey or something? I'm busy. We have a gardener, sure, but I don't know his address—my husband pays all the bills—"

"If you could look it up, please, we'd be obliged."

"Oh, for goodness' sake! Why you have to come wasting my time on this right now—I suppose it'd be in Bert's account book—heavens above, and we pay taxes so police can waste their time like this, with the crime rate up, burglaries and murders all over—" She went on grumbling in the living room as she looked, finally came back and dictated an address. It was just called Greene's Gardening, and it was based in North Hollywood.

This afternoon, switch to the other half of the job and try to get a look at all the gardeners.

But police work was never static: as things came up, they had to be looked at.

At twelve-thirty an incoherent female voice had asked for police at an address on Cleveland, and the patrolman took one look at what was there and called the front-office boys. Varallo and Forbes went out on it just after getting back from lunch.

It was an old English-style stucco house, with a nicely maintained front yard. Inside it was a shambles. The ambulance was already gone. "I didn't like the looks of either of 'em," said Patrolman Steiner. "Thought they ought to go in fast."

By that time the girl who had called was more coherent, but she kept saying she had to get to the hospital, she'd called Mother and Daddy and they'd be there but she had to go, to find out how they were. She answered a few questions hastily. Her name was Marion Burns, and she'd come to see her grandparents, they'd had an anniversary on Saturday but she couldn't come to the party because she'd had to work, she worked for the phone company and the hours were always peculiar, and when she got here the front door was open and she heard groaning, so she ran in—and she had to get to the hospital—

The householders were Ray and Pearl Burns, aged sixty-nine and sixty-seven. "It looked as if somebody had worked them over," said Steiner, "and you can see the place has been ransacked."

Forbes surveyed the living room and said gloomily, "We know the words and music."

This was a modest place inside, good solid furniture but nothing fancy, and old. But it was a house in a good area of town, well kept up; and the old people lived alone. They'd find out from the family whether there was apt to be much cash around, any valuable loot; but it looked to both of them like just an ordinary place. The rumor did so often get around, old people must have money stashed away— or it could be that they'd been picked just because they were old and couldn't fight back. You paid your money and took your choice.

The place was a mess. Every drawer had been pulled out and dumped, pictures torn off the walls, the clothes from closets yanked from hangers. In both bedrooms the beds had been stripped and the mattresses slashed open. The kitchen cupboards had been emptied, and there was smashed china on the counters, the floor. There was, of course, no telling what loot the ransackers might have got; they'd have to see the family.

They got a mobile lab unit up to start dusting for prints, and went down to the hospital. They saw a doctor briefly; he was busy. He told them that Mrs. Burns had a broken hip and various head contusions. Mr. Burns was in more serious condition; he had a fractured skull, and they would be operating to relieve the pressure. He couldn't say whether the man would live; he hoped so. And they couldn't talk to Mrs. Burns yet. Maybe tomorrow. They'd be kept informed.

They saw the Burnses' son and his wife, who were shocked and upset but coherent. They said the Burnses never kept much cash in the house.

"There isn't much to keep," said Harold Burns ironically. "Dad's got Social Security and a little annuity he bought years ago. We help them out with the taxes."

"We'd like you and your wife to have a look through the house, see if you can spot what's missing."

They said they'd do that; there wasn't much they could do here now.

Eventually, of course, the Burnses might be able to tell them who had beaten them up and wrecked the house, but probably at best all they could offer would be a description, which might or might not be helpful.

They got back to the office at three-thirty and tossed a coin for who should do the report. Varallo lost.

When Meg and Tammy came home at a quarter to six there was someone sitting on the front step of the apartment. It was old Miss Kemp, disheveled and distraught, and on her lap was the convulsed dead body of the little tan dog. She looked up at Meg with dull reddened eyes; she had stopped crying a while ago, but the tear marks were still on her withered cheeks.

"Oooh—" said Tammy.

"Darling, you run upstairs quick and get Stan to let you in. Scoot, now. Miss Kemp—"

"He's dead, Petie's dead. I don't know what to do."

"Oh, Miss Kemp, I'm so sorry. How did it happen? Couldn't you get him to a vet?"

"I don't know. It must have been poison—I don't know. We were just over by the park, such a nice day we went out again this afternoon—I saw he'd picked up something, but I never thought—and then he started to have convulsions and he cried and cried, and I picked him up and tried to hurry home—but he was dead. When we got here. I don't have a car, I couldn't— Oh, Mrs. Burgess, I want him buried decently. I don't know what to do."

"You just wait, I'll—I'll think of something," said Meg. She ran up the stairs. "Oh, Stan, poor Miss Kemp—her little dog picked up some poison and he's dead. The poor soul's in a state about getting him buried, and all I can think of to do is call Mr. Glidden." She sat down to the phone hurriedly.

"That's a damn shame. I wonder what he got?" Tammy was pulling at his arm, something she wanted to show him; she'd taken a great fancy to him, the little she'd seen of him. Poor baby, thought Meg, she'd never known many men: a father.

Mr. Glidden was instantly sympathetic. "Now that's an awful shame. I know what store she set by that little fellow. I wonder what it was?—and I'll bet I know, at that. The P. and R. people shouldn't be allowed to use it, or at least they ought to warn the public—that damned snail bait they put out, it's death on dogs. I nearly lost a dog of my own once with that stuff. Unless you get 'em to a vet fast, it's no good." He ruminated. "She's worried about burying him, you say. Tell you what I'll do. I'll come over and see he's put away—there's that little bed along the back, just right, and some pretty flowers there. You think she'd be satisfied about that?"

"Oh, I'm sure she would. It's awfully good of you. He was all she had. I'll go and tell her, thank you."

And strangely enough, in her sympathy with Miss Kemp, who was old and alone and hadn't had anyone but Petie, it wasn't until she came upstairs again that any other aspect of it struck her. She found Stan Pollard standing in the middle of the room, his hair ruffled where he'd been running fingers through it. "I wonder what killed him," he said.

She repeated what Mr. Glidden had said. "Oh," said Stan. "Is that so? Well, maybe."

Suddenly Meg felt cold. "What—do you mean?"

"I don't know," said Stan. "But he was a good watchdog, wasn't he? Barked at strangers every time. Feisty little dog."

"Yes," said Meg. "Yes, he was." They looked at each other.

"Don't forget to fasten the chain."

"I could ask you to stay for dinner. It's not much—meat loaf and gravy and potatoes and some odds and ends."

"Half a loaf," said Stan. He sounded uneasy. "All right. Can I go and get anything? Ice cream for Tammy?"

"Ice cream!" shouted Tammy, bouncing up and down.

"Well—" said Meg.

"I'll be back in half an hour. I think I'd like a word with Mr. Glidden," said Stan.

Burt looked in as Varallo was finishing the report and said, "Don't know how much good we'll do you at that place, in the way of prints. Gene's still there hunting latents. Hell of a lot of places to dust, and I've known 'em to turn up in some funny places, you've got to be thorough. One thing we have got for you, though, and it'll make some dandy evidence in court if it ever gets that far."

"What is it? "

"A beautiful footprint," said Burt. "I've got a honey of a moulage —it came out just the way it's supposed to when you're practicing in police science class, only it seldom does. This is a classic."

"Stop raving about it and tell me what it is."

"Well, it was in the kitchen. You never saw such a mess, by the way—"

"I saw it."

"Yes, well, in the course of ransacking the cupboards he'd managed to upset a canister of flour all over the floor. And then he stepped in it. And his shoes were wet."

"How come? It's dry as a bone—that predicted rain faded away."

"I asked," said Burt. "The family had landed there by then and of course we couldn't let them in to look around until we were finished, so they were just standing there. And it seems when the granddaughter came and found them, the front sprinklers were on—that was another thing alarmed her right away, because she could see they'd been on way too long, water running down the gutter. After she called us she turned them off. It looks to me as if the ransackers got in last night. Maybe just before or after dark, and the old man had the sprinklers on. There were lights turned on all over the place. Anyway, his shoes were wet and he made this nice print in the flour. It's a big one, Vic. About a size thirteen—a sneaker with a ridged crepe sole, and there's a crack right across one ridge on the heel. If you locate it, the moulage will pin it down."

"Very helpful," said Varallo. "Now give us a couple of latent prints and a name so we know where to look for the sneaker."

"Keep your fingers crossed," said Burt.

There was a subdued commotion outside now, around the headquarters building, as the Traffic shift changed at four o'clock. The squad cars came heading into the lot, as the new shift of men who'd be on until midnight were briefed at roll call. Five minutes from now, or ten, the squads that needed it would be gassed up and ready to roll, and the new Traffic shift would pour out to separate on their respective ways.

Varallo was reading over the report when a uniformed man came in; it was a rookie by the name of Adams. "Say," he said, "I thought I'd better tell you—I think I spotted that British Lotus right at the end of shift. But—I'm damned sorry—it got away."

"You don't say. Where?"

"I was out on Glenoaks heading toward Burbank when I saw it going the other way, across the center divider. I'm pretty sure—when we were told to watch for it, I looked up a picture of it, and it's a sort of individual car. And then the color. But by the time I got to where I could make a U-turn, it was too far ahead to catch—nobody said to use a siren on it."

No, because of course there could be more than one around; Delia's old lady could have been much mistaken. "Well, at least we know there's one somewhere around town," said Varallo.

"I'll keep an eye out, when I'm around that area."

—And he didn't know much about the mechanics of this, but any intelligent man could learn basic principles from a little study. His mind jumped back to college—always been good at getting a subject all packed into his mind the last minute before an exam; it might go out of his head next day, but he had the grade. Quick study, that was it.

He had been sitting here in the library most of the day, taking notes, looking at drawings. It was coming clear in his mind, the plan all precisely worked out—now he had a free hand. He could take all the time he wanted. He could see the way it would go now.

And this was quite simple—much simpler than he had thought it would be. Partly a matter of mathematics, and he'd always been good at that too—old man deviling him into that damned dull course, but it had been a snap— Most things easy to him, he'd always had a better-than-average brain.

This was going to be it—had to be it—and if it was just a trifle less safe, it was still safe. He had absorbed all the books told him, and it was going to be an accident. An accident, not even a very unusual one. A nice, safe, tragic, nasty accident. Nobody's fault. Nobody's crime.

And another nice thing about it, nothing to buy under the counter: nothing dangerous to buy that could be checked back. But not here. He didn't know this damned place, this network of city that seemed to stretch out in all directions forever, but by what the book said—*agricultural operations*. That wasn't city. This damned place. Somewhere out of the city, and that meant a little trip. A day, two days. And then, take his time setting it up. This one was really foolproof. But safe.

He sat thinking about it, of all he had to do, to get, the cold shrewd brain moving here and there. The obsession was a twin obsession in him now: he had to get them, the bitch and her kid who were responsible for all his bad luck and loss and four years out of his life, they had to be paid back for what they'd done to Wayne Burgess, but in the paying he must not risk himself. They'd never get him to shut him up anywhere again.

And so all the plans, the two that had missed (how the hell?) and this one, didn't call for plotting anything that would look like a crime. It had taken some thinking out, but he had it clear now.

He folded his notes methodically and went out to the old car in the library lot. And, he thought, keep the cover sweet—it would only be two days, three, and then it would be done. Finished. Like the bitch and her kid. Good and finished.

When the woman came into the apartment, he said casually, "Guess what, doll? My agent's lined up a bit part for me. On location tomorrow."

"Gee, that's great. You be gone long?"

"A day, two maybe."

"What's it in, a bigtime show?"

"I don't know yet. I'll tell you when I get back."

He'd be damned glad to get away from her, the fat whore.

When Rhys and Hunter came on, among the other routine matters called to their attention, left over from the day watch, was a bench warrant just handed down today. It was for one Donald Biggs, and as

Hunter glanced over it he said, "I hope I never meet him when he's in anything with wheels." The slow-moving processes of the law had finally put this and that together on Donald Biggs. Over a period of four months he had collected an impressive array of nine moving-violation tickets, all for speeding, three more for illegal turns, one for running a light. He had failed to appear in court on any of them, ignored repeated requests to appear, and was now subject altogether to about a thousand dollars in fines and the revocation of his license for one year. Somebody—it looked like Forbes's writing—had appended a note. As if they hadn't enough to do, they'd had a look for Biggs at his known address on Burchett Street; he'd rented a room there and had moved out last week, and the owner didn't know where.

They didn't get a call until after ten o'clock. Then a squad called them out to a mugging downtown.

It was a big, fairly new motel, three-storied, with a generous-sized parking lot that stretched away from the main building. The parking lot was on a side street, not as well lighted as the main drag at right angles. There was no telling when it had happened, but at any time after dark a lot of the motel tenants would be out for dinner, and those who weren't were probably in the motel dining room on the other side of the building; the mugger had likely had the parking lot all to himself and his victim.

The ambulance was pulling out as they came up. Patrolman Judovic said, "His pulse wasn't too good—whoever clobbered him didn't pull his punches. His wallet's gone, pockets cleaned out—no watch. Standard mugging. He was staying here—another couple found him when they drove in."

The night manager was agitated. They'd never had such a thing happen before—right downtown, it didn't seem possible— They could have told him it happened anywhere.

The manager could tell them his name, and that he was registered as from Kansas City, but that was all he knew; didn't know what his business here was, who he might know here.

He let them into his room, but there wasn't anything helpful there: no address book. An extra suit, some shirts and underwear, socks and ties and handkerchiefs, all good quality but anonymous. He had left a batch of traveler's checks in the safe in the manager's office.

"I suppose there's somebody to notify," said Rhys.

The manager had been standing around looking helpless, but now brightened. "I do remember that he made a long-distance call last week—it was on his bill, of course. The switchboard will have a record of the number."

The switchboard did, and it was a number in Kansas City. Rhys glanced at his watch and said, "Well, it'll be something else for the day watch to take care of. It's now two-thirty A.M. in K.C."

When they got back to the office he called the hospital. The man had a severe concussion and a possible skull fracture. The hospital wanted to know the name of a relative or someone responsible—for the bill, Rhys mentally added to that—and of course he couldn't help them there. All they could do was leave a note for the day watch.

The first thing that came in on Tuesday morning was a call from a doctor at Memorial Hospital, Mrs. Burns's doctor. The old lady was competent to be interviewed, and very anxious to talk to the police.

"And how is he doing?" asked Varallo.

"Not so good. He came through the surgery well enough, but his heart's not in very good shape."

Varallo took Delia with him to talk to the old lady. She was sitting half propped up in bed, her gray hair rather wild about her face, and she gave a little gasp of relief when Varallo showed her the badge. "Now we don't want you to get excited and upset, Mrs. Burns, but anything you can tell us—"

"Oh, yes!" she said, and she gripped Delia's hand like a vise. "Oh, yes! Because it was too cruel, you've got to find out who those two men are and lock them up! I'm so frightened for Ray. Harold and Mina have been here and they keep saying he'll be all right, but how can he be? Just last Saturday was our forty-fifth wedding anniversary—"

"We just want you to tell us exactly what happened," said Delia calmly. "Just take it easy, there's no hurry."

"Must tell you—yes. So you can start looking for them—catch them —so they can't hurt anyone else." She struggled to sit up higher. "It's all right, I'm not excited—just want to tell you. Oh, dear, I hope Ray is all right. It was Sunday night they came. It was about seven o'clock. Ray was just going out to turn off the lawn sprinklers—as a matter of fact we'd both forgotten they were on, and it was after dark —when the doorbell rang. We'd been sitting there reading, you know. And—and when he opened the door they just came pushing right in— and Ray said what did they want and the big one just hit him and knocked him down." She paused for a moment. "I just turned round in time to see that, and I must have screamed, the other one came over and asked where the money was, and I said we didn't have any money in the house, and he said they knew we did and where was it— and then he just—just yanked me up out of the chair and hit me in the face with his fist—" They could see the bruise dark on her jaw. "And I fell down against the coffee table—that's when I broke my hip. I couldn't move. I tried to call out to Ray, but he was just lying there—I was so afraid he was dead—"

"Now take it easy," said Varallo. "Can you tell us what they looked like?"

"Oh, yes! They were both black men, one was a lot bigger than the other, he was huge—the other one wasn't quite as black—and they had on filthy dirty clothes and they *smelled*. And I couldn't move! I just had to lie there while they went all through the house, I could hear them smashing things in the kitchen and opening drawers—oh, it was awful! And it was even worse after they went away—I couldn't reach the phone, get any help—and I kept calling to Ray, but he just laid there—I was sure he was dead—I don't know how I got through the night, I must have kept fainting off—I just don't know— Oh, but I didn't tell you—the other one, the smaller one, he called the big one a funny name. I heard him say it twice. Lonzo, he called him. Lonzo." She looked at them anxiously.

"Well, that's very helpful, Mrs. Burns, thanks. You'd better get some rest now."

"Are they telling the truth about Ray? Are they? Please tell me—is he alive?"

"Yes, he is," said Delia. "He's alive, Mrs. Burns. And you're going to be all right."

She sank back on the pillow. "But why—why did they come and do that to us? We hadn't any money in the house. I don't think Ray had five dollars in his wallet. Why?"

They couldn't tell her why.

Tammy had taken a fancy to Stan, about the only man she'd ever known at all. "Stanny not comin'?" she asked.

"I don't know, baby." He'd got sick of it, of course; he thought she was an idiot. No, he'd believed her about Wayne. Just not about the rest. It was after eight o'clock. They were all ready to leave, the breakfast dishes cleared away. Couldn't keep this up forever, of course; he thought it was silly, and he'd—

She couldn't stand here vacillating forever either. Finally she took up the phone. She got, after delay, the manager of the motel.

"Mama—do I goin' to school today? Mama? You feel bad like you did?"

"Yes. No," said Meg. "Come on, baby, you're going to school." She picked up her bag; the ring of keys was beside it and she dropped it into her jacket pocket. They went out to the hall and she locked the door behind them, seeing in her mind's eye that long safe deadbolt sliding into its niche in the wall. Safe. Secure.

She drove Tammy up to the nursery school and then back downtown to the police building on the corner of Isabel and Wilson.

"Because you're going to listen to me this time," Meg said to Delia. "I've got to make you listen to me. All of you. You've got to see—how queer it is about Stan. Oh, my God, poor Stan—I brought that on him too. It's not just an accident—just coincidence. How could it be all coincidence? Just happening? I called the hospital and they wouldn't tell me anything, they just kept asking if I was a relative— After I told them Mr. Pollard's address they just hung up. And there was the dog—" She pounded one hand on Delia's desk. "It's all being *planned*—can't you see it?"

Varallo got up and collected the night watch report from O'Connor's desk; O'Connor would have looked it over, but the name wouldn't have registered with him. "The dog," said Varallo.

"Miss Kemp's Petie. He was poisoned yesterday—somehow—and he was such a good watchdog. He let everybody know—if there was a stranger around. And she's there most of the time, you know—only goes out for an hour in the morning, for a walk, and the rest of the time she just took Petie out around the apartment building. Such a good watchdog," said Meg.

O'Connor had come over and was listening. She ignored him; she was talking to Varallo and Delia. "Oh, you proved to me—you tried so hard to prove—those two things were just accidents. Because the locks are so good. Maybe they were—you thought I was a nervous fool, imagining things—and maybe I was. But it was because I knew, all along, that Wayne was out there—waiting, and planning. That he was going to try to kill us, somehow. Only this time he'd be careful— about his own skin. I *know* he can't get into the apartment—but those queer things happening, at least I thought they were queer—and Stan was kind, he said he'd stay there days to make sure. And now he can't—he's been put out of the way, don't you see? I wish somebody would call the hospital and find out how he is, they'd tell you. And I told you, I knew in my bones, it was Wayne who killed Carol Sue."

"What's that?" said O'Connor.

"I knew it. He thought she was Tammy. But you wouldn't listen to me."

"Let's hear about this," said O'Connor deliberately, "in words of one syllable. Not you." He hushed her with the flat of one big hand, and pointed the other at Varallo.

"Delia knows more chapter and verse on it."

O'Connor swung Katz's desk chair around and sat down, and it protested as he leaned back. "Shoot," he said. "All of it."

Delia obliged. When she came to the end, he sat massaging his jaw for a long minute.

"I wish somebody'd call the hospital," said Meg. "It's my fault he got hurt. And we ought to call Mr. Pollard." She still didn't look at O'Connor, probably because she hadn't the faintest idea that O'Connor was anything but what he looked like, a very tough, crude, unimaginative cop.

He said, "That was the break in the pattern. A big way one way, a little way another. Just a mite out of the original area. And no rape— just a kill. They graduate to getting the kick that way, but not always." He looked at Meg. "Both watchdogs," he said. "Both watchdogs at once. The same day."

"That," said Delia, "stretches coincidence—or does it?"

"Coincidence," said O'Connor, "can cover a lot of goddamned things, but I don't think it covers both the watchdogs. It's too neat. Too pat. Too smug."

"Smug," said Meg. "That's—Wayne. He knows it all. He's the smart one. Can we call the hospital?"

"Bob got a number in K.C. from the motel." O'Connor ran a thoughtful hand through his curly black hair, and then abruptly went into action. Characteristically, he made Meg a growled apology first. "I didn't buy you and your ex, but I don't like too many coincidences either." He laid a hairy fist on Varallo's phone and got the hospital. "You've got this Oliver Pollard's address?" he asked Meg. She remembered it and told him. He conducted a short conversation with the hospital, browbeating whoever he was talking to unmercifully, and put the phone down. "He'll be O.K. eventually. Out of it now, concussion, bruises and so on. And if I know the goddamned hospital, so anxious to be sure the damn bill's going to be paid, I'll bet they've been on to Uncle Oliver before you were out your apartment door. We'd better talk to him—he'll want to know what's going on." He looked up the area code and dialed. He said to Meg, "Whose department covered the homicide area?"

"What? I don't know what—"

"The homicide, the homicide. His parents. K.C. or a suburb? The police force, damn it."

"Oh," said Meg. "Oh, it was Kansas City, I think. Yes, I remember the sign on the patrol car—" But O'Connor had now got Uncle Oliver. He rolled the desk chair across to his desk and stabbed a forefinger at the amplifier, and Uncle Oliver came through firm and clear.

The hospital had called, he said. He had demanded full details, and was satisfied of his nephew's condition, but wanted to know all they knew about the affair. "I can't get away here—I have a lawsuit going on and several other things I can't leave. As long as Stanley will be all right—I presume you have considered Wayne Burgess in connection with this. I am, of course, conversant with what's been going on out there. Stan asked me to try to trace him, but the private detective— Is Mrs. Burgess all right?"

"And we'll try to see she stays that way. Yes, we'll be in touch with you." O'Connor looked at Meg. "The two watchdogs is what sells me. I don't know that I buy any more of it. Carol Sue—" He lit a new cigarette thoughtfully and looked at it. "But I'll go along, Mrs. Burgess—somebody's planning something, putting your two watchdogs out of the way." He took up the phone again, and this time told the desk to get him K.C. police headquarters. Eventually he got connected with a Captain Hurst and talked to him quite a while.

Meg was sitting there staring at him. Delia touched her arm. "It's going to be all right, you know. I told you, if he contacted you, made another threat, we could do something. Well, you could say, by implication, he has. This one we believe."

O'Connor put the phone down and swung around to them. "Let's lay it on the line," he said. "Burgess is here, and planning to make some kind of attempt on you. You and your little girl. We don't know what. And there's not a hell of a lot we can do, but we'll do it. K.C. still had his mug shots on file, of course, and they're wiring some out pronto. Now, you know you're safe when you're in your apartment behind those good locks. You believe that?"

Meg nodded.

"And God knows we haven't got the manpower to detail a twenty-four-hour guard on you—"

"Shutting stable doors," said Delia.

O'Connor scowled at her. "And this place you work, it's a public building, people all around. And you say he'll be careful not to get caught this time, so he's not likely to just walk in with a gun?"

"I don't think so," said Meg weakly. "Besides, he wants Tammy too."

"Um," said O'Connor. "Those mug shots ought to be in by noon."

"What—what can you do?"

"This and that. Circulate those mug shots to every man riding a squad. Use Traffic detail, with the mug shots, to cover every motel in town, ask if he's there. Of course, if he's grown a beard or something—"

Meg said, "No. He wouldn't. When we were married he grew a mustache, and he hated it. He wouldn't."

"Is he a drinker? Gambler? Like to bowl? Like porn?"

"No, why? He—he always will chew gum," said Meg. "It looks so vulgar, I never could stop him— *Why?*"

"Look everywhere he might be. The point is," said O'Connor patiently, "let him know, if possible, that we know he's here, we're looking for him. So—being careful of his own skin—he'll maybe give up his little ideas about you. At least he won't make any move once he knows that."

Meg said, "I didn't even call Dr. Burton. I'll be getting fired."

CHAPTER NINE

By noon that day, Wayne Burgess' official photographs, taken at the time of the murders four years ago, had come in by wire from Kansas City, and been sent to the lab for copies to be made up: a lot of copies. They would be distributed to the Traffic men at the four o'clock roll call, and at the other shift changes. And O'Connor went into a huddle with Lieutenant Rinehart, who headed Traffic detail, arranging coverage of all the motels, the few hotels, in town, all the nearby restaurants. Each squad car would contact those in its normal cruising route. "And," said O'Connor, "tell 'em not to be discreet about it. Crude and open, we're looking for him."

Katz had got interested in this, and said, "I wonder if he showed up anywhere around that apartment. And what about service stations?"

O'Connor said he was already ahead of him. "We can't cover every station in town, but the squads will take the ones nearest the motels. He's got to be driving something." From now on, the desk would call Meg Burgess' office every hour during the day, to check on her. And she didn't think there was any way Burgess could get at the child in that nursery school.

"I wonder what plan he's got in his head," said Katz.

"Something at the apartment—on account of the dog—the two watchdogs," said O'Connor sardonically. "Of course the easiest thing to do would be to set up a fake robbery. Make it look as if he'd intercepted her as she came home, forced his way in—tie them up to make it look like accidental strangulation. He'd need the dogs out of the way for that."

Delia said, "She didn't think he'd try anything like that again when it didn't work for him before."

"They tend to follow routine the way we do," said O'Connor

dryly, "and why else do we go by M.O.'s? Though this one sounds like a fairly wild one. The point is, whatever he's got in mind, if she's right, he wants to keep it strictly anonymous. And if he's around, where else will he be but a motel? He doesn't know anybody here, and the chances are he doesn't intend to stay long. Why would he rent an apartment? And when he gets the word that police are asking about him, by his right name, know he's here, he'll back off fast. It's the simplest way to handle it. And, for God's sake, we've got other business on hand."

That they had. Owing to the Burns thing turning up yesterday, they hadn't yet looked at the actual new gardeners they had found out about, and Varallo and Katz split those names up and went out on that. They were doing a lot of driving at that piece of routine; they hadn't yet found a lone gardener or garden service that was based in Glendale.

Varallo started out for North Hollywood to see Greene's Gardening. The address turned out to be a big nursery, and a busy one; it was a while before the owner, Douglas Greene, could give him any attention, waiting on customers alone. "What the hell do cops want with me?" he asked genially. "Glendale cops yet?" He was a big man about forty, with biceps like a boxer's. Varallo said it was just a routine piece of investigation, and Greene looked interested and skeptical but asked no more questions. "Yeah," he said, "there's good steady money in it, and at the same time you're providing a good service. You get enough regular jobs, it adds up. Contract to take care of people's yards weekly, it's usually thirty, forty bucks a month —you got to charge that on account of the gas, running all over." He employed three men at that—"Matter of fact I just took on the third one, the wife's brother from back East—he needed a job and I got the work, just added four new jobs." They were all out on their regular gardening jobs now; he told Varallo where. Burbank, Tujunga, Glendale.

Varallo caught the two in Burbank and Tujunga on the jobs, and neither of them looked anything like the description they had. By the time he got back to Glendale it was past five o'clock, and that one had long finished his gardening job and departed. Varallo went back to the office and found O'Connor sitting at his desk with his feet up on Forbes's desk chair reading a report. He told him briefly about the gardeners, and O'Connor said, "And we are all wondering if this is a great big fat waste of time, aren't we? Well, at least we've wrapped one up. The lab can be useful."

"What have we got?"

O'Connor passed over the report. Three of the latent prints picked up in the Burns house—from the kitchen counter, a bedroom mirror, and the counter in the bathroom—had been identified as belonging to Billy Lee Hall. He was in Glendale's records on only one count, arrested two years ago for B. and E., but his address then had been Los Angeles; so Thomsen had checked with LAPD and he had a long pedigree with them: burglary, assault, narco possession.

"Now isn't that just ducky," said Varallo bitterly. "Always at the end of a day. So more overtime tonight. But damn it, Charles, I'm going home first to have dinner. I do like to see my wife and family occasionally."

"And all these damn gardeners," said O'Connor, "look like a dead end."

They met back at the office at seven-thirty and took O'Connor's Ford. "You just got that baby compact so you never have to ferry suspects," grumbled O'Connor.

The address was down near Echo Park, Allesandro Street: an old, tired, shabby section of downtown. It was a block of old frame houses, with no lawns or plantings to soften outlines. A chocolate-colored little girl about eight answered the door and said sure her Uncle Billy was here, she'd get him.

He came to the door and looked at the badges and said, "Oh, hell. What you guys want now?"

"You," said O'Connor, and crooked a finger at him. "Come along like a good boy."

"Damn it, I was just havin' dinner. I ain't done nothing."

"Oh, yes, you have, Billy. You left some very pretty fingerprints someplace they shouldn't have been."

He looked ready to cry. "Oh, *hell*," he said despondently. "I guess I better tell my wife where I'm goin'." They went in to keep an eye on him while he got a jacket and broke the news; there were about a dozen people there, and a birthday cake for somebody on the table. They took him back to Glendale headquarters.

Rhys and Hunter sat in on talking to him. "Make it short and sweet," said O'Connor, leaning back and loosening his jacket so the .357 Magnum showed. "Do I have to tell you where you left the prints, Billy? You and some pal named Lonzo broke into a house on Sunday night and beat up a couple of old people. Before we book you for it, we'd be interested to know who your pal is and why you picked that particular place."

Billy Lee Hall looked at them sullenly. He had had enough experience of police and courts to know that the prints nailed him; there might be a reduced plea, he might get off with a minimum sentence, but some kind of sentence there would be. He was a thin, rather light-skinned Negro with an Oriental cast to his eyes. He said disgustedly, "Oh, for God's sake. Get busted just for that, and we got a lousy four-twenty out of it! In the guy's wallet. That goddamn stupid chick doesn't know from nothin'—it was a real dismal caper."

"What stupid chick? Who's your pal?"

"Ah, this Sally—Sally Eggers, I been making a little time with her. She just got a job at that place, doin' housework. She says they're loaded, lotsa jewelry, and the guy always has a wad of cash, stuff all over the place we get a good price for. Sure I tell you who Lonzo is— you think I'm goin' to the slammer alone? Lonzo Wade, he's a good friend o' mine, I cut him in on the deal. But there wasn't nothin' in the place! Just nothin'!"

"I suppose," said Varallo, "that Sally told you where to go, how to get there?"

Hall was still mulling over his disappointment. "What? Yeah, Sally wrote down the number, so we find it O.K. And there wasn't—"

"You still have it on you?"

"What? I guess so." He looked down at himself. "I had the same clothes on—" He felt in his jacket pockets, found a scrap of paper. "Stupid goddamned chick," he said.

O'Connor unfolded the scrap. "Who's so goddamned stupid, Billy? It says here, eighteen-oh-three. You landed at thirteen-oh-three."

Hall looked stupefied. "We did? Well, I'll be damned."

"Very probably," said O'Connor. "I do get tired of dealing with you dumb bastards." He took him over to the jail while Varallo checked with R. and I. at LAPD. Alonzo James Wade, of course, had a pedigree with them too, and he got an address. Tomorrow would be time enough to pick up Wade, and tomorrow was his day off. He hoped to get all the roses sprayed for aphids, finally.

Overnight there was a professional heist job at a market on North Central, two men walking in just at closing time, 11 P.M. Rhys's report was on O'Connor's desk on Wednesday morning, and the market manager and the one stock clerk who had been there came in about nine-thirty to make statements. The manager, Frank Teed, was a little red-haired man, and he was still seething and swearing. The stock clerk was a stolid middle-aged man named Earl King, who said the company had insurance. It was a chain market.

"Goddamn it, that's not the point, Earl! Sure to God there's insurance, and just how damned high the premiums are I can guess, just because there's so damn many of these punks running around loose—and you needn't tell me," he rounded on O'Connor and Forbes fiercely, "it isn't your fault! Catch 'em when you can, and then the goddamned fool judges turn 'em loose to go and do it again! If I could've got my hands on those bastards—"

"But you didn't. We'd like to hear whatever you can tell us about them," said O'Connor.

"They had on masks," said King.

"Well, what size were they? Any foreign accent? Any marks?"

"Yes," said Teed. "I don't know if you'd say they had any inside knowledge—for God's sake, it's posted on the front of the store, weekday hours eight to eleven. Anybody could guess that after we closed I'd be clearing the registers, putting the money away in the safe. They didn't know where the safe is, I think they expected it to be in the back storeroom, because that's where they jumped us. They must have been hiding behind some crates or something back there. The first I knew was when one of them stuck a gun in my back—the other one had already collected Earl in the back room—I was just on my way there to stash my apron in the laundry hamper."

"They had stocking masks on," said King. "They tied me up and made Frank hand over all the cash from the registers, and then they tied him up. I thought he was going to have a stroke."

"I hadn't even counted the take—you'll have to get the register tabs—my God, when I think of those bastards just walking out with—

at a guess," said Teed in something like a snarl, "eight, nine thousand bucks, I could—"

"The sizes," said Forbes patiently. "Dark? Light? Negro? Mexican?"

"How the hell would I know? They were white—and there's just one thing I can tell you. The one who tied me up had a tattoo. Maybe that'll do you some good, I hope. A goddamned tattoo right on the back of his hand—his right hand—mostly in red—fancy letters, and it said BORN TO RAISE HELL. And that is God's truth."

"It might be helpful," said Forbes. "That's a funny one, Mr. Teed."

"I can think of other words for it," said Teed. "The time I had getting loose—and this big lummox," he looked at King—"when I asked him to chew the cord, he has to say his teeth don't fit!"

"Well, they don't very good," said King. "These new dentures. They're kind of loose, I didn't think I could get a grip, like." The thin nylon cord used to tie them, apparently brought by the heisters, was at the lab. "But I can tell you about the gun. One of them anyway."

"What?" demanded Forbes and O'Connor together.

"This gun the other one had, the one without the tattoo," said King. "I got a good look at it while Frank was getting the money. It was a Harrington and Richardson Guardsman thirty-two."

"You sure about that?" asked O'Connor.

"Oh, sure. Guns I know—they're my hobby, sort of. You know that one, it's got a kind of square barrel. A six load."

"You're absolutely sure? Well, thanks. That's something anyway," said O'Connor.

Forbes typed the statements and they signed them. He and O'Connor went down to Records and had a look for the tattoo via the computer, but there wasn't any sign of it in their records. They sent a query over to LAPD.

In late afternoon, O'Connor went down to the hospital to see whether he could talk to Stan Pollard. The nurse said he had been conscious, but only briefly. They'd taken X-rays and didn't think there was a skull fracture, but he had a broken arm—apparently he'd landed on it when he fell—and a couple of broken ribs, as well as the concussion.

O'Connor looked at him lying there in the hospital bed. Pollard didn't look to be conscious, but O'Connor bent over and spoke his name, and after a minute Pollard's eyelids twitched. He opened his eyes halfway and they focused on O'Connor with difficulty. "Mr. Pollard, can you hear me?"

"Who—in hell—'re you?" mumbled Pollard.

"Police. Do you remember anything about how you got hurt?"

"Car," said Pollard after a struggle. "Just—out. Bang. Couldn't tell —a thing." He shut his eyes again and O'Connor thought that was all, but after another long minute Pollard muttered, "Wayne—Wayne Burgess? Never laid eyes—" He opened his eyes again and squinted up. "You—take care—Meg."

"We'll try to," said O'Connor, but Pollard was unconscious again.

So far, and it was over twenty-four hours, none of the patrolmen circulating Burgess' photographs had come across a smell of him. The manager of a second-rate motel on Colorado had said doubtfully that it looked somewhat like a young fellow who'd stayed there two or three nights a couple of weeks ago, but he couldn't be sure. He'd been pressed to look up the registration, but that proved to be of no use; they hadn't expected Burgess to be registered under his own name, but the initials didn't match, and that was usually the earmark of an alias.

It had been even easier than he had thought, no sweat at all, and he got back to town that afternoon. A kind of triumphant excitement was filling him up steadily; this one was going to be it, this time he was going to do it.

But everything had to be just so; he was going to have plenty of time for arranging it just so, but he had to be sure of every detail, because this was something he'd never done before.

He had come back to the little secret hole he had made for himself here, and he was looking over his meticulous detailed notes when the woman came in. She was dirty from her day's work, he saw fastidiously; she annoyed him, being there. Her loud cheerful voice grated on him, but he had to answer her.

"Gee, good to see you back, lover. You never said what TV show it was. What kinda part did you hafta play?"

"Oh, a waiter," he said. It was going to be a delicate little job, and it had to be just right.

"Where'd you hafta go?"

He didn't know this country. "The desert somewhere."

"Gee, that's a funny place to play a waiter." She was fussing around in the kitchen, came back to sit on the couch with a can of beer. "God, I'm glad it's cooled off. It's murder, work in an air-conditioned place all day and then come home to this crummy pad. But rents, gee, outta this world." She wouldn't stop talking, asking questions. "Whatcha doin'? You got another part to learn?"

"That's it." He put the notes away; he supposed she could read, whether it would mean much to her or not.

"You got enough bread for us to go out and eat, lover? I just don't feel like getting anything. Maybe we could go to the corner place, have a couple drinks—"

Fat whore, fat whore, said his mind. Just a little while now, do it, have it done, and be rid of you. Them and you forever and forever. But she wouldn't stop talking at him.

"You never said what TV show it was. What was it?"

He'd never watched the tube very much: for a blank moment he couldn't remember the titles of any dramatic programs at all. She was repeating the question, foolishly insistent, and he dredged up a title from memory, one people had talked about. "It was 'Party Wives.' A new episode."

"Oh," she said, sounding surprised, "but that's not going to be on next season. It went big awhile, but it got dropped by NBC. I saw it in *TV Guide*. They're not making that one any more."

He was irritated at the clumsy little mistake. "Maybe it's got another sponsor or something. Anyway, it was."

She put the can of beer down and came over to him. "There wasn't any TV part, was there? Where'd you go? What for? I might've known I'm not good enough for you—"

"Oh, for God's sake shut up," he said.

"Well, I like that! You big jerk! You think you can just do anything and I put up with it—I'm not that big a fool. Maybe I did a little thinking while you was gone—you think I can't see you're just usin' me and my place? College-boy smoothie, think you walk all over me! You been playin' me for a sucker, and now you can't even pretend to be polite—"

She was like a fly buzzing around him, not important but a nuisance, and he wanted, here and now, just to sit and think about this, get all the details straight in his mind. Buzz, buzz, buzz, she went.

"Well, isn't that so? Isn't it?" She let out a strangled sob. "I shoulda known I don't mean a damn to you—but you might at least answer me—"

"Shut *up!*" he shouted, and gave her a casual belt across the side of the head. Eyes wide in surprise, she staggered and fell against the coffee table and just lay there.

He went on thinking. He was doing it inside his head, all the moves one by one, everything lined up straight, just the way it had to be. So everything would happen just the way it was supposed to.

After a while, ignoring her, he went out. Later, when he was feeling more like it, he'd sweet-talk her back. He only needed another day; then he could forget her.

It wasn't until much later that he realized he'd made a little complication for himself.

Varallo had accomplished something on his day off: his roses got sprayed. A silly sort of hobby for a cop; the things had been here when they bought the house, and with Mr. Anderson next door egging him on, he'd got interested. This year the damned aphids hadn't been quite as bad as usual; the roses were doing fairly well.

Laura brought the baby out in the back yard in the afternoon, and Ginevra chased butterflies, and Gideon Algernon Cadwallader made pounces after imaginary mice in the rose bushes.

He hadn't, however, had time to feed them, and it was now the next thing that had to be done. Maybe next week. And he thought about all the people who, working an eight-hour job, took it for granted that they got the weekend off, and he sighed. But there was the seniority building up again, and he wasn't getting any younger.

On Thursday morning, with Delia off, he caught up with the status quo before going out anywhere. LAPD couldn't produce anybody out of their records with that BORN TO RAISE HELL tattoo. O'Connor had now asked Pasadena and a few other departments. Siegler was up for arraignment tomorrow; Hall and Wade probably on Monday.

That was a stupid thing, even a little more stupid than the things they generally saw. He wondered how Mr. and Mrs. Burns were doing. It was in the cards they wouldn't be capable of living alone in their own little house any more; two independent lives shattered, for a stupid criminal's stupid little mistake, reading a 3 for an 8. Thinking about that, looking over the night report, he asked O'Connor suddenly, "On Hall and Wade—did you think about—"

"I'm ahead of you," said O'Connor. "Delia and her stable doors. I thought it was only neighborly. Yeah, I saw the people at that other address on Cleveland. Their name is Wray." That much farther up Cleveland, of course, the houses were newer and more affluent. "I told them it might be a good idea to fire their new maid. Well, it's possible the D.A.'s office may want to charge her too, but I doubt it. The courts don't like the conspiracy bit much."

Varallo laughed. Katz was out with Forbes on the heisters: the market job. He still hadn't finished checking on the men from Greene's, one other gardening outfit. One man from Greene's he had missed on Tuesday. He called Greene and found out where he'd be; his name was Clarence Reame. It was an address on Spencer.

He got there about nine-fifteen. There was a small pickup truck in front, with a gas lawnmower in the street behind it. The gardener had finished mowing the lawn, was trimming a low privet hedge around a flowerbed in front. Varallo parked the Gremlin behind the truck, got out and walked up the drive.

"Mr. Reame?"

The man straightened. "Yeah?"

Varallo only needed one look. Wondered if all this was a waste of time: if the LAPD lab had led them astray for once. But here he was, turned up by the meticulous lab work and the tedious routine. Here he was, Mary Lou Turner's grabber described so graphically. He was about five-ten, with narrow stooped shoulders, and he widened out to a fattish stomach and broad hips. He had on rimless glasses. He had sparse brown hair. And as he opened his mouth to speak the one word, Varallo saw the gleam of a gold tooth. He might be thirty.

"Yeah?" he said again, and Varallo brought out the badge.

"We've got some questions to ask you down at headquarters."

The narrow shoulders sagged. Reame stood looking at the hedge shears, and after a minute he said dully, "I ain't finished the job. I can't leave the truck."

"That'll be all right," said Varallo. "We can call Mr. Greene."

Reame put the hedge shears down carefully on the front porch. For the first time he looked directly at Varallo. "He won't like it," he said. "He won't like it atall." But he was quite docile and meek; he got into the Gremlin and rode quietly all the way back downtown.

When Varallo brought him into the detective office O'Connor took one look and a small, satisfied, grim little smile touched his mouth. He got up. "What's his name?"

"Clarence Reame."

They took him into an interrogation room and he sat down on the hard chair and fixed his gaze on the table. "You know," said O'Connor, "we had a pretty good description of you—from the little girl who got away from you. And here you are, big as life, just the way she described you. Do you remember that one?" O'Connor leaned over him, and now his mouth was hard and straight. "The one who got away?"

Reame nodded jerkily.

"But the other three didn't get away, did they? They weren't so lucky. The little five- and six-year-olds you forced into your car and raped. What about it, Reame?"

He looked up sideways at O'Connor and said in a thin, miserable voice, "Ena's goin' to be awful upset. She didn't know about it. I'm sorry. I've always been sorry about it, but it just seemed like after a while I couldn't help myself. From doing it. See, I thought I could get kind of a new start here, maybe straighten out and—and not have to do it any more. And Ena and me, we never was much for the letter writin', a card at Christmas and maybe a birthday card. She knew I was in jail but not what for. I—I told her it was a hold-up, I got awful broke once and didn't know what else to do. She was way out here, how'd she know? But she kind of promised Mom to look after me, she's nearly ten years older, see. And—so I wrote her and asked could I find a job here—and she wrote back, the guy she's married to give me a job. A good job."

"So," said O'Connor.

"I never meant to do it again. But the yards I go to work in—up there—there's schools. Where the little kids go. Two different schools. I—I see them walking along, the little kids."

"And you got the urge to do it again," said Varallo. "Where was it before? Where were you in jail?"

"Indiana. It was French Lick, I was workin' for a carpenter there. I got in the Indiana pen. Ena didn't know what for. I was in four years."

"All right," said Varallo. "Now, the first one here. Sandra Tally."

"I never knew their names. I just saw her walking along alone—"

"You'd been on one of the gardening jobs up here?"

"No, sir," said Reame. He shuffled his feet. "I figured they'd remember the truck, all the tools in back and all. I went back and got my own car. I got a little apartment in Burbank, and I got a old car."

"And just why," asked Varallo, "did you stick to just that area, this one part of town, to pick up the little girls?"

Reame glanced up at him briefly. "I never been in California before. I don't know the streets in all these towns. I just know how to get to all the jobs I got to do. But up there, see, with them two schools, there'd be a lot of little kids around."

As simple as that. They'd never thought of the two elementary schools in that area.

O'Connor said quietly, "There was another little girl, Reame. Carol Sue Wiley. Riding her tricycle, almost in the dark, in front of that apartment on Grandview. She didn't get raped, did she? She got dead."

"No, no," said Reame; he kept shaking his head; he was sweating now. "Not that one. That was why—why I didn't do no more. You got to believe that. I—I—it's an awful wrong thing, but I'd never go to *kill* one of them. The little kids. I'd never do that. I don't read the papers, but I heard the other guys talk about that—say the place it was—and I—I was scared, you find out I did it to the other kids, you think— But I never, I never done that. I wouldn't do a thing like that."

They straightened from him and looked at each other.

"Now I do wonder," said Katz, "if that girl could be right. The vindictive ex-husband?"

"I don't know," said O'Connor shortly. "It's up in the air. I do know that Reame's kind are chancy, and they can be violent in more ways than one. But we've got to wrap it up for the D.A. The courts do like all the T's crossed."

They found his apartment, located his car—an old blue Ford—and towed it in. Varallo called Greene, who went straight up in the air, and then had another fit when he heard about the Indiana pen; if he'd known about that he'd never have touched the guy with a ten-foot pole— Not wanting to be responsible for a divorce action, Varallo hastily explained that his wife hadn't known why her brother was in the pen. Probably if she had—

"In the pen at all," said Greene violently, "was enough! She tells me he's kind of a weak character is all, she promised her mother to look after him! By God, I'll look after him—"

"No, we will," said Varallo. "You'd better come and get your truck."

Pasadena obliged them, on Thursday afternoon, with the pedigree of one Richard Thorson, who had a little string of charges ranging from petty theft to narco possession, and also had the legend BORN TO RAISE HELL tattooed on his right hand. He didn't sound too likely for the pro heister with the stocking mask, but Varallo and Forbes went looking for him. They found him in the hospital in traction; he had borrowed a pal's motorcycle a couple of days ago, with disastrous results. That wasted a little time, but that was part of the job too.

Thomsen sent up the report on Reame's car on Friday. Just as expected, the laboratory evidence showed: stains, blood, and semen, and some of the blood was of the same rather unusual type as that of the first rape victim. That would tie it up tight.

"And you know," said O'Connor crossly, "that I'm going to have to lay that whole rigmarole in front of the D.A." He looked almost accusingly at Delia sitting at her desk across the room. "Stable doors!" he said.

"Well, it's not my fault," said Delia.

"When there's any shadow of a doubt, Reame can't be charged with that homicide. So just what do we do with it? Make a separate case file?" He lit a cigarette angrily. Varallo and Katz exchanged a glance.

"So some damn smart-aleck deputy D.A. says to me, 'So what about this Wayne Burgess? Have we got any evidence? Have we got any information?' and I've got to hand him this nebulous mess? There's not one iota of evidence on the Wiley kid, and I don't see there ever will be."

By then they had seen Clarence Reame's record, from three places in Indiana and two in Iowa. He had the usual beginning pedigree, stealing underwear, indecent exposure, culminating in the rape of a six-year-old girl in French Lick, Indiana, five years back. It said nothing, one way or the other, on Carol Sue Wiley.

Now the patrolmen had reached every motel and hotel in Glendale, the restaurants and service stations nearby, and there had been no smell of Wayne Burgess anywhere. And there were two things about that that they discussed back and forth. Was he here? Had he ever been here? And if he was, why hadn't he made a move?

The desk was still checking Meg Burgess' office by phone, every hour. She reported that nothing unusual had happened.

Stan Pollard was sitting up in the hospital bed and taking slightly more notice, but he was still shaky and they were going to take more X-rays.

"Damn it," said O'Connor querulously, "if he is here—if he was here—where else would he be but a motel? And damn it, they're not all like that fancy one where Pollard got clobbered. The second, and third-rate ones—I can see a desk man passing it on as a warning, not an excuse to kick him out—police asking for you, by a different name. It was the only way to try to do it, protect the girl, but has he already been scared off? And if he has, we'll never know."

Goddamn it, goddamn it, the bad luck and delays he'd had— This meant he couldn't do it until after the weekend. The weekend when the little bitch and her kid would be home, around that apartment. The weekend stretched out before him like two months instead of two days—days when he couldn't get at her. Goddamn that sniveling bitch, nothing but trouble in the end.

But it had meant he had to get out, and he was still nervous of motels. It could give anyone a handle on him, even with another name.

Everything in the car, he had found it took time—too damned much time. Places asking references, no. And he didn't know the damn town, which address might be in the right part of town for him, the old cheap part where not much notice was taken.

It was Friday afternoon before he found a place: an old shabby house north of town in another community, where the woman was just anxious to rent the room. She hadn't expected to get a young, handsome, charming tenant, and she never asked a question. It didn't matter what he told her; it passed out of his mind nearly as soon as he had put out the automatic charm—not sure of getting a job here, thought he'd like to try California, he was from Illinois, he was applying for a job tomorrow. It didn't matter. Two days to get through, and then on Monday he would have a clear field to set it up, and it would be done. The bitch and her kid—foolproof this time.

That fat blowsy whore, making all this extra delay. All her fault.

He wasn't much of a drinker as a rule, but tonight he felt savagely that he'd like to get drunk, and stay drunk the next two days, until the time he could start to do it, set it up—

But he couldn't do that, because of the new cover here—and on Monday he would need his mind quite clear—quite clear, his brilliant mind always a quick study at new things, always keeping him ahead of other people.

How to pass the time, the long dragging time until Monday—he'd never been a reader, never found books interesting, had to use them for studying, but that was all. The books of fiction, nothing. Nobody in the books was as alive, as brilliant, as interesting, as he was himself.

Pass the time—and it would pass. Monday—

On Friday afternoon Varallo brought in Luis Martinez, not feeling that anything much would come of it, just doing the routine. Martinez had a little pedigree of narco possession, grand auto theft as a juvenile. He wasn't very interesting, but Burbank's records told them that his older brother, Alfredo, bore a tattoo reading BORN TO RAISE HELL on his right hand, and Alfredo having a slightly stronger pedigree and not being at home at the moment, it seemed expedient to ask Luis if he knew where he was.

Luis was a handsome young fellow in sharp sports clothes; he worked part time at a middling-good men's-wear store in La Crescenta. He said, getting out a cigarette, "God's sake, that all you want to know? I don't mind telling you. Al's gone up to 'Frisco. He picked up with a real slick dish, she had some deal hanging up there, I don't know what. Anyway, that was three, four weeks back, if you were thinking he pulled something here. Were you?"

"If we were, we aren't now. So thanks very much," said O'Connor.

Luis sat there beside O'Connor's desk, in no hurry to go away. "This is my lucky day," he said, showing white teeth. "That's all you wanted to know. And so you're a real straight force, no fuzz on the take here, not a chance, there's still a grapevine and it'll go out you were looking for Al, reason you brought me in. My lucky day."

"How come?" asked O'Connor.

"So I can sit here nice and private and tell you something you like to hear, and nobody but me and the fuzz know where you heard it. You interested, *compadre?*"

"Depends what it is," said O'Connor.

"It's about half a million bucks' worth—wholesale—of coke and H and stuff due to change hands. It got delivered a couple days ago, the middleman's supposed to pick it up tonight or tomorrow night." He rattled off an address: an apartment on Salem Street. "Rico Guttierez, that's his pad. The front right apartment. Him and his chick Maria. You play it right, you get a nice haul, him and her and the middleman. So we're all happy."

"And what's your interest?" asked O'Connor.

"That's my business. I'm just telling you. You want to listen, fine. You don't, your loss." Luis got up. "Tonight or tomorrow night, sometime before midnight." He divided a grin between O'Connor and Varallo. "And all you ever asked me was about Al—we all know that." He sauntered out casually.

"Goddamn it to hell!" said O'Connor forcefully. "A stake-out yet! More overtime!"

"You told me not long ago," said Varallo, "that we picked the job because we're too stupid to know better."

That was at three o'clock, and O'Connor had gone over to see Rinehart about rearranging a few Traffic routes so he could call some back-up in a hurry if he needed it on the stake-out.

The routine had come to a little standstill for once; various heists had got filed away as unsolvable. They were still waiting to hear from a few other forces in the county about that tattoo, which sometime might turn up the right X on that market job.

At five o'clock Delia talked with the desk briefly and said to Varallo, "They just called Mrs. Burgess. Everything fine—she's just leaving."

The phone cut across his reply. There was a new homicide down. Nobody else was in; she went out with him on it.

It was a narrow, shabby old street in an old part of town, a little street called Fernando Court off San Fernando Road not far from the railroad tracks. The address was a ramshackle frame apartment building of about twelve units. There was a little crowd of people out staring at the squad car, and Patrolman Tracy was trying to calm down a buxom female who was just short of hysterics.

"Now, listen, ma'am—just take it easy—the detectives will want to talk to you—" He looked at Varallo with relief. "It's the left rear on the top floor. Homicide all right. She found it. Friend of hers, I gather."

They went up to look. The door was open. It was a shabby, tired place—four small rooms, counting the bathroom. The corpse was lying at one side of the little living room, beside a coffee table: a woman. She'd been in her mid-thirties, brown-haired with a henna rinse; she was a little too plump. She was wearing a tan uniform dress zipped up the front.

Varallo felt one arm. "It's a while. Could be rigor's come and gone." They didn't waste much time looking around; there weren't any obvious clues to be seen. They went back to the street and called up a mobile lab unit from the squad car. Tracy had the woman in the front seat now, and she was a little calmer and more coherent. Her name was Lorna Patching.

"I never had such a shock—Lil—oh, my God—but I got to tell you—" She was a plump bleached blonde, and she was wearing the same kind of tan uniform as the corpse. "I got to tell you—see, we work at the same place, Bob's in Hollywood on Santa Monica, and Lil always picks me up in the morning, I don't have a car—well, her name's Lil Stanton—only she didn't yesterday, and I figured maybe she just didn't feel so good, took the day off, I had to get the bus, I was late. But I couldn't get her on the phone last night. And when she didn't show this morning, I said to Gus—that's my husband, he's got the Shell station on Los Feliz at San Fernando—I said it was funny, not like Lil—so when I got off work, I took Gus's car and come to see, and the door was open and— Oh, my God!" She burst into tears all over again, and she blubbered, "You just find that new boyfriend of hers—he's got to be the one did it—Gus and I always thought there was something funny about him—"

CHAPTER TEN

There wasn't much they could do here until the lab men were finished. She agreed to drive up to headquarters, answer some questions— "Only I better call Gus, tell him where I am."

They weren't about to go overtime on it; tomorrow morning, see what the lab men could tell them; but she filled in a little background. She'd known Lil maybe six, seven years, met her when they both worked at a pancake place in West Hollywood, Lil was married to her second then; well, she'd been married a couple of times but it didn't take, Lil liked to be independent. "It's kinda different with Gus and me, I mean we get along O.K., but people are all different." Lil had been about thirty-six, she thought, and really didn't look it, except she wanted to take off about ten pounds. And they'd sure better look for that new boyfriend of hers, he was probably the one did it. His name was Ricky Arnold and there was something funny about him anyway. She didn't know where Lil had met him.

Varallo thanked her and said, "We'll probably want to talk to you again."

"That's O.K., anything I can do to help. Gus could tell you about him too, we went out with them a few times."

After she'd gone out Delia said, "I'll do the report in the morning." She got her handbag out and fished for keys. This looked like the usual rather sordid little homicide, just posing more paperwork.

It was after six, but Varallo didn't move for a minute, lazing back in his chair, his crest of tawny blond hair a little untidy. "How come you did pick the job, Delia?" he asked seriously. "It's uphill for a female."

Delia hesitated. They were alone in the office. She'd worked with all these men for nearly six months, and she liked them; they were good men to work with; she thought they liked her. She liked

Varallo; and he was a little older than the others, even the lieutenant, had been a cop longer than the rest. She very nearly started to tell him about Alex, and then she didn't. It might be a silly way to feel, but Alex Riordan had been something of a legend in the LAPD, and she felt if they knew, it would be as if she was boasting about it, trading on his name; and she had to make good at the job as herself, on her own. She just said, "Oh, I had a relative in the LAPD, I thought it sounded like an interesting job. Sometimes it is, isn't it?"

They went down to the lot together, and she got into Alex's old Mercedes and started home.

On Saturday morning O'Connor came in already swearing before he saw the night report. He and Rhys had sat on that damned stakeout, he said, on Salem Street, until 1 A.M., and nothing had showed; and then when he got home the baby had colic or something and yelled all night. "Katy can sleep days, but I feel as if I'd been dragged through a knothole." As usual, his tie was already crooked. "Well, we'll see if anything shows tonight." At least nothing new had showed up overnight, or not much: a heist at a drugstore.

Varallo got onto the lab and talked to Thomsen. "I know it's early to ask, but if you could give us some idea, what you might get on that new body."

"You're not exactly early," said Thomsen, "because we're going to get nothing. Which maybe says something to you right away. There wasn't a print in the place. And by what it looked like aside from that, she was a pretty sloppy housekeeper—the place was a pig sty and had been for a long time. Dirty dishes in the sink, sink dirty, mouse droppings in the lower cupboards, every drawer a mess, the refrigerator hadn't been cleaned in years, I'd guess, and the bathroom—that toilet— But every surface that'd take prints was polished clean. There weren't even any of hers, except on the beer can on the coffee table."

"*Ven—va via!*" said Varallo.

"What?"

"I said, that's very peculiar. And interesting."

"Yes, we thought so," said Thomsen. "It seems to argue that somebody knows his prints are on file somewhere."

Varallo thought about that for a minute, took up the phone again and got Goulding. "Have you looked at our latest corpse yet?"

"Is there any hurry? Sure, I can get to it this morning. There's nothing else on hand."

Delia was still busy on the initial report, but Varallo said, "That can be finished later. Let's go do some legwork instead." He told her what Thomsen had said, and she was interested.

"That says something all right. Where are we going?"

"To see Lorna's husband. Just from what little we heard, I don't think Lorna is quite the emancipated female Lil was, it's possible Gus wears the pants in the family and can tell us a little more."

Gus Patching told them quite a lot. The Shell station on that corner was a big and busy one; there were four mechanics and a couple of teenage kids pumping gas. Whatever education Gus had or hadn't, he was a successful man. He looked at Varallo's badge, looked at the Mercedes, and said, "That baby's seen some miles go by. I been wondering if you'd want to talk to me. We can go in the office." It was surprisingly neat and clean; he pulled up two straight chairs for them, sat at the desk. "Naturally I heard about it from Lorna. Hell of a thing." He was older than Lorna, a man about forty-five, thin and bony, with shrewd gray eyes and a big Roman nose. "I couldn't tell you anything about the murder, the last time I saw her was last Saturday. We met them at a place for drinks and dinner."

"Them, yes," said Varallo. "The boyfriend. Your wife says he's the one killed her. What do you think?"

"It wouldn't surprise me," said Patching. "That kind, Lil I mean, they go around asking for it. Don't get me wrong, I don't set up to pass judgment on anybody—we all got our faults. Lorna liked Lil, well, they'd known each other awhile. Just at work, casual, I mean she wasn't a close pal. Lorna never was the kind to go picking up men in bars, even before we was married, or I wouldn't have married her, if you take me. Well, Lil had oughta known her way around, married twice. But I don't think she knew anything about that guy, and it was"—he thought—"funny. Lorna and I both said so."

"Funny how?" asked Delia.

"Well, you'd understand what I mean, miss. Lil was in her thirties, maybe she'd been a good-looker ten years back, but she wasn't no movie star. And this guy couldn't be over thirty, kind of handsome, he could've found some slick chick his own age anywhere, something better than Lil. It seemed funny he took up with her. I had a couple thoughts about it."

"Which we'd like to hear," said Varallo.

"He said he was a TV actor. You know, just starting out. Well, a lot of those people are mixed up with the dope bit. I wouldn't swear he wasn't on something, few times I saw him—kind of a glassy stare, and withdrawn like they say. I had the idea maybe he'd got on the outs with a dealer or something, even the Syndicate, and wanted to lie low for a while." He shrugged. "Don't know if there's anything in it."

"His name is Ricky Arnold."

"Yeah—or he said so."

"You think he was living there? Moved in with her?"

"Oh, sure. If it's any use to you, I can give you his plate number," said Patching casually.

"The hell you can," said Varallo.

Patching grinned a small tight grin. "I've got what they call a photographic memory for letters and figures. Sometimes it's handy. Like I say, a couple times Lorna and I met them for a few beers, dinner. He's driving an old white Ford four-door, and the plate number's WFB-960."

"Are you sure?" Varallo looked at him doubtfully.

Patching grinned again. "Try me. They stick in my mind." He didn't look around. "The Buick out there, the brake job, it's DWF-722. The VW getting gassed up, JFL-418. Your Merc is CJL-800. Am I right?"

"On the nose," said Delia, smiling.

"Well. That's his plate. He struck me," said Patching, "as a hair-trigger kind of guy. You know your own job, but I said to Lorna, it's possible he got doped up or drunk or something and killed her without any reason. That could happen."

"It could indeed. That's very interesting, and might be helpful," said Varallo.

"Might?" said Delia, back at the wheel of the Mercedes. "That plate number could go halfway to breaking the case, Vic."

" 'Could be' isn't 'will,' " said Varallo cautiously. "But we cer-

tainly want to talk to Mr. Arnold—if that's his name, which I doubt.
A TV actor. Would you have any kind of guess how many actors'
agents there might be in Hollywood and environs?"

"I was never any good at higher mathematics."

"No. I think before we waste about a week calling them all to find
out which one has Ricky Arnold as a client, we'll take a shortcut and
ask Sacramento about the car."

Besides the other gadgets in the Communications office, there was
a telex that was hooked up to a computer at D.M.V. headquarters in
Sacramento. It took about fifteen seconds to work, after you'd fed it
with either a name or plate number, and in its time had saved a lot of
work and cut a lot of corners. They fed that plate number into it, and
presently it uttered some busy little clicks and jerked out a terse mes-
sage on its typewriter-like platen.

The plate number belonged to a 1967 Ford, and it was registered
to Arthur Michael Moseley at an address in Huntington Park.

Nobody else was in. Sergeant Duff said the D.A.'s office had
hauled O'Connor down there again, and he'd gone off swearing a
blue streak about wasting time. Forbes and Poor were out on the
new heist, and probably Katz. "Yes," said Varallo inattentively.
"You'd better finish the report, Delia. I doubt very much if I'll find
Mr. Moseley at home in Huntington Park, but I may hear something
about him."

The address there proved to be a newish apartment building with a
manager on the premises. He looked very surprised at the badge, and
even more so at Varallo's questions. "Arthur Moseley? He's never
been in any trouble with the law, far as I know—nice young fellow.
Rent a little bit late sometimes, but he worked steady, always had a
pleasant word for you."

"He's moved?"

"Last month. No, he didn't leave any forwarding address. He told
me he'd got kind of fed up with the climate here, he was going up to
Washington or someplace, and naturally he wouldn't know any address."

"He quit whatever job he had here? Do you know where he was
working?"

"I suppose so. He was working at the Pep Boys Auto Supply over
on Santa Fe Avenue." That was all he knew. Moseley had lived there

for about two years, been a quiet tenant, never any drinking or noisy parties. And he hadn't had many people come to see him. They had heard a rough description from Lorna—"Kind of tall, dark hair and pretty good-looking"—and he heard about the same now from the manager. This was a rather funny little rigmarole.

He tried the Pep Boys Auto Supply store. It was a big one, with six or eight clerks and two proprietors. One of those expressed the same surprise at questions about Moseley; he'd been a good worker, everybody liked him, the proprietor would certainly be surprised to hear he was in any police trouble.

"It's a little something to do with his car," said Varallo mendaciously.

"Oh, just some red tape, hah? Well, I've got no idea where he's moved, but you might ask Bob Wise back there—he's got a customer right now—the blond guy in the truck accessories. He was pretty thick with Moseley, I think they got together sometimes out of working hours."

Wise reacted to the badge like an amateur actor in a melodrama. He backed up, turned first white and then red, and said he didn't know anything, anything at all, about Art Moseley. Interested, Varallo said, "Your boss said you were a good friend of his."

"Oh, just in the store," said Wise vaguely. "I don't know where he's gone." He looked at Varallo with a flash of resentment in his eyes. "I didn't know they used police on a thing like this."

"A thing like what? Why did he quit his job and move?" Wise looked around and said there were customers waiting, he couldn't— Varallo backed him up to a counter of rearview mirrors and told him gently that if he knew anything about Moseley's whereabouts he was obstructing the law to withhold information. Wise snarled at him and said he couldn't tell him anything.

"Obviously you know something," said Varallo. "Now, I can take you back to headquarters and make this an official questioning, you know. Would you prefer that, Mr. Wise?"

"Oh, for God's sake," said Wise. He got out a handkerchief and wiped his mouth. He said, "Look, there isn't one damned thing I can tell you that's going to give him away—wherever he's gone—and I suppose you'll keep on at me until I tell you what I do know. It's time for my coffee break—we can't talk here."

He led Varallo a couple of doors away to a little restaurant and they ordered coffee. Wise was looking more confident. He lit a cigarette and began, "I don't know what the hell police are doing in this, I didn't know the courts used you on stuff like this. I suppose you know Art was in a hell of a bind. His ex-wife's been on his neck, and he was fed up but good. Art's a hell of a nice guy, but there's no denying he's got kind of a hot temper. They got in an argument once and he sort of beat up on her, and she divorced him and got a judge to award her one hell of an alimony. Art was always behind with it, and no wonder, and he got sick of it, that's all. He was going to get out from under, that's all. She knew his address, see, and he told me he was going to need all the dough he could scrape together—he didn't say where he was heading, so I couldn't tell anybody—and he wasn't about to pay her last month's alimony, so he just ducked out of sight. He had to hang around until that insurance check came in—"

"What was that?"

"Hell, he'd been waiting for it three, four months. A guy banged into him back in November, did about five hundred bucks' worth of damage to his car. But the company said he ought to get the check before the fifteenth, he was just waiting to pick it up and then light out. I don't know where, and that's all I can tell you." Wise drank coffee. "Art's one for the chicks all right, and I've known him to tie one on, but to send police after him—" He was resentful about that.

One for the chicks, thought Varallo. That was interesting. Absently he asked the name of the insurance company. This made a little story that hung together. Moseley hanging around waiting for that check before splitting; with not much money, so looking for a cheap pad to hole up in: and it looked as if Mr. Moseley of the hot temper had got himself into more trouble than a court order for back alimony could give him.

"Do you know if Moseley was ever in one of the services?"

Wise looked surprised. "Yes, he did a tour in the Navy just after he got out of high school."

And that was interesting too. Varallo left Wise drinking a second cup of coffee and found the nearest post office. The badge got him a little more information. Moseley hadn't left a forwarding address, but he'd rented a post office box for the minimum length of time, and temporarily his mail was going into that. So he could get the check, of course.

When Varallo got back to the office he found Forbes there, one hip perched on Delia's desk, talking about the new heist. He passed on the information about Moseley and Forbes said, "Sometimes an answer drops right into our laps. But talk about out of the frying pan into the fire."

"Yes, it looks, that way." Varallo took up the phone and told Communications to put out an A.P.B. on Moseley and the Ford. If the insurance check had come in, Moseley would be long gone; but they knew he'd been here—when? Wednesday? Thursday? And despite the hot temper, Moseley was no fool: he knew his prints would be on file with the government—that tour in the Navy—so he got rid of them.

A lab report came in after lunch on the nylon cord used on that market heist; it was a rather unusual type, manufactured locally, so Forbes and Poor went out to consult the manufacturer, which was in Van Nuys, about retail outlets.

Dr. Goulding looked in just after they'd left and said there was nothing very abstruse about that corpse. "She got a knock on the head, sustained a fractured skull and died of it. It looks as if she could have fallen, or been knocked down, against a sharp edge of some sort—a table or something. If she was struck with a weapon, it'd be a two-by-four or something like that."

"I think your first guess was better," said Varallo, thinking of that shabby apartment and where the body had lain beside the coffee table. "Can you pin down the time?"

"Hardly to the hour. Rigor had come and gone—long gone. I'd say any time Wednesday afternoon or evening," said Goulding.

"Yes, it works out about as I thought it would," said Varallo. "Stupid people doing stupid things. Thanks so much." He laughed. "And if we pick him up, it'll be called second degree."

Goulding had just wandered out, and Varallo was saying, "I'll bet Charles is fit to be tied, caught downtown listening to the lawyers argue about plea bargains," when the phone on his desk buzzed and he picked it up. "Varallo."

"This is Adams." The rookie patrolman. "I thought I'd call direct instead of using the radio, sir. I just spotted that Lotus again. I got it this time." Varallo reached for a pen. "I did just what we were told—pulled him over and told him we were running a spot check for expired licenses. Silly sort of excuse, but a civilian wouldn't realize it. Anyway, he's an Edward Norwood, and the address is Beverly Hills. He said he was heading home."

Varallo took it down. "Funny he was over here, or is it? After all, anybody can have friends anywhere—"

"I wouldn't know," said Adams, "but he's funny all right. I mean the way he acted. I don't know if he was high on something, he seemed to be handling the car all right. But he was—queer. As if he didn't care why I'd stopped him, or—or if it was Tuesday or Christmas. Well, anyway, that's the address."

"Beverly Hills," said Varallo to Delia. "I wonder if there is more than one of those old racers around. And if your old lady was woolgathering. We are getting around the county these days. Let's go see Mr. Norwood."

"You're not kindly giving me experience," said Delia. "You're just getting out of all the driving."

This time of day, traffic wasn't bad, and they got out there by three o'clock, started hunting the address. It was a square and stark new condominum complex on Tower Road, and Edward Norwood had one of the top-floor units. There was a rank of elevators, very discreet, very quiet. The hallway was wide and the carpet felt feet thick.

"Rags to riches," said Delia. "We don't usually move in this kind of society."

Varallo pushed the bell; they both half-expected a uniformed servant to answer it, but instead the door was jerked open and they faced a slight, fair young man wrapped in an exotic black silk jacket over gray slacks. "Mr. Norwood?" said Varallo.

"Oh, yes." He looked at the badge blankly; then comprehension dawned, and he asked, "What do you want?"

"A few minutes of your time, if you don't mind."

Without a word he turned his back and walked across the room, and they went in. It was a huge room decorated in shades of pale gray, rich carpet, velvet drapes, a mahogany bar at one end, square modernistic cubes of furniture. "It's about your car," said Varallo.

"Oh, the car. One does like to be different—anybody can drive a

Caddy or Jaguar, don't you think?" He hadn't sat down; he didn't ask them to; he stood looking out the window at the magnificent view over the city.

"Very distinctive," said Varallo. "I wonder if it's the only one in the county."

"Oh, it is, it is indeed. It is really such a bore, having so *much* money," said Norwood. He moved jerkily, nervously, flinging around from the window. "Nothing to do that's interesting, when you can do anything you please. It was amusing, looking for a car nobody else has. For a while."

Varallo said baldly, "There was a man shot up in Glendale the other day, and we have a witness who says the man who shot him got into that green Lotus and drove off."

"Oh." Norwood fingered his upper lip. He looked at them sideways, furtively, walked over to the bar, stopped and turned. "It is such a bore," he said rapidly, "and I've often thought if my grandfather hadn't left so much money, life might have been more interesting. I don't know if you understand that. One tries everything, and gets so tired of it—the liquor, the women, the kicks, everybody says try the tricks, the greatest—coke, acid, grass—but really it gets to be a bore too, and one feels so hellish the next day. You know?" He wandered back to the window again. "I've never tried getting married, of course."

"Mr. Norwood, have you taken any drugs today?" asked Varallo sharply.

"What? Oh, no, not today, not today," said Norwood. He cocked his head with a queerly coy effect and said, "But of course it would be a new experience—not that I suppose much would come of it—and of course you could get a search warrant for this place, couldn't you?"

"Very likely," said Varallo.

"And there *is* that gun in the bed-table drawer. I have not a very practical mind," said Norwood. "I expect if I had had to earn a living I would have. But new experiences—I suppose if I tell you about it something would happen. Something different." Suddenly he gave Delia a gracious smile. "Your secretary may take notes if you like."

"What were you doing in Glendale?" asked Varallo, watching him.

"No, I don't think I'd ever been there before, or had I? That was strange. My uncle has just died. Not quite so filthy rich as the rest of the family, but he had a house somewhere above a place called Sunset Canyon. The lawyers are dealing with it, of course—oh, everything was left to me—but I had to decide what to keep from the house. He fancied antiques, there are some rather nice things there—" His gaze wandered around the room. "I've been thinking, throw all this out—" he gestured jerkily—"and have all period pieces. It would make a change. What was I talking about? Oh, the gun. Yes. I came across it that day—quite a nice gun, and all loaded. Probably on account of burglars, would you think? We never have them here. I rather liked the feel of it, I took it along. And I'm afraid—I told you it was strange territory to me—I went out of my way, going home. I was," said Norwood simply, "lost."

"You parked the Lotus on a side street off Brand Boulevard," said Varallo carefully. "Why?"

"My dear fellow, I don't know where I parked it," he said. "I was in need of a men's room, and I noticed one at a service station on a corner. I parked, I went in. I came out. How it does remind one of Omar, doesn't it? 'Came out by the same—' I had the gun in my pocket. And ever since I had found it, I had been wondering how it would feel to kill a man. Now that was something I had never done. I wondered. If there would be some great huge wondrous feeling—as if one was a god—" He sighed. "But it was nothing. Nothing."

They watched him. "You saw two men outside the bar there," said Varallo, "and you walked over and shot one of them?"

"Yes—yes. Wondering how it would feel. And it meant nothing—nothing," said Norwood disappointedly. "He fell down and I saw the blood, but the colors are brighter on acid, and I had no sensation at all. I turned away and left. It was a sad thing."

There he was quite right. It had been a sad thing for Al Montez, that ordinary workingman with a family. "Where is the gun, Mr. Norwood?"

"In the bedroom, as I told you. I have no use for it now."

Varallo found the bedroom, which was approximately twenty-five feet square, and found the gun. The lab would tell them it was the H. and R. which had killed Montez. He went back to the living room, found the phone, and got the local headquarters, explained, asked for a squad car. The sooner he got this one booked into their jail, the happier he'd be.

"Mr. Norwood, you'll have to come along with us now."

"Now?" Norwood was surprised. "I am going out for dinner. To-morrow, perhaps—" He looked at Varallo and laughed. "My dear fellow, you don't suppose you'll be able to keep me in *jail?* Six million dollars doesn't stay in jail. Or commit crimes. No, no. The lawyers will see to it. I must call old Hutchinson."

He refused to change his clothes, and the Beverly Hills men, after some discussion with Varallo, took him off as he was.

They shut the door of the condominium behind them. "And he could be right," said Delia. "You can't electrocute a millionaire, or can you? My God, what a thing."

"Nobody's going to electrocute him anyway," said Varallo. "I have a bet there's permanent brain damage there—the LSD probably —and he'll end up in Atascadero. But we'll have to get back to base and start the paperwork on it."

O'Connor and Rhys sat on the stake-out again on Saturday night, with a short-wave radio to keep them company; and about ten-thirty a closed van drove up, parked in front of the apartment on Salem Street, and three men got out of it and went up to the door of Rico Guttierez' apartment in front.

They were sitting in O'Connor's Ford across the street, and had a clear view; there was a bright porchlight over the door. Rhys spoke into the radio. "Give 'em time," said O'Connor, "to get the goods on display, and we'll go in and see what we've got. Unless this is a practical joke on us and they're sitting around playing dominoes." Five minutes later three squad cars pulled up silently from two different directions. The squad car men went down the side drive to locate the back door; O'Connor and Rhys went over there and rang the doorbell.

It wasn't answered, but things began to happen at the back; a man came out into the drive from that apartment, spotted the uniformed men, yelled and tried to run for the van. One of the patrolmen felled him from behind and slapped the cuffs on.

The front door opened and two men ran out. Rhys collared one and they fell in a rough-and-tumble fight on the sidewalk. O'Connor called on the other one to halt and he kept on running, so O'Connor snapped off a shot and brought him down. The uniformed men were in the apartment by then.

They looked to see what they'd got, and the man on the ground was groaning and clutching his upper thigh. "My good Christ," said O'Connor, holstering the .357 Magnum, "I need some practice on the range, I aimed for his ankles." They called an ambulance for him.

They found a little more than they'd bargained for; a miscellany of drugs worth about half a million in street value. One of the men had a Texas driver's license on him made out to Samuel Wiener, and when they got back to the office a query to NCIC placed him as a much-wanted wholesaler. The other two were probably bodyguards to ride shotgun on the merchandise. The van was registered to Tim McCully in Hollywood, so they brought the LAPD in; and the thing kept widening out.

In the Guttierez apartment they had come across a list of names and addresses, mostly in Hollywood and L.A., which an educated guess could pinpoint as the buyers. They were probably expecting delivery Sunday or Monday, and might all be at home waiting for it; so tomorrow O'Connor and the top brass from LAPD Narco would be plotting all the simultaneous raids. In the end, it might come to over a hundred arrests, and the very thought of all the paperwork on it was enough to make O'Connor damned grateful that Glendale was sharing it with a lot of other men.

He got home at daylight, and Maisie, sound asleep on the living-room couch, mistook him for a burglar and raised the roof, waking Katharine and the baby, who went on howling for the next hour.

Meg took Tammy to the park on Sunday. She knew they were safe while they were inside the apartment, but it was such a lovely day, and Tammy begged to go; Meg had felt guilty at keeping her cooped up. The unreasoning, intuitional fear had been in her for a long time; she never fastened the chains on the two doors without that solid reassurance filling her: *now we are safe.* Yet, curiously, this beautiful golden spring day in the park, the fear receded and she just felt peaceful and calm.

She had been to see Stan Pollard yesterday. He was sitting up, talking like himself, and he said his uncle was getting the decks cleared to come out and shepherd him home. That he'd want to see Meg too, probably. "I guess it was worth getting clobbered," he said soberly, "when it made the police sit up and take notice and believe you."

And perhaps—that was what Delia Riordan had told her yesterday, that the lieutenant thought all their activity had warned Wayne away. Because if he knew they knew he was here, he wouldn't risk getting caught again—even to get back at her and Tammy.

She watched Tammy playing in the swings, and she thought, as soon as she could save up some money they'd leave this place. That wasn't home any more. Start fresh somewhere else, and just forget about the Burgess money. She could look after Tammy herself.

She sat there quite a long time; it was nearly five o'clock before they went home and she shut them in securely and fastened the chain.

Nothing much useful had developed on the nylon cord. For once Sunday night had been quiet, and there was a lull that Monday morning, nothing much to do for a change—except for O'Connor's wholesalers. He had taken Forbes and Katz along to join in planning the raids, over at the Hollywood precinct.

But that afternoon the Santa Monica force got around to sending up some information on one Willard Hubbard, who had a pedigree with them of B. and E., robbery with violence, and assault; he had the BORN TO RAISE HELL tattoo on his right hand. It was a little queer, thought Varallo, how many of those had turned up. It seemed rather unlikely that he'd have come all the way to Glendale to heist a market, but you never knew. And by the time he got down there, hopefully found him to talk to, it would be after six and he'd be late again.

He found the address, and an anxious-eyed, weak-faced woman answered the door. She looked at the badge and said, "Oh, dear, is Will in trouble again? I'm so worried about it—don't know what gets into him—and just lately he's been getting thick as thieves with that cousin of his, Henry Grady over in Glendale, and Henry's a nice boy, I wouldn't like to think Will was influencing him to—"

You never knew where the next lead was coming from, and sometimes they came easy.

He got back to the office just at quitting time. Delia was just standing up, getting out her keys. He told her about Henry, she said that was gratifying, and they were at the door when the phone rang.

"Why always at the end of shift?" Varallo wondered, and picked it up.

"Tracy's just picked up Moseley on that A.P.B.," said Hamilton on the desk. "But something funny—he said you should meet him in the lot, he thinks you'll be going for a ride."

"Now what the hell—all right. We've got Moseley," he told Delia, "but I'm damned if I'm going to question him tonight. And what Tracy thinks he's up to—" They went out to the lot in the deepening dusk, and three minutes later the squad car pulled in and Tracy got out of it and hauled his capture out of the back seat. He had cuffed him, now unlocked the cuffs.

"Spotted him in a station along Glenoaks," said Tracy. "When I got a good look, I thought you might like to show him to somebody. I was in that detail showing those mug shots."

In the shadowless light of the arc lamps, the prisoner stood looking into space: a tall dark man with sleek black hair, a cleft chin, a strong nose, thick eyebrows. Delia let out a little gasp. "That's—" she said.

"So it is," said Varallo gently. "Thank you so much, Tracy. You were quite right." He took Delia aside. "We think we want him for Pollard. We just might be able to break him down to admit that. But we'd better get the positive identification. I think it is, you think it is, but—"

"She won't," said Delia, "be thrilled to see him. Yes."

They put him into the Mercedes, Varallo in back with him, and drove up Glenoaks to Grandview. He never said a word; he was like a man in a state of shock. He sat impassive, rigid, looking straight ahead. When Delia parked, and they got him out, he went between them like an automaton up the little walk until they came to the step, and then he looked around, looked up, and he said, "No. No, oh, no, no."

"Come on," said Vallaro, and took his arm.

He was like a statue there. In the street light they saw his lips pull back from his teeth in a ghastly little rictus. He began to back up down the walk, moving delicately, and in one queerly irrelevant gesture he raised his left arm and looked at his watch.

Varallo took one stride and got hold of him again. "Come—"

With the little fixed smile still stretching his mouth, the man said in a soft voice, "That thing's due to blow in three minutes—" And with the effect of slow motion turning back to normal, he whirled and ran.

In that split second Varallo and Delia whirled and ran. They didn't have to consult each other. Behind her, Delia heard the familiar roar of that faithful engine as the Mercedes turned over and caught—keys left in—Varallo went pounding up the stairs and beat on the door marked BURGESS, beat on the door marked CHILDS. "Mrs. Burgess—hurry—it's police—" He could hear Delia pounding on the doors below, calling. "Mrs. Burgess—"

The chain was unfastened slowly; she peered out. He thrust the door wide, seeing the wide-eyed little girl across the room. He made a dive, scooped her up in one arm. "The Childs—"

"They're not home yet. What—" He grabbed her under his other arm, swept her down the stairs. Delia had old Miss Kemp by one arm.

"I can't get them to answer—"

"Come on!" said Varallo roughly, and they were out the door, into the street, and across the street, and then it went up. There was a giant's cough from somewhere in the building, and it went up in bright flame and, a long moment later, a puff of black smoke.

Curiously, in that moment none of them spoke or made any sound. Meg caught the little girl in her arms silently. Miss Kemp sat down suddenly on the grass in the parking strip. Then doors and windows began to open and people came out along the block, running and shouting.

Delia said, "I couldn't get them to answer."

"Not your fault."

"He took the Merc. He took Alex's Merc."

Someone had called the fire department and police. The first squad car came bucketing around from Glenoaks and Steiner got out of it. As Varallo came up he turned and stared. "What the hell are you doing here? My God, what's going on? I just passed the worst mess you ever saw, up there at Pacific—I was on my way here, I called it in. My God, an old Mercedes and a Ford van, all mixed up together and starting to burn—nobody walked away from that one. My God, what happened here?"

And Varallo came to life suddenly; he thought, the garages—cars full of gas— He turned on Meg. "Have you got your keys?" he snapped.

She produced them from her jacket pocket. And as he took them, she turned her face up to him in the street light, and her eyes were the eyes of a drowned woman, wide and dark and empty.

Wayne Burgess had been thrown cleanly through the windshield of the Mercedes, his throat cut wide. Donald Biggs, ignoring the red light at Pacific, had hit the Mercedes broadside, and both cars went up in flames.

The Wileys were dead in the fire, of smoke inhalation, and the autopsy would say later that they'd both been drunk.

And it was later too when Varallo said to Meg, "He had a key to your apartment on him, you know. That minute you handed your keys to me—" and he hadn't got her car out after all—"you thought of something, didn't you? You realized—how he'd got in?"

She nodded dumbly. Oliver Pollard had arrived by then, and installed her in a suite at the Glendale Hotel. "It never—entered my mind—when you were all asking. When I wear anything with pockets, I've got a habit of dropping my keys into the pocket. Handy. They're in my handbag any other time. And Wednesday mornings—when there aren't any patients coming in—the doctor not in—I wouldn't bother to take my handbag to the ladies' room, put on fresh lipstick. If he was watching—"

"Which he was. In the office, your jacket left hanging on your chair. Two chances, and one of them paid off," said Varallo. "Where was he watching from?"

"There's—a men's room right across the hall."

"And you told us he chewed gum. About thirty seconds, after he got hold of your keys, to get an impression of all the likely ones, obvious house keys. And in any slum section of town he'd find a locksmith to make one from that."

"It was a very cute little job," said Burt; and that was later too, after they'd been poking around what was left, the lab men interested, and the fire department interested as to what they'd find. "If you didn't know it had been set, it would probably have been put down to a slow gas leak—he'd arranged a little break in the gas line coming in, on the back porch. I think we can show it's an artificial cut—"

"It doesn't matter," said O'Connor. "But interesting. It would have looked like an accident?"

"That's just what. It was kind of cute. A time bomb in a way, alarm clock works I'd guess—there's not much left. And no dynamite, no obvious explosive. He'd used the commercial fertilizer—"

"What?"

"A nitrate-based fertilizer—oh, you were thinking about that LAPD lab report," said Burt. "Funny at that. But a nitrate-based fertilizer combined with fuel oil makes just a dandy explosive. I don't know, if the blasting cap had been found, whether somebody might have suspected—but we couldn't find it. The chances are it'd have been written off as an accident."

"And who the hell would have thought," said O'Connor, "that he'd have picked up that floozy just to have a temporary roof? And end up killing her instead of who he meant to?" He laughed suddenly. "As far as Art Moseley goes, let his wife hunt for him, and good luck to her."

"You suppose," wondered Katz, "the girl's going to marry that Pollard fellow now?"

Delia laughed and shook her head. "I should doubt it. She's been through one rough marriage, she won't be in any hurry again. I should think she'd come in for some of the Burgess money. She can take her time deciding on a new place to live."

O'Connor looked at the stack of reports on his desk. "I just hope to God nothing breaks to make us a lot of legwork. I'll be busy on this narco thing the next week, damn it."

As they all dispersed into the parking lot at end of shift, Varallo found Delia parked next to the Gremlin. He said, "New car?" It was a dusty green Ford.

"No, I'll have to get one. This is a renter." And then she laughed, her rare full-throated laugh, infectious. "The poor old Merc," she said. "Alex said it was an honorable end for an old veteran."

"Alex?"

She was getting out the keys to the rented car. She said suddenly, "I'd like you to meet my father sometime."

She came in the back door of the old house. It was a chilly evening, and driving in she'd seen that Steve had lit a fire on the hearth, smoke coming out the chimney. She stood in the kitchen and inhaled thoughtfully. Pot roast with vegetables around it, browned potatoes. And—she looked—there was a crusty apple pie in the oven.

She went down the hall. They were in the living room, Alex reading *Master Detective* and Steve *True Detective*.

Delia smiled at them tenderly, that moment before they realized she was here. It was nice to be home.